I0578420

NICHOLAS CULPEPER
and the MYSTERY of the PHILOSOPHER'S STONE

Copyright © Dr Michael Noble 2019
Published by the Buon-Cattivi Press, 2019
Adelaide, Australia
ISBN (paperback) 978-1-922314-00-0
ISBN (ebook) 978-0-9953661-9-0

Book design and cover illustration
by Andrew Crooks

NICHOLAS CULPEPER and the MYSTERY of the PHILOSOPHER'S STONE

MICHAEL NOBLE

Buon-Cattivi Press

Adelaide, Australia

Contents

Publisher Acknowledgments vii
Foreword ix
About Dr Michael Noble xi
Author's Note xiii

*Nicholas Culpeper and the Mystery of the
Philosopher's Stone* 1
Nicholas Culpeper's Parting Words 203

End notes: Contingencies, Life Choices
and Power-Relationships 204

References....................................... 234

Publisher Acknowledgements

Buon-Cattivi Press would like to acknowledge the hard work of the many people involved in the production of *Nicholas Culpeper and the Mystery of the Philosopher's Stone*.

We would like to thank the dedicated assistance of Amelia Walker, Ruth Trigg, and Louise Niva while entrusting us with Michael's novella. We would also like to thank Gretta Koch, Simone Stewart, and Trevor Morrison for their immense friendship with Michael and assistance in his academic scholarship. We'd also like to extend thanks to everyone who has offered their support and ideas that helped make this novella a reality.

Our final thanks and acknowledgement are to Dr Michael Noble, without whom this novella and its introduction to the work of Nicholas Culpeper would not exist. Michael was a wonderfully insightful and caring person, we hope our care of this novella has done his work justice.

Royalties from the sale of this book will be donated to Intersex Human Rights Australia as requested by Dr Michael Noble.

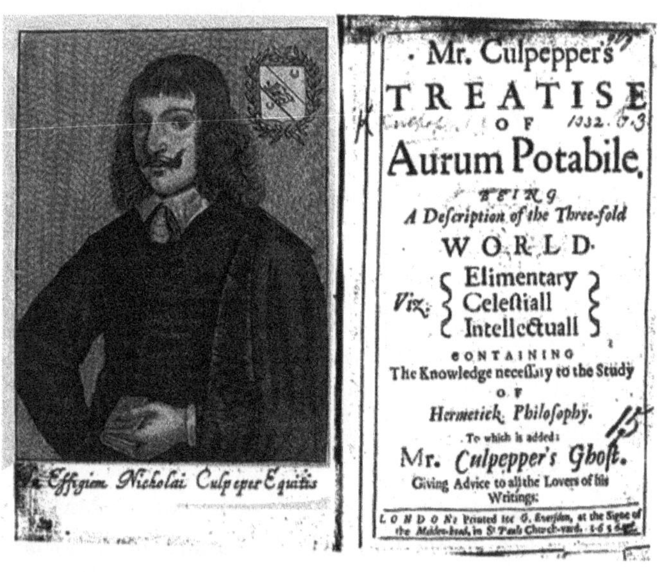

Figure 1: Title page of *Mr Culpeper's Treatise of* Aurum Potabile (1656)

Foreword
By Ruth Trigg

This work does not sit alone. It is one part of Dr Michael Noble's PhD, comprising a novella and an exegesis (thesis). Michael's novella is profound and elegant, and to read this novella against the pristine, extended control of the academic thesis genre is to throw more astonishment and credit to the brilliance of this work. Each style is so different it is hard to reconcile they came from the one writer. I urge you to find Michael's thesis elsewhere and revel in it, to immerse yourself in exemplary scholarly writing and analysis of the highest order. It is a superb evocation of the British philosopher Nicholas Culpeper's dilemma: how to share deep knowledge, and how to resist its base exploitation.

About Nicholas Culpeper

Most of us have barely a fleeting knowledge of Nicholas Culpeper, perhaps only as a 17th Century herbalist. Culpeper's life was short—1616 to 1654. His contemporaries were Galileo 1564-1642, Shakespeare 1564-1616 and Milton 1608-1674. The English Reformation was challenging the accepted wisdoms of the ancient past, shifting power from top-down authority structures through church and state to offer slightly more equitable access to ideas, knowledge and literacy through printed books, monographs and handbills.

Michael had a deep passion for Culpeper, his era, his works and in particular, his revolutionary medical philosophy. In his note to his novella, Michael clearly states:

The aim of this novel is to establish empathy with and understanding of the subtle and intangible aspects of his life, especially his ideas and beliefs.

For this purpose, Michael's novella perfectly illuminates the difficulties Culpeper experienced in his life through his determination to provide healthful herbal and medical knowledge to everyone, principally the poor and oppressed. The social and medical systems of that era kept medical knowledge closely guarded through the use of Latin, hence accessible to only the most learned within the College of Physicians and Association of Apothecaries. Culpeper translated ancient texts and urged his readers to observe nature and learn from it themselves. Practicing well away from the jurisdiction of the College of Surgeons, he sought the deepest truths of the Universe and created a system of thought which he encoded in his writings, available only to those with the desire to seek and find.

Michael, with his beautiful sense of humour and his disciplined understanding of epistemology and story-telling, has carefully and sensitively crafted a replication of Culpeper's processes of both hiding deep truths in codes, yet revealing these secrets to the most dedicated searcher. His novella will set your foot upon a path of beguiling investigation.

About Dr Michael Noble

Dr Michael Noble really was born out of his time—he loved cross-stitching, restoring antique writing boxes and bringing balance into his life through a passion for bushwalking and gardening.

In his later years, he trained as an English as an Additional Language (EAL) tutor and found this deeply rewarding. He always enjoyed making time to help other university students with assignments and research—many have said how he contributed to their study success and outlook on life.

Despite being frequently ill throughout his life, flattened by fatigue and often depressed, he managed to complete an exemplary five degrees, culminating in his ground-breaking PhD *"Nicholas Culpeper and the mystery of the philosopher's stone: recovering and enhancing subjugated knowledges through historical fiction"* in 2017. In the end, his 30-year meditation practice sustained him well through his short battle with cancer in 2018. He is greatly missed.

Author's Note

The events described in this historical novel are entirely fictional. The detective-like character, Zachariah Jenkin, is a product of the author's imagination. Hence, Zachariah's investigations into the authorship and veracity of the book *Mr Culpeper's Treatise of* Aurum Potabile never actually happened, even though archival evidence suggests that contemporary associates of Nicholas Culpeper (1616-1654) speculated as to whether he had actually written the text.

The novel does not seek to recreate actual or verifiable events. Rather, the genre of the realist historical novel serves, in this instance, as a medium that enables me to examine religious ideas and philosophical currents commonly believed, observed and practised by Culpeper and his mid-seventeenth century contemporaries. The medium also enables me to speculate on the influences these beliefs and ideas had on Culpeper's motivations and actions, all of which are verified in the archival sources. Endnotes indicate passages and sentences often copied verbatim from the cited archival sources and textually transformed into dialogue, as well as occasionally providing additional information on specific topics that may encourage further reading. In relation to the novel as the artefact component of the thesis, the endnotes presented are comprehensive in order to inform the examiners of the archival location of the texturally transformed references.

Set in the summer of 1656, two years after Culpeper's death, the aim of this novel is to establish empathy with and understanding of the subtle and intangible aspects of his life, specifically his ideas and beliefs. The novel also explores Culpeper's intentions and motivations for the drafting of his *Treatise*, while speculating on the text's meaning and function, especially in relation to his life and its significance to his other published medical and esoteric texts.

I. We went to School to Nature,
to see which way things were made in
a Naturall way, and guided being
made; and we suppofed, that way we
might come to know their Natures, by
knowing of what matter, and by what
means they were made.

II. We viewed the fignatures in things
that were made, we fearched if that
we might finde their Natures thereby;
we perceived work enough in this for
a man to bufie his head about all the
dayes of his life, and yet learn fome-
thing every day.

Figure 2: Extract from *Mr Culpeper's Treatise of* Aurum
Potabile, 1656, p. 83

NICHOLAS CULPEPER
and the MYSTERY of the PHILOSOPHER'S STONE

MICHAEL NOBLE

Prologue

Nicholas Culpeper's Study
Spitalfields, London
Friday, 2nd January 1654

William Ryves stared through the window searching a horizon obscured by misty rain. It was a dismal afternoon, the second day of the new Year of Our Lord 1654[1]. There had not been any celebrations in this house. A fire in the hearth sputtered feebly, seemingly unable to warm a room shrouded in a cold, dank atmosphere of impending death. He listened to the labouring breath of his employer and friend, Nicholas Culpeper, sleeping fitfully on a cot behind him. His lungs filled with the blood and phlegm characteristic of the consumption wracking his body, it was obvious that Nicholas would soon succumb to his illness.

During the closing days of the previous summer, Nicholas still possessed his characteristically lean physique and swarthy complexion, his dark curly hair framing a lightly-bearded intelligent face.[2] In the space of only a few months, at thirty-seven years of age his ravaged face was now that of an old debilitated man. His once quick piercing eyes were now sunken into bruised sockets, dry yellowed skin stretched tightly over hollow cheeks. His bluish lips were cracked and often speckled with drops of blood coughed up in fits of wracking spasms.

"

Nicholas's health noticeably beginning to deteriorate by late November, Nicholas had a portable cot installed in his study under the large western-facing window. Here he could enjoy the warmth of the afternoon sun. He wanted to be near his books, manuscripts and writing materials so he could continue to work, even though ailing.

An apothecary or maker of medicines, Nicholas also studied and practised medicine, natural philosophy[3] and astrology, as well as translating texts from Latin into English. His unauthorised translation five years earlier of the College of Physicians' *Pharmacopoeia Londinensis*, under the title *A Physical Directory*, caused an uproar.[4]

William chuckled softly as he recalled the vitriolic response from the Royalist press:

> Mr Culpeper is a most despicable, ragged fellow, and yet he looks as if he has been stewed in a tar-pit, being a drowsie-headed coxcomb not worth the name gentleman and scholar.[5]

'What amuses you?' Nicholas asked.

Roused from his reminiscence by the weary, strained voice behind him, William turned his attention to his friend. Glancing up, Nicholas witnessed the compassion in William's striking sad blue eyes. No wonder, Nicholas mused, that the business relationship that had begun when he no longer had the strength to transcribe his notes had developed into such a deep and trusting friendship.

Bending down to help his master into a sitting position, William replied, 'Oh, Sir, I was just thinking about the stir caused by your translation of the *Pharmacopoeia*. It seems only yesterday.'

'Bah!' Culpeper spat. 'For all their prancing and strutting

indignation and their hypocritical claims, one might suppose my translation from their Latin tongue would harm people who sought to make their own herbal remedies to treat themselves? No! The real reason for their buffoonery was that their pockets would suffer. Their outcry just confirmed my claim "the doctors' practice is to ask for gain, even at a time when men cry out in pain.'"[6]

Both men laughed at the now familiar aphorism Nicholas had written in the preface of his translation, which helped fuel the outrage of the College. Laughter changed to wracking coughs as the exertion took its toll on Nicholas's body, a sound now sadly familiar as it reverberated throughout the house.

Searching his bedside table, Nicholas said, 'William, where are my pipe and tobacco?'

'I have taken it upon myself to remove them, sir, because their effects worsen your condition.'

'Ah… I suppose so, William. After all, tobacco was the greatest enemy to my health, but I was too accustomed to it to leave it,' Nicholas conceded.[7]

Nicholas settled into his pillow. Seeking to change the subject lest William continue to harp on about the evils of tobacco, he said, 'And how many times have I told you not to call me 'sir'? My friends call me Nicholas and you are my dearest friend.'

'Yes, Mr Culpeper,' William replied. He had been in awe of his employer for so many years and held him in such deep respect he could not bring himself to treat Nicholas as an equal.

Nicholas smiled and sighed, realising he would never win this battle. During these days where it seemed he was surrounded by dishonest men who wished to steal his works or worse, profit from his name, he knew William was a man he could trust. He was determined to reward such dedication and friendship. Nicholas had already given William much of his personal reference library, some of the drafts of his own works, and piles of astrological charts.[8] The books and old manuscripts were well-thumbed, stained with ink, their margins covered with his scribbled annotations. Some of these old books and manuscripts were falling to pieces with over-use. But he knew William would value these over any monetary reward; he was one of only a few who knew that within those tattered pages lay secrets and questions and answers men vainly searched their whole lives to grasp.

Nicholas eventually realised William had spoken. These days it seemed his mind was anywhere other than in the present.

'Sir… sir, Mr Heydon will be arriving soon. Are you able to meet with him?'

Nicholas's young lodger, John Heydon, had requested an audience in order to introduce an acquaintance and discuss a matter he claimed was of great importance. Heydon had recently taken up residence at the invitation of Alice, Nicholas's young wife. Having persuaded her that he was descended from European royalty, Heydon tried to ingratiate himself with his landlord.[9] But Nicholas had known from the first that he was a fraud, as subsequent events would prove.

Professing an interest in the new concentrated alchemical medicines now competing with traditional herbal medicaments, Heydon had wasted no time in trying to persuade his landlord to assist him in becoming established in this lucrative trade. Even though Nicholas had published some tracts that mentioned alchemical medicines, he resisted Heydon's approaches and refused to discuss the subject of alchemy altogether.

Both men already knew the topic Heydon wished to discuss. Several days earlier while drinking in the local tavern, William had overheard Heydon discussing the subject with a man unfamiliar to him. Obscured from view by an oak pillar, his interest had been roused when he heard Heydon mention his employer's name.

'... I have seen these manuscripts myself,' William recalled Heydon whispering to his companion. 'He keeps them in a book closet adjacent to his study. But once, when Mr Culpeper was absent from the house, I took the opportunity to investigate the secrets hidden behind the door he had forgotten to lock. In those brief seconds, I saw manuscripts written in Mr Culpeper's hand,' Heydon had whispered as he furtively looked about the tavern, fearful he would be overheard. 'On the cover sheet of a tattered manuscript were scrawled the words *aurum potabile*. While quickly flicking through the sheets, I spied a phrase that leapt from the page, for it read:

> We desire philosophers to view this with a heedful eye, the exact knowledge of which is infinitely necessary to the attainment both of *aurum potabile* and the philosopher's stone.[10]

'What knowledge? Does this mean he knows the secrets behind the making of the universal elixir?' his companion had asked.

'I do not know. Thus far he has been so secretive about these manuscripts, I suspect it will take a great deal of persuasion before he agrees to my recommendation that he either publishes them himself, or better still, gives them over to my care,' Heydon replied.

William had immediately reported the conversation to Nicholas, who then demanded Heydon be evicted from the house. He was forced to relent following a heated exchange with his wife, who refused to consider their boarder's intrusion was at all sinister. And, anyway, as she had argued resentfully, Heydon's rent money helped support them. Nicholas had suspected for some time that Alice's interest in their boarder was more than financial, but he also realised that soon she would be a widow and would need someone to care for her. And, considering the manner in which she had brought Heydon into their home and his dubious character, he believed they deserved each other!

Before Nicholas could respond to William's question as to whether or not he was able enough to receive guests, they heard a loud rap on the front door below.

'Well, it would seem that I have no choice,' Nicholas said as he straightened his night-clothes and smoothed down his wispy, dishevelled hair. 'Please invite them in, William.'

As William approached the door, it burst open and a child tumbled into the chamber. 'Papa, papa, Mr Heydon is here with another man,' she shrilled excitedly.

Rushing towards the bed, she stopped short as if remembering she must be gentle with him.

As father and child gently embraced, William thought of how Nicholas, who had devoted his life to trying to alleviate sickness in others, had himself lost six children in their infancy. This child, Mary, who was the true picture of her father, was his sole surviving issue.[11]

Miss Jane, once Nicholas's nurse and now managing his household, asked for leave to enter. Ushering the resisting child from the room, she said, 'Mr Heydon and Dr—'

'Mr Culpeper, good afternoon,' a young man said, as he barged past Jane and Mary, almost knocking them into the doorframe.

Posing in the middle of the room as if he expected on-lookers to admire his sheer presence, no-one could avoid noticing this prancing dandy. Twenty-four years of age, slim as a willow, long wavy black hair and superior hawked nose, Heydon wore the latest fashion of garishly coloured pantaloons and a flowing gown, all made from expensive silk and linen, and edged with crisp white ruffled lace. His crisp linen attire spoke of elegance and breeding, all a ruse to deceive, Nicholas silently mused.

'Mr Culpeper, I trust you are well?' Heydon said in his annoyingly nasal and over-friendly tone. 'May I introduce my associate, Dr William Freeman?'

Dr Freeman approached Nicholas. In contrast to Heydon's opulence, the doctor's simple black linen garb aimed to present an aura of self-discipline and modesty, qualities dedicated physicians tried to cultivate in order to impress their clients. However, Dr Freeman's demeanour and sneering expression suggested arrogance and indifference.

Concealing his wariness and extending his hand, Nicholas cordially replied, 'It's a pleasure to meet you, Dr Freeman. May I introduce my secretary and friend, Mr William Ryves?'

Barely acknowledging William's presence, Dr Freeman strode forward and lightly grasped his host's frail withered and yellowing hand. His cultivated demeanour of the learned physician was instantly betrayed, as he could not conceal his disdain at the sight of the sickly figure of Nicholas reclining on the cot.

'It is a pleasure to eventually meet you, Mr Culpeper. Your work and reputation are well known,' Dr Freeman said in an artificially jovial tone. Withdrawing his hand, he discreetly wiped it on a kerchief as he took the stool furthest from the bed.

'Mr Culpeper,' Heydon began hesitantly. 'We have spoken before of the new chemical medicines recently introduced into England from the Continent and even though you have claimed in some of your texts that you have some reservations as to their safety, I am sure you agree they are more effective than the crude herbal compounds the College of Physicians use. So, I am confident that, with Dr Freeman's assistance and expertise, you could publish texts instructing your readers in their proper preparation. They are crying out for more of your texts; and consider the benefits for your wife who, I am confident, will be able to continue to enjoy the financial security derived from your worthy publications—'

As Heydon inhaled a well-overdue breath, Nicholas took the opportunity to respond to the flood of his guest's persuasive argument.

'Most of the texts I desired to be published are now available for purchase,' Nicholas said. 'I have exhausted myself and my library. Nor do I require assistance in learning the correct making and uses of chemical medicines. Lastly, I am sure my wife will profit from the extra editions and be able to live a comfortable life without having to hire out her rooms to boarders!'

Apparently oblivious to his landlord's barb, Heydon turned to his companion, silently encouraging him to speak. Clearing his throat, Dr Freeman explained that he had recently returned from the Continent where the making of chemical medicines by the most respected alchemists was far more advanced than in England.

'I am confident that with my expertise and your good name,' he continued, 'we could profit by the dissemination of the knowledge of making and using of these new medicines.'

Irritated, Nicholas replied, 'Dr Freeman, I do not require your expert knowledge on this subject as I have studied the various alchemical theories extensively. I will state once again, I have not included chemical recipes in my texts. Such preparations are often made from metals and compounds in such concentrations they are more likely to kill than to cure. I prefer herbs and other natural remedies because they are most proper and effectual against disease.'

'Yet,' Dr Freeman stated confidently, 'I have recently obtained information from a reliable source that you have written a manuscript on the preparation of the most profitable of alchemical medicines, *aurum potabile*, or as the sellers of such wares call it, the philosopher's stone.'

The atmosphere of the room chilled instantly. Nicholas's furious gaze cut deeply into Dr Freeman's marrow. Barely controlling his temper, Nicholas replied briskly, 'I too have been reliably informed that you are aware of the contents of my private library. Yet, do not presume to associate me with those quack alchemists who boast they know the secrets of *aurum potabile*, or claim they can distil gold out of horsedung, or—'

His words were cut short by a violent bout of coughs, Heydon and Dr Freeman recoiled, fearful of being sprayed with bloody phlegm. Rushing to Nicholas's aid, William placed his open palm against the ailing man's chest and gently pounded his master's back with his fist. Once the spasm had passed, William assisted Nicholas in taking a draught of syrup of citron and rosemary, a soothing cordial that Nicholas himself had made in his apothecary shop. Casting a withering look upon the men who had upset his friend, William ordered them from the study.

Nicholas gasped, 'No, William, I would like to know exactly the purpose of my guests' visit.'

Trying to repair the damage done by Dr Freeman's tactlessness, Heydon said in his best ingratiating manner, 'I apologise for my friend's presumptions, Mr Culpeper. Having been on the Continent these past few years, he is unaware of the high esteem in which you are held by the common people of England who would never associate your work with quackery. We have come here today to encourage you to publish your alchemical works simply because I believe that, in order for people to identify the charlatans from the dedicated and genuine alchemists, a person such as yourself is needed to protect and uphold the reputation of that fine art.[12] People will think twice before accusing you, a learned scholar and gentleman, of being a swindling mountebank.'

Nicholas hesitated and contemplated the men standing nervously before him. For all his flattering words and claims of seeking the secrets of alchemical medicine for the good of mankind, he knew Heydon was motivated by self-seeking, material profit. Heydon and his associate believed the philosopher's stone was made in an alchemist's furnace, an object to possess. Blinded by greed, they would never discern the deep alchemical secrets that were known only by a few and so would forever be denied the true gift that is *aurum potabile*.

Clearing his throat, Nicholas articulated to ensure his meaning was clear, 'I appreciate your faith in my reputation. Nonetheless, my concern is not about being wrongly associated with quack doctors and alchemists, but rather that the entire subject of alchemy is widely misunderstood by all but the most dedicated adepts. If I do choose to share my work, I have instructed William to deliver the manuscript to scholars who will recognise its significance and value, and may employ its contents appropriately. Therefore, as far as I am concerned, gentlemen, our business is concluded.' With an unequivocal gesture of dismissal, Nicholas requested William to usher Heydon and Dr Freeman from the chamber. Resisting at first, the two men glanced at each other as if silently agreeing that, as far as they were concerned, their business was not at an end.

'I am sorry you have declined our offer, Mr Culpeper', Heydon huffed, barely concealing his fury. 'Dr Freeman and I will not trouble *you* again on this matter.'

Striding purposely from the study, Dr Freeman graced William with a withering look of contempt.

***

Chapter One

Wakehurst Place, Surrey
Thursday, 7ᵗʰ April 1656

Rounding a bend in the road, the manor house came into view. Zachariah Jenkin was relieved to have finally reached his destination.[13] Although Cromwell's Major-Generals had cleared the highways of thieves and claimed to have re-established peace in the counties, Zachariah felt anxious travelling the lonely muddy roads without an escort, a luxury he could ill afford.

Dismounting, Zachariah led the horse to a small lake a short distance from the road. An apothecary accustomed to gathering his own herbal ingredients for his salves, pills and decoctions, he was constantly aware of the bounty surrounding him as he travelled throughout the countryside. Resting on a log under the shade of an ancient willow tree, he absentmindedly gazed upon the watercress and lilies floating lazily on the water. Behind him, comfrey and goldenrod grew on the banks. From the rushes at the water's edge, he heard frogs chirping and the soft buzz of insects.

Slipping the now well-thumbed note from his pocket, he read its contents once again:

Refolding the paper, Zachariah speculated again on the possible reasons for this summons. Sir William Culpeper's titled family had owned much of the land around the village of Ockley in Surrey for generations.[14] Zachariah had been the preferred apothecary to the family for nearly twenty years. Even though he had met Sir William socially on a few brief occasions in his youth, over the years their intercourse had become reduced to merely his medicinal services to the family. Lady Jane Culpeper or one of her servants would most often consult Zachariah at his shop in the market town of Crawley in Sussex.

His lordship rarely travelled to London in these troubled times. Rarer still did he invite guests to his family estate, Wakehurst Place. Sir William avoided the political intrigues that had engulfed the country following the execution of King Charles, six years earlier. A member of the ruling elite, Sir William should rightly have supported the royalist cause. His reticence in openly supporting either side caused him to be viewed with suspicion by both the Royalists and Parliamentarians.

Thus, Zachariah was surprised when he received an invitation—or more precisely an instruction—to attend

Sir William at his ancestral home. Sir William's note was confusing. He suggested the possibility of securing Zachariah's services, but other than providing medicaments and some simple medical treatments, what other skills did Sir William assume he could offer?

Standing by the water's edge, Zachariah glanced down at his reflection. People commented on his sanguine complexion being a true reflection of his temperament. He was of medium height, fleshy but not fat, and even though he had reached his fortieth year, he had retained his mane of blackish brown hair that curled about his shoulders. As was the fashion for a man of his station, his beard and moustache were clipped modestly. As always when attending his patron, he wore his best black breeches and white linen shirt.

Bracing himself for the anticipated meeting, Zachariah decided to walk his horse the short distance to the manor. Strolling along a wide gravelled avenue bordered by tall poplars, he glimpsed the manor's ornate dormer windows peaking above a copse of trees. Erected in 1590 by Sir William's father Edward, Wakehurst Place was a large, square-shaped edifice built from local honey-coloured sandstone.[15]

Surrendering his horse to the stable-boy, Zachariah made his way to the eastern servants' entrance where he was welcomed by the housekeeper.

'Greetings, Mr Jenkin,' she said. 'Sir William is in his library. Here, let me take your bag. I will see if the master is ready to receive you.'

Zachariah waited in a long oak-panelled gallery, family portraits gracing its walls. Soon the servant reappeared and gestured to him to enter. Furtively gazing about the library at the many book cabinets lining the walls, Zachariah spotted Sir William standing near a west facing window, his features illuminated by a narrow shaft of sunlight.

Turning to face his guest, Zachariah saw Sir William had changed little since they last met. The squire was tall and lean with a melancholic-choleric complexion. In his late fifties, he had receding brown hair and an angular, beardless intelligent face. Dressed in severe but expensively cut black woollen garments, the cuffs of his linen shirt were decorated with silk embroidery. Sir William's ramrod posture and bearing, his hands clasped lightly behind his back, marked him as a refined and respectable nobleman.

'Good afternoon, Mr Jenkin,' Sir William said in his characteristically haughty tone. Not waiting for a response, he invited Zachariah to enter the chamber. As if trying to alleviate his guest's nervousness, the squire smiled and said in a softer tone, 'Here, take this seat near the window, the warm sunlight is so inviting in these chilly cavernous rooms.'

Offering Zachariah a glass of white wine, Sir William asked, 'Did you meet with any trouble? The roads continue to be unsafe, but I have not heard of any highwaymen around these parts.'

'No… err, my… err… Lord,' Zachariah replied nervously, dipping his head deferentially. He was taken aback at his host's familiarity and didn't know how to respond. Usually on meeting in public, Sir William had remained aloof. But now, in the privacy of his library, he was treating Zachariah as an acquaintance of equal standing.

Collecting a sheet of paper from his desk, the squire settled into an ornately carved and leather-lined padded chair. He stared coolly at Zachariah as if weighing him up. With the initial familiarity having evaporated, Zachariah's attention was drawn to the paper in Sir William's hand. Recognising it was a printed handbill, Zachariah's brow creased in consternation. Advertising wares or announcing upcoming events, these cheaply printed bills were commonly pasted dozens deep on walls or any flat surface where people congregated. Why was this one so important to Sir William?

In a slow measured tone Sir William said, 'I suppose you have wondered why I have asked you to the manor, Mr Jenkin? Firstly, neither I nor the members of my family require your medicinal services. Rather, I have asked you here on a delicate matter that, I believe, considering your background as well as your past and present business associates, you are the best person I can approach with this task.'

Feeling bewildered, Zachariah waited while Sir William appeared to be struggling to articulate his thoughts.

'As you may recall,' he continued, 'I secured your services soon after you had completed your apprenticeship following a recommendation from my now deceased relative, Mr Nicholas Culpeper. He had introduced us during one of his visits to the manor a year or so earlier, I believe.'

'Err… yes, I recall our first meeting,' Zachariah replied cautiously. 'Nicholas was eager to introduce me to his mother who lived in Isfield. We took the opportunity to visit Wakehurst Place. He told me that, whilst you were a distant relative, he preferred to think of you as a patron…' Zachariah's explanation trailed off, as he suddenly realised that he was being too familiar with his lordship.

Zachariah never really knew how Sir William felt about

Nicholas and had always avoided reminding Sir William of this friendship. Nicholas had, after all, sullied the ancient and titled name of Culpeper by his support of Cromwell and the Parliamentarians against the monarchy during the early years of the Civil War. If that wasn't bad enough, Sir William's wayward cousin came to prominence just after the execution of the King in 1649 following his translation of the College of Physicians' medicinal books. The reactionary and provocative comments Nicholas inserted in the prefaces, usually directed against supporters of King Charles and the professions, caused uproar amongst Nicholas's gentlemanly peers. Nicholas's behaviour often resulted in adverse reactions from Sir William's family, who felt their social standing was threatened by the antics of their radical and outspoken distant relative.

'How well did you know Nicholas?' Sir William asked, interrupting Zachariah's reminiscences.

'We were associates and friends,' he replied tentatively. 'But, as you would well understand, the war disrupted many people's lives. While I chose to focus on establishing my apothecary practice and trading company in Crawley, Nicholas became heavily involved in the parliamentary cause, and due to a lack of funds he was unable to complete his apprenticeship.[16] Soon after the events of '43 when the Parliamentarians began to organise and train men in readiness for war, I left London to establish my practice in Crawley. So, my close association with Nicholas naturally waned.'

'Yes, I recall your arrival in Crawley all those years ago. Does this mean that you did not maintain contact?'

'We established a regular correspondence and, on occasion, we would meet in London. I understand he continued his illicit apothecary practice, as well as providing remedies and medical advice to the poor. Following his success with the translation of the College's *Pharmacopeia*, he embarked on the translation and authorship of other medicinal books. His books were easy to use because he provided simple instructions on self-treatment and the use of herbs from local fields and gardens rather than having to buy expensive medicines from apothecaries or rely on the advice of physicians.'[17]

'Yes, yes, but what of his attracting the attention of the Society?'

'It was reported in the *Mercurius Pragmaticus*[18] of the College of Physicians' hostile response to his translation of their *Pharmacopeia* into English,' Zachariah offered. 'I do believe the Society of Apothecaries welcomed the translation, even though they never admitted it publicly. Many apothecaries cannot read or write Latin and so the translation provided them with access to the physicians' medicinal and herbal secrets.'[19]

Satisfied with answering Sir William's questions honestly while defending his friend's name and reputation, Zachariah waited apprehensively for his host's response.

Yet Sir William remained silent, seeming to observe his guest while weighing in his mind whether to proceed.

'Sadly, I had not seen Nicholas for more than eighteen years,' he began. 'Nonetheless, I am aware of his translations and had read in the gazettes of the controversies they generated. However, for the moment that is not why I asked you here.'

Sir William offered Zachariah the handbill. 'Do you

know anything of this?'

Wiping his sweating hands on his breeches, Zachariah took the paper and tried to decipher its faded and smudged lettering. Feeling somewhat inferior in the company of a man who was known for his scholasticism, and slowly forming each word individually, Zachariah spoke the title:

> *Virtues, use and variety of operations of the true and philosophical Aurum Potabile. Now made and sold by Dr Freeman, as also by Dr Harrington, and me Nicholas Culpeper, in Spitalfields.*[20]

Zachariah nervously glanced up at Sir William. Impatiently, he gestured Zachariah to continue reading. Feeling stricken and confused, his now trembling hands making reading even more difficult, Zachariah laboriously deciphered the text:

> This precious jewel of *aurum potabile*, which Dr Freeman and myself have attained to the perfection thereof, is now only in the hands of Dr Freeman and myself and Dr Harrington, who hath long and often tried and known the virtues, use and manner of operation thereof, to the great comfort of many who have diseases, which otherwise might have proved inseparable and incurable—[21]

'Here, let me see that,' Sir William snapped impatiently, grabbing the handbill from Zachariah's grasp. Scanning the page, he confidently read snatches of its contents:

> It cures all agues ... cures diverse people of that most horrid putrid fever ... cures gout of all sorts perfectly ... It's a universal fortification for all complexions and ages against all sorts of degrees of pestilential and contagious infection[22]

'You can read it in more detail later, Mr Jenkin,' Sir

William said as he placed the handbill back on the table. Gesturing at the bill, he asked, 'So, Mr Jenkin, what do you make of it?'

'I don't know what to say. I don't believe Nicholas was involved in the production of the kind of alchemical medicines sold by street charlatans and quack doctors. I just do not really know…' his voice trailed off.

'Do you know Dr Freeman and Dr Harrington?'

'I don't recognise the names,' Zachariah stated emphatically. 'After I moved to Crawley, over time my contacts with Nicholas increasingly became few and fleeting, mostly restricted to correspondences. We met for the last time about five years ago, and then only briefly. I don't recall him ever mentioning those names. I hadn't even been informed of his death. Instead, I found out from his obituary in the press.'

Feeling confused, Zachariah gulped his wine, his hand trembling so much he feared spilling the expensive liquor.

Aware of his guest's discomfiture, Sir William responded kindly, 'Mr Jenkin, I realised many years ago that you felt uncomfortable discussing Nicholas in my company. I assumed it was because you feared my views of his involvement in the war as well as his subsequent association with political sectarians and radicals.' Smiling reassuringly he added, 'Yet, unbeknownst to you, I was sympathetic to his position and he understood this. Did you know that he had dedicated one of his publications to me?'

While Sir William was busy searching his shelves, Zachariah took a large draught of wine in an attempt to calm his nerves. Always prone to sweaty hands when nervous, he once again wiped them discreetly on his breeches.

Sir William returned with two large leather-bound books. He offered the smaller to Zachariah. Opening the cover, Zachariah scanned the title: *Catastrophe Magnatum, the Fall of the Monarchie … by Nicholas Culpeper Gentleman, Student in Astrology and Physic.*[23] Bemused, Zachariah glanced up. Sir William gestured to him to continue. Lifting the book closer to his face and peering at the letters before him, Zachariah continued:

> 'To the right worshipful Sir William Culpeper Knight and Baronet, Nicholas Culpeper wishes health wealth and peace in this world, and a crown of glory in that to come.'[24]

Taking the book from Zachariah, Sir William turned the page.

'I will not read the entire epistle,' he said. 'Briefly, Nicholas acknowledges the close association that had existed between my father and his, and the subsequent friendship that developed between us during our youth. He also mentions that while we had not seen each other for many years, we maintained links through other members of the Culpeper family.'

Closing the book and placing it on the table, Sir William continued, 'My patronage continued a long tradition between our families, which began when one of his predecessors fell into debt. Nicholas's father and grandfather before him entered the Church, and my family provided them with a parish and small rectory in Ockley.[25] Nicholas was supposed to have followed their example, but as you know, his life took other avenues.'

Glancing towards the window, Sir William paused and sighed.

Turning his attention back to his guest, he continued, 'As

you may know, Nicholas never knew his father, the Reverend Nicholas Culpeper. He died just prior to his birth. I regret to say my father, Sir Edward, was not very charitable to the Reverend's widow, Mary. He withdrew his patronage, forcing her to return to her father's rectory in Isfield in Sussex.[26] Later, he tried to make amends by inviting the young Nicholas to Wakehurst Place, where he was trained up as a gentleman, but the stain of his conduct bothered him.[27] Hence, when Nicholas approached me to be his patron, I knew he was in financial difficulties, so I agreed and when he died, I continued to provide some monetary support for his widow, Alice.'[28]

Abruptly changing the subject, Sir William grasped the handbill and said, 'The servant who found this informs me that it has only just appeared on the streets of London. But did you notice the date at the bottom? It is January 1st 1653. Just over a year before Nicholas's death. What do you make of this?'

'Sir William, I reiterate I do not believe Nicholas would stoop to the level of the mountebanks who ply their dubious wares on every street corner, promising universal cures for halfpenny a dose. My only explanation for the early date is forgery. These quacks have used his good name to sell their wares. As you well know, any book claiming to be by Nicholas Culpeper is assured excellent sales. The date of Nicholas's death would be well known, and so to put such an early date on that bill would have been for the sole purpose of seeking legitimisation for this advertised potion.'

'So, are you suggesting that the contents of this bill are current, but it has been backdated through an act of deception? This would suggest Dr Freeman and Dr Harrington are selling this elixir *aurum potabile* in Nicholas's home in Spitalfields where his widow Alice continues to reside. It would appear, Mr Jenkin, that Alice is supporting herself very well on the proceeds of this universal medicine.'

Ah! Zachariah thought, so Sir William was concerned that his widowed relative was receiving money from her husband's family, when in fact she was making a significant profit from Nicholas's publications and medicinal recipes, supposedly of his own concoction. Zachariah wondered if Sir William expected him to intervene in this business arrangement. Why, he had no idea. Sir William could simply cease providing the funds himself without assistance from anyone.

His tongue loosened by too much wine, Zachariah blurted, 'If you are concerned the widow Culpeper is taking advantage of you, why don't you simply cease providing her with funds?'

Sir William reeled back in his chair as if Zachariah had physically struck him. His face darkened with fury, Sir William shot back, 'Mr Jenkin! Do not presume to tell me how to attend my business.'

A shocked silence descended. Zachariah's nervousness transformed into terror so profound he was rendered speechless. Even though the son of a very wealthy merchant and having in turn succeeded in his trade, Zachariah understood his station was well below that of a titled nobleman.[29] Accustomed to speaking his mind in the company of his peers, he had momentarily forgotten that he was, after all, only Sir William's servant.

Sir William abruptly rose from his chair, turned and

gazed out of the mullioned window. Zachariah sat silently berating himself for his rudeness.

Eventually Sir William returned to his seat and said, 'I will overlook your indiscretion, Mr Jenkin. This time!'

In a more congenial tone he continued, 'I think you misunderstand me, Mr Jenkin. Over the years, I have purchased all of Nicholas's publications. He claimed in his earlier works that his intention was to create a new method of medical practice by blending astrology with medicine.[30] The success of his later works indicates that he had achieved his aims. Unlike the allegations of the College, Nicholas was not one of these charlatans who swindled the unwary. Certainly, he was not formally qualified, but he was well versed in medical knowledge and practice. Furthermore, my studies into his new methods suggest that he may have actually discovered a recipe for a wondrous universal medicine. What do they call such an illustrious elixir? A philosopher's stone, as claimed by his widow.'

Offering the other book he had retrieved from the cabinet, he continued, 'Have you read his most recent publication?'

Titled *A New Method of Physic, or a Short View of Paracelsus and Galen's Practice*,[31] Zachariah noticed the book was dated 1654, the same year as Nicholas's death. Remembering that his friend had died in the second week of January that year, this tome must have been one of the first of many posthumous publications attributed to him. Concerned that his patron may not be aware of this, Zachariah asked if he was confident the book was actually one of Nicholas's, explaining that some unscrupulous stationers were publishing books in his name, but which he actually didn't pen or translate himself.

'I also suggest the handbill has been fraudulently dated to make it appear authentic,' he added.

Sir William nodded in agreement, but gestured to the book they were examining, as if the matter of the bill was settled. 'If you read the epistle, Mr Jenkin, you will see the book is an English translation from Latin, originally authored by the German physician, Partlicius. Nicholas wrote that he had completed the translation in 1651, but chose not to release it for publication. Apparently, he was concerned that as the Parliament had not finalised laws to protect original work, other authors would appropriate his translation for their own ends.[32] Unfortunately, before he had time to complete a full translation, his health began to deteriorate. If you turn to the end of the epistle, you will see that it is dated the twelfth of November 1653.'

Sir William took the book from Zachariah and quickly flicked through the pages. 'Ah, here it is. What do you make of this?' he said:

'Of the nature of physic and alchemy … The body of physic is the content of a huge sort of precepts gathered together and founded upon certain principles, where they are either congruous to one another, or at least seem to be. That which we call the second is either the first, or the daughter of the first. The first is practice: the daughters of the first are either the eldest or the youngest. The eldest as rule and hermetic philosophy …'[33]

Running his finger down the page, he resumed:

'Hermetical philosophy was invented by Hermes Trigmegistos and others in our times, it is as it were revived from the dead by Paracelsus and seems now like a new model of physic.'[34]

Bemused, Zachariah didn't respond.

'Are you familiar with the subjects of Hermetic philosophy and Paracelsus, Mr Jenkin?' Sir William said.

'I do know Nicholas referred to the philosophy in his medical texts,' Zachariah replied. 'But I never really understood how it was related to his astrology and physic.'

He explained to his patron what little he knew of Paracelsus, that he was a German physician and apothecary who, during the previous century, had developed new ways of making medicines using alchemical methods in order to improve their effectiveness. Even though these methods were embraced by the Europeans, in England they were often criticised because the language of alchemists was associated with religious sectarians and political radicals.

'I have not read very much on Paracelsus or the Hermetic philosophies,' Sir William admitted. 'But I am aware that, while resisted here in England, they do hold currency on the Continent where aspects of his chemical and philosophical theories have been put to practical uses. That is why I believe Nicholas may have discovered a new universal medicine!'

Zachariah's silence prompted Sir William to state specifically the purpose of summoning his apothecary to the manor.

'As you well know, Mr Jenkin, from the first publication of his *Physical Directory*, just over seven years ago and up to the present day, the name Nicholas Culpeper has generated controversy. Opinions of him and his publications vary considerably, especially among the middling sort and traders.[35] Much has been written on billboards, published in the press, and discussed in the taverns. Even in the Parliament, the universities and the pulpit there has been much discussion about Mr Culpeper's character, his motivations for writing, translating and publishing, his medical expertise, and his astrological predictions, not to mention his involvement with sectarians and Cromwell's cause. Yet, very little commentary or opinions have been published about his new model of physic[36] and whether or not his ideas are valid. I believe they are. I believe the controversy surrounding this universal medicine may be concealing or diverting attention away from the possibility that Mr Culpeper did create a recipe for a universal elixir or philosopher's stone. But I need evidence this is so.'

Pausing, Sir William waited for Zachariah to respond, but he just stared back.

'Have you any experience in the making of alchemical medicines, Mr Jenkin?' Sir William prompted.

'I know how to prepare and apply such wares. I also order chemical medicines from London and distribute them to my customers throughout this region. But I prefer not to prepare them myself,' Zachariah said. 'The process involves the use of distilleries and furnaces. As my workshops are at the rear of my living chambers in the High street, I fear I may cause an explosion that could harm or even kill my family.'

'Did your trading associates have any connection with Nicholas? And if so, do you they think may have any reliable information on this universal medicine?'

'Yes, they did and I believe so,' Zachariah replied warily, as he began to suspect why he had been summoned.

'If this medicine proves to be a universal elixir, I am

prepared to maintain my support for the widow Culpeper as well as her attempts to continue her deceased husband's business,' Sir William explained. 'Yet, I am concerned the unfortunate reputation Nicholas created for himself may obstruct people's acceptance that he did indeed discover the secrets of the alchemical philosophers. I therefore require a reliable person to undertake an investigation into the perceptions and opinions of the people who knew him. He will need to be able to assess the validity or worthiness of Nicholas's associates' and critics' views, and especially if they are able to provide any reliable information on his alchemical knowledge and practices.'

Allowing Zachariah a moment to digest his comments, Sir William eventually broke the silence by asking, 'Do you think you are capable of undertaking this investigation, Mr Jenkin?'

Zachariah was startled by Sir William's request for his assistance. Not knowing how to respond, he hesitated.

Seeking to persuade Zachariah further, Sir William added, 'I do not think it appropriate that I undertake this investigation myself. Firstly, people will tell a person of my station that which they believe I wish to hear rather than speak the truth. Secondly, I need someone with knowledge of chemical medicines who can competently determine if people are speaking the truth. Lastly, I need a man whom I can trust and who knew Nicholas. You, Mr Jenkin, are that man.'

Flattered by Sir William's comments, but feeling over-whelmed and unsure he was as confident as Sir William presumed, Zachariah stuttered, 'Err... um... Sir William, I am at a loss as to how to respond. I believe I could determine if the universal medicine were genuine, but it may take weeks to investigate these other matters. While my apprentice and Mrs Jenkin could manage the shop and my trading business, London is an expensive city—'

'If you undertake this task, I will provide you with all the funds you require,' Sir William interrupted. 'Furthermore, I will pay for your time and, if you can provide evidence of its worth, I will instruct you to notify the widow Culpeper of my business proposition. If she accepts my offer of further patronage, I will insist that you be charged with its distribution.'

Startled at such a generous offer, Zachariah was speechless.

Smiling, Sir William rose from his chair. 'I think it best I leave you for a few minutes to give you time to consider my proposal.'

Zachariah watched as Sir William strode confidently from the chamber. He remained seated for several minutes. Gazing out of the window, he mulled over Sir William's proposition. From personal experience of being accosted by travelling mountebanks claiming to possess universal medicines supposedly made from powdered gold and other mysterious and exotic ingredients, he was dubious of this latest concoction. All of the preparations he had seen thus far not only did not extend life, they often contained poisonous ingredients that actually shortened it.

For all of his faults, Zachariah knew his friend had been an honest man who had often condemned the sellers and makers of such elixirs. If Sir William was correct and Nicholas was well versed in Paracelsian and alchemical medicines, as well as this Hermetic philosophy, he may have discovered such a recipe. Furthermore, if the investigations were productive, and this universal medicine was proved genuine, then he would also profit. After weighing the issues in his mind, Zachariah decided that he would accept the proposition.

When Sir William returned, he asked gently, 'Have you come to a decision as yet?'

'Yes, I have decided to accept the task,' Zachariah replied. 'It would also give me the opportunity to try to understand a man who was a friend, companion and confidant during my youth, but in the light of this matter over this universal elixir, it appears he was someone I never really knew. If, as you suspect, there is some truth in the claims about this universal medicine and you are able to persuade the widow Culpeper to accept your continued patronage and my right to distribute the medicine, then I would be a fool to refuse your request.'

Appearing very pleased with Zachariah's comments, Sir William replied enthusiastically, 'Oh, I believe that we will all benefit if you can achieve the outcomes I seek. I would like to be able to counter the allegations and condemnations he received throughout his life, not just for the benefit of his memory, but also as it would ease the problems he has caused for his extended noble family. If we can provide evidence that he was not a charlatan, but rather that his new model of physic was and remains effective, then all the people who rely on his medical texts will also benefit. Most especially, the College and Society of Apothecaries will no longer be able to besmirch his memory and continue their sullying of my noble and distinguished name.'

Sir William withdrew a cloth bag and a folded piece of

paper from a polished wooden box. 'I believe three pounds will cover your expenses,' he said as he offered the bag of coins to Zachariah. 'If you require any extra, send me a message and I will arrange additional funds with my banker in London.'

Three pounds! That is the amount I spend on my entire household in a month, Zachariah thought, trying to conceal his surprise.

Sir William then offered the paper. 'While I would prefer discretion, if you believe you will not gain admittance or that others are thwarting your efforts, you can present this letter of introduction which I believe will loosen the tongues of those who may be reluctant to assist you. While its contents inform that you are acting on my behalf, it does not elaborate in what capacity. I encourage you to be tactful. During your investigations, please practice caution and only reveal our association if it is absolutely necessary. Do not broach the subject of the universal medicine too soon.' Raising his eyebrow, he added, 'I believe you understand my meaning?'

Quailing at the thought of the quest before him, Zachariah could only nod in agreement, not really sure he did understand his host's comment.

Sir William smiled reassuringly. 'I think I have said enough. Also as Lady Culpeper has asked for your counsel about medicinal matters, I believe we should bring this meeting to an end.' Escorting Zachariah from the library, Sir William paused. 'Oh, before you go, I will lend you my copy of *A New Method of Physic*. Read it carefully, as I suspect it may contain clues to this elixir. Feel free to purchase any other books you feel may be useful.'

'Sir William, I will travel to London as soon as possible

and try to gather the information you have requested. If needed, I will send word. I assure you I will maintain a record of my encounters and discoveries.'

As he rode northwest back to Crawley, Zachariah reflected on the strange conversation. Considering further on the issues involved, he decided he could collect information on Nicholas the man by approaching his associates and friends in London. However, he was not confident of discovering the secrets behind the universal medicine, or the mysteries that surrounded Mr Nicholas Culpeper.

***

Chapter Two

Dolphin Inn, Aldgate
Monday, 28th April 1656

The young ruffian grabbed Zachariah's packs.

'Hey you,' he shouted, lunging for the boy. He had only just arrived at his destination and it seemed he was already being robbed.

'Ya dun'na understand,' the boy cried, struggling in Zachariah's grasp. 'The mistress ain't here, so she told me to take guests to der rooms.'

Letting him go, Zachariah turned and inspected the premises where he expected to spend the next few days. The Dolphin Inn was on the main highway just outside of Bishopsgate, north of London. It was within walking distance of Nicholas's house in Spitalfields, as well as convenient to London's other main thoroughfares.

Zachariah followed the servant through an alley between street-front shops, wide enough to accommodate delivery carts and hackney coaches.

'Ya room's up there, sir,' the servant shouted, pointing to an open gallery running the entire length of the second storey of a large half-timbered building.

Zachariah heard snatches of music and revelry coming from a dining room below. From the single-storey kitchen an inviting aroma of roasting meat caused his stomach to complain. But a whiff of a cloying odour from the latrines soon stayed his hunger.

Turning his attention back to the servant, he saw the boy was already up at the gallery, leaning over the rail, staring impatiently down at Zachariah.

On his reaching the landing, the boy said to Zachariah, 'Tha mistress says ya to 'ave one of our smaller chambers to ya self.'

Zachariah was relieved. He didn't relish the idea of sharing the standard dormitory found in most inns, even those of better quality, especially considering that stored away in his bags was the valuable book Sir William had given over to his care.

'Ere's ya key, suppa's at sundan,' the boy said backing out of the room. About to close the door behind him he turned and said grinning, 'Oh! Ya've missed da mid-day meal, but dere's food sellars down near tha gate.'

Finally alone, Zachariah inspected his chamber. Above one of the two beds was a niche suitable for the storage of books. Two pewter candlesticks and a glass-fronted lantern rested on a small pine table between the beds. Above the table, dappled light leaked through shuttered slats shielding the single glass-paned window. The only other pieces of furniture were a couple of stools and a large, iron banded oak chest secured with a strong lock and key.

Carefully removing Sir William's book and two of his own medicinal texts from their protective cloths, he placed them neatly on the shelf. Authored by Nicholas, Zachariah had read his copies many times, but he planned to reread them in a new light in the hope of discerning any clues as to

Nicholas's association with the alchemical arts.

Under his feet, Zachariah felt the resonance of music and singing. The rollicking ribald tune from a balladeer helped dispel a morose mood beginning to descend upon him. For a moment he thought of joining in the merriment, but quickly changed his mind. He was too fatigued from a long day of travel. Instead, he put his mind to planning how he would approach Alice Culpeper the next morning. She had not responded to his letter notifying her of his impending visit. He would go to Spitalfields anyway. If he was successful and she could answer his question, Zachariah hoped his stay at the Dolphin Inn would be very short indeed.

* * *

It had been many years since Zachariah had walked the narrow lanes of Spitalfields. Where paddocks once bordered Bishopsgate Street, now rows of brick and wooden buildings leaned out over a rutted muddy thoroughfare. Turning east down a lane, he soon came to a large field where cattle grazed. Opposite, he spied a familiar pair of houses.

Zachariah examined the dwellings Nicholas had built with his young wife's dowry. He had chosen this inconvenient site because, as it was outside London's walls, it was beyond the jurisdiction of the College of Physicians. This enabled him to operate an unlicensed apothecary shop without fear of prosecution. The southernmost house had tall, wide mullioned windows which filled the rooms with afternoon sun. It had served as Nicholas's apothecary shop while his study and consulting room were on the floor above.[37] The adjoining house was the family's residence.

'Well, Zachariah, this is it! Stay calm,' he whispered through clenched teeth. Steeling his nerves, he knocked on the residence's front door and waited. No response. Disappointed, he thought his trip was a waste, as no-one seemed to be home. Walking over to the shop, he rapped loudly on the door. As a tattered bed-sheet covered the shop window, he feared he would not receive an answer.

'Who is it?' a muffled voice cried out.

Startled, it took a moment for him to reply. 'Er… it's Mr Zachariah Jenkin from Crawley, Surrey. I sent word of my visit a week or so ago. I am here to pay my respects to the widow Culpeper.'

The door burst open. Standing before him was a tall, gaunt woman. An expression of sheer delight lit her care-worn features.

'Oh, it's you, Master Jenkin,' she said raising her arms in welcome. 'I can't recall the last time I set eyes upon you. Let me think… ah… it must be more than seventeen years.'

Standing aside and ushering in her guest, she continued, 'Come in, come in, that way, down the hall to the workroom. I trust you remember the way.'

Speechless, Zachariah could only nod his head in confusion as he was bundled in and propelled down the narrow hall. It was not until he had almost been thrust onto a stool that he had time to orientate himself.

Zachariah stared up at the woman looming above him. His gaze was drawn to a bruise extending from her right cheek to her ear. Most people would have thought the blemish was caused by an angry husband. But Zachariah knew better. He recognised that bruise. The woman fussing over him was Nicholas's childhood nurse and, later, his mother's companion, Miss Jane Wilson.[38]

'Hello, Jane,' Zachariah said meekly. 'Please forgive me. I was rather taken aback at seeing you here after all these years.'

Smiling silently, Jane turned her attention to a pan simmering on the hearth.

Thinking he had disturbed her in the middle of preparing a herbal infusion, Zachariah sat quietly observing his surroundings. He recognised the chamber. It hadn't changed much since he had been there last, nearly twenty years before.

He was sitting in Nicholas's workshop. Early morning sunlight streamed through the window, dust motes dancing in its beams. Bunches of bound herbs hanging from hooks filled the air with a myriad of scents. Bulging sacks leaned haphazardly against the walls; boxes stacked under tables; shelves straining under the weight of pewter and earthenware containers of all shapes and sizes. Dominating the room was a sturdy pine table littered with utensils, its surface polished from years of use.

As he gazed about, he detected another distinct aroma—sweet vanilla tobacco. He remembered. Nicholas! In all his years of enduring the choking clouds of tobacco smoke in taverns and other diverse chambers, in only one had he ever smelt this particular odour: Nicholas's residence. Preparing his own tobacco mix, Nicholas had added expensive vanilla and other select spices to produce a milder, sweet blend he had claimed was gentler on his ailing lungs. Having spent so much time in his residence and apothecary chambers, Zachariah mused, the smoke must have well-penetrated the beams and walls, and lingered still. The notion comforted

Zachariah, because it was as if his friend's spirit remained in residence, looking down on his family.

Zachariah thought of the last time he had seen Jane. It was during one of his visits to Nicholas's childhood home in the village of Isfield in Surrey. Then, Jane's face had been fleshy and, while blemished, her skin glowed with a healthy rosy hue. Now her hooked nose dominated pinched features with dry thin skin stretched over sharp jaw bones. The red birthmark had darkened to an old bruise.

Sensing that Zachariah was staring at her, she turned and their eyes met and held for a few seconds. Embarrassed, Zachariah glanced away and then down to his feet.

Zachariah silently berated himself for goggling at Jane's blemish. Years past, Jane had masked much of her face with a close-fitting starched linen cap that concealed her ears and much of her face. She had tried all kinds of herbal treatments to bleach the stain to no avail. But her attitude to the blemish must have changed over the years. Now her cap wasn't large enough even to hide her tightly bound grey hair. Also evident was a change in Jane's attire. Her bodice and skirt were made from thread-bare russet wool, patched and fading, a state of dress she would not have tolerated back in Isfield.

Offering a mug of water to Zachariah, Jane settled on the bench opposite. Zachariah gazed at Jane in silence, her presence in Nicholas's shop disorientating him.

'You are wondering what I am doing here, Master Jenkin?'

'Err. Yes. And please call me Zachariah. After all, while we may have lost contact many years ago, my memories of the days we would spend wandering the meadows around Isfield are some of my happiest.'

'Ah, Isfield,' Jane said. 'Yes, I recall those hot summer days when we would escape the rectory.' Laughing, she added, 'And Nicholas would make his apologies to his grandfather—who had wished to read him some new sermon—with the excuse that you and he needed to learn more about the local medicinal plants.'

They both laughed as their shared memories began to heal bonds frayed by years of separation.

'Nicholas once told me that his generosity of inviting me down to Isfield was actually an act of self-interest', Zachariah said. 'My presence was supposed to act as a foil against his grandfather. Nicholas called the old man an over-zealous conservative Puritan. Such a domineering and controlling figure must have made Nicholas's life in the rectory almost unbearable—'

'Oh, the pan!' Jane interrupted as she jumped from the bench.

Reaching for the pan, Jane poured the boiling liquid into a clay vessel filled with green leaves and began to vigorously stir. As he watched her prepare the herbal concoction, Zachariah reminisced over those days long past when he first encountered Nicholas's grandfather, the formidable Reverend William Attersoll.

Nicholas had told Zachariah of his grandfather. Upon meeting him, Zachariah concurred with his friend's descriptions. Well educated, the Reverend had written several treatises on theology. He held extreme conservative theological views, which led to him being ostracised from both his own family and his parishioners.[39] A fervent believer in predestination, he lectured his parishioners and grandson that God had already separated the saved from the damned. A person's natural behaviour and tendencies were evidence of their status. So many people spent their lives obsessively self-reflecting, seeking evidence of their election, or conversely, damnation.[40] Attersoll would therefore have condemned any wilful act of Nicholas's as evidence he was beyond redemption and so would forever be separated from God.

While Zachariah's parents had been observant Puritans, they had never threatened him or his siblings with terrors of eternal damnation. Even so, as an adult, doubts over the fate of his soul sometimes caused him nightmares. How it affected a young innocent and vulnerable mind was beyond contemplation. From Nicholas's occasional episodes of fervent religiosity, evidently it left indelible marks. Unbeknownst to him at this time, Zachariah would soon learn the life-long consequences Reverend Attersoll's fanatical sermons on predestination had had on the mind of his grandson.

Her task completed, Jane returned to the table, whereupon Zachariah continued his reminiscences. 'I remember Nicholas telling me that he was inspired by his mother's skills in the finding and use of local herbs. I must admit, I was rather sceptical at first, but a few days with you and his mother changed my perception of the knowledge of local wise-women. I had been taught such women were superstitious and ignorant. It was a rude shock to realise that not all wisdom was contained in books.'

'Ah, Zachariah, I don't agree. Do you remember how Nicholas took it upon himself to teach me my letters by reading from a book on herbs and then instructing me to follow?'

Chuckling, Zachariah replied, 'More to the point, he

would confuse you by making you read a passage and then tell you the author was an ignoramus who didn't know a herb from a tree!'

Their laughter petered out into a comfortable shared silence. Zachariah felt a warm glow suffuse his body as he remembered how Jane would fuss over him as much as she did Nicholas, as if he were a naughty boy needing guidance and direction.

Jane's voice drew him back to the present. 'Zachariah,' she said kindly, 'do you recall Nicholas's mother becoming sick while he was still an apprentice? He persuaded her to move to London so he could try to alleviate her affliction? Naturally, I accompanied her. I then nursed her till she succumbed to the disease that quickly consumed her body.'[41]

'I recall that time, Jane,' Zachariah replied wistfully. 'Nicholas wrote to me of those events. Against his better judgement he sought the services of a physician from the College, who prescribed an ointment made from red lead. He made up the ointment himself. I recall he said you applied it daily.'

'The biting and burning ointment only made things worse, Zachariah. I tried to persuade Nicholas to use soothing herbs, but he was in such a distraught state he wouldn't listen. Eventually, the lump burst. Soon after, in great pain, Mary died.[42] After her burial I returned home to spend time with my brothers in Isfield. But they made it clear they could not support me and I could not secure regular employment.'

Jane rose, collected the mugs, and rinsed them in a basin beside the hearth. Zachariah sensed she was agitated.

'Hearing of my situation, Nicholas was kind enough to invite me into his home. Soon after my arrival in '44, he became embroiled in the battles and was shot in the chest.[43] Alice couldn't cope, so I nursed him like I had nursed his mother.'

Jane lapsed into silence as if these memories brought back all the pain. Sighing, she continued, 'Zachariah, he never really recovered from his wound. So, I began to assist him here, preparing medicines and serving in the shop. I also managed his new household and cared for Alice's succession of sickly children. Nicholas made provisions for me on his deathbed. He made Alice promise that my place here was secured.'

With an obviously strained and forced laugh she turned to face him and said, 'So here I am!'

Zachariah suspected Jane was withholding something. There was a discrepancy between what she was saying and her agitated state. Whilst the smile remained on her lips, her eyes betrayed a sense of distress.

'So, enough of my story!' she deflected, 'What brings you to London, Zachariah?'

Zachariah hesitated, unsure of how much he should confide. During his youth, he had liked and respected this woman who was nearly twenty years older than he. She had been deeply committed to Nicholas and his mother. Yet, what about now, where did her loyalties lie? Not wishing to deceive this kindly woman, he decided not to mention his true task until he could determine if she was sympathetic.

'I am in London for the next few days acting on behalf of a distant relative of Nicholas's, Sir William Culpeper,' Zachariah began. 'You may recall that Sir William was Nicholas's childhood friend and later his patron. He asked me to visit his widow, Alice, to see how she is faring.'

Jane's response was intriguing. Looking away, it was as if she were embarrassed, her face held a frozen smile. Suddenly, she rose from her stool, poured the now cooled herbal mixture into a large stone mortar and begin to grind with a heavy pestle. While concentrating on her task, she said with deliberation, 'Zachariah, it's obvious you don't know. It's no longer the widow Culpeper. It's Mrs Alice Heydon. Alice recently married a Mr John Heydon.'

'No… no. I was unaware she had remarried,' Zachariah replied, shocked at this unexpected information. Sir William had not mentioned Alice's recent marriage. He surmised that Sir William must also be unaware of Alice's new circumstances. If he had, his financial obligations towards her would have been immediately severed. More intriguingly, she married the man who was implicated in the promotion of the elixir.

Putting the pestle down a little too hard on the table, Jane turned to face Zachariah and said, 'I fear, Zachariah, there are quite a few things you don't know about. May I speak plainly? I trust you are the same man whom I knew when you visited Isfield? I hope so, because I'm putting my faith in you. So I beg of you, don't repeat what I am about to tell you.'

'Certainly Jane, I will respect your confidences.'

'I remember you were a close and supportive friend of Nicholas's during your apprenticeship together. I know his mother wished he had as much good sense and discernment as you. She always trusted you, Zachariah, and now I am putting my trust in you.'

Taking her seat again, Jane explained how she had tried to raise her concerns with Alice about her new husband's intentions, but was quickly put in her place.

'Alice has been seduced by Mr Heydon's charms and believes every tale he weaves. She will not hear of any criticism against her new husband. I don't even bother trying to talk to Nicholas's so-called friends and associates. They seem more concerned with trying to profit from his books and steal away his manuscripts. They claim they have Nicholas's best interests at heart, but really, I don't trust them. I tried to talk to Nicholas's secretary, Mr William Ryves, but he is reluctant to become involved, claiming no-one has the power to stand up to Mr Heydon. So, I haven't had anyone to turn to.'

Glancing away, trying to hide her distress, she took a deep breath and said, 'While Alice was a widow, my position in this household was safe as she depended on me. Also, her young daughter Mary thinks of me like a grandparent. But now Alice is married, I fear attracting Mr Heydon's attention, lest he decides my services are no longer needed. I am too old to find another position and I don't have anywhere else to go.'

'Jane, Jane, please do not fret. I can assure you I will not betray you. I am here to support you and I believe my task would have met with Nicholas's approval.'

Jane's quizzical expression suggested to Zachariah that he had inadvertently admitted that there was more to his presence than just visiting Alice.

Appearing somewhat encouraged, Jane rose from her stool, strode toward the window and stood with her back to Zachariah. Without turning she said, 'Zachariah, there is something not right going on in this house, which has had the effect of sullying and besmirching the good name of Nicholas Culpeper. And,' she continued, pointing to something beyond Zachariah's sight, 'it has something to do with that new building.'

Zachariah approached the window. The scenery had changed significantly. Gone was the muddy forecourt littered with broken bricks, stacks of timber and roofing shingles. The yard was now paved. To the rear were stables. Beyond were overgrown and neglected fields. Near the stables was what appeared to be a recently constructed brick building, its slate roof dominated by a large chimney stack.

'What is it?' he asked, his breath misting the window glass.

'Do you recall I mentioned that I gladly worked for Nicholas in preparing his medicines? I still do so here in this rear chamber, but Mr Heydon and his associates have taken over the selling of the wares in the front shop. I am no longer allowed in there, nor to serve customers. Nor am I allowed to enter that building,' she said, pointing accusingly at the strange new construction. 'But something is going on in there that's not right. They are making something and selling it in the shop, claiming it's a universal medicine that will cure all ailments. Mr Heydon rarely speaks of his business in my hearing. But I have seen the handbills pasted on walls and posts all around London. He is promoting a new medicine he calls 'orrum potabal', or something like that. And worst of all, Mr Heydon asserts the medicine is from a recipe discovered by Nicholas that he has published in a book of the same name as this mysterious elixir.'

If Zachariah hadn't been completely flabbergasted by the news of Alice's recent marriage, he certainly was now. Without having to pry or persuade, Jane had revealed exactly what had bought him to London. He could also understand why this woman, whom he had remembered as having a shy but happy disposition, was now haggard and melancholic. He realised he may be the first person to whom she felt she could unburden herself of these recent events that she believed were besmirching Nicholas's good name. No wonder she was so eager to share her concerns, he thought.

Zachariah gently placed his hand on Jane's shoulder and said, 'Jane, you have honoured me with your confidence. It is only right that I offer to you the reasons why I have called upon Alice… Heydon.'

Guiding her back to her stool and drawing another up to sit beside her, Zachariah briefly explained the task with which Sir William had charged him. In the light of Jane's comment about Nicholas's friends profiting from his name, he refrained from mentioning Sir William's vested interests.

'My aim is to discover the truth behind John Heydon's claims and especially if that book he has published under Nicholas's name really does contain such a recipe. If this involves unmasking Heydon then, unfortunately, that will have to be.'

Eager to inspect the building in question, but concerned about the consequences of being caught snooping, Zachariah added, 'By the way, Jane, where are Alice and Mr Heydon? No-one was home when I called next door. When are they due back?'

'Oh, Zachariah! I am sorry. With the surprise of seeing you, I forgot to say. Alice and Mr Heydon are away. Alice took her personal maid with her to look after her daughter, so that is why the house is empty. And before you ask, I am no longer informed of the wherefores and whereabouts of the master and mistress of this house. All Alice told me was they would be away for a week or so. That was a fortnight ago. I am expected to keep the house ready for their return. But don't worry, Mr Heydon usually sends word when they arrive back in London, just so that when they reach Spitalfields I have a hot meal waiting for them. I have not received any such notice as yet.'

Zachariah silently voiced an expletive. His hopes of completing his task quickly and being back in Crawley within the week seemed to have been thwarted. Oh well, he thought, while he waited for their return, he could undertake further investigations, beginning with this new brick building.

Offering to assist him, Jane led the way through the rear yard. Zachariah stopped to admire the well-tended garden beds.

'I try to keep up the maintenance of these plots. Medicinal herbs are over there, coltsfoot, horehound, balm and woundwort, and here are my spring vegetables,' Jane explained, pointing out the various plots.

Zachariah was only half listening, for his attention was focused on the outbuilding. On closer inspection it was sturdily built, made entirely from brick with a slate roof. The door was strengthened with iron bands and secured with a padlock. Walking around the structure, he saw one of the shutters was slightly ajar. With the help of a stick, he prised it away from the window.

'Phew, that smell! Jane, this is certainly some kind of workshop. There is a distinct sharp odour of sulphur seeping through.'

Dragging a chopping block up against the wall, he clambered onto it and peered in. 'It's very dark in there, all I can see are shadowy shapes,' Zachariah said, as he precariously held onto the window sill. Moving his head aside to allow the sunlight to penetrate more deeply, vague shapes appeared. 'Hold on, I can see… err… what seems to be glass. Yes, there is a distinct glint of glass. And I think there is some kind of tripod there on the hearth. That hearth is big, Jane. It has some kind of bellows attached.'

Losing his grip, he stumbled off the block and fell backwards into the long grass.

'Oh, are you all right, Zachariah?' Jane cried as she bent down to help him.

Struggling to his feet, he said, 'Well, from what I could make out, it seems Mr Heydon has built another apothecary workshop for himself. For what purpose, I wonder?'

Realising that he was not going to learn anything more here that day, he decided the best course of action was to seek information elsewhere.

As Jane saw him out, Zachariah asked, 'Can you recommend anybody who may be able to answer my questions regarding that book on *aurum potabile*?'

'Orrum what?' Jane repeated scowling.

'That elixir you saw advertised is pronounced "or-rum pot-ah-belee",' Zachariah explained.

'Orrum pot-ar-billie,' Jane repeated, trying to get her tongue around the unfamiliar words.

'It is Latin for drinkable gold. Often it is called the philosopher's stone, or the elixir of life.'

'Oh. I can't read Latin. I just skip over those funny looking words when reading my herbals,' Jane replied sheepishly.

'To tell you the truth, I can only read and understand Latin when it's related to my trade. That is why Nicholas translated the *Pharmacopoeia*, because most apothecaries cannot read Latin.'

'Well, Zachariah, at least you mastered the skill of writing. I may be able to stumble through my herbals, but writing is beyond me.'

Taking a small commonplace book and pencil from his pocket, Zachariah said, 'Well, you can save your fingers by telling me the names of the people you think may be able to help me.'

'I think you should begin with the bookseller, Mr Nathaniel Brooke. He was a frequent visitor and friend of Nicholas's. He published most of Nicholas's astrological books. I've heard he has publically condemned Mr Heydon.'

'Do you know why they are in conflict?'

'From Mr Heydon's angry outbursts, it seems that Mr Brooke has disputed his claims about that elixir. Considering Mr Brooke's expertise, his comments may suggest the elixir is fakery.'

'What other avenues should I explore?'

'Mr Brooke's rival, Mr Cole, is currently in Alice's favour. Of late he has been a frequent visitor to Spitalfields. He encouraged Nicholas's anti-royalist pursuits and they were both involved with the Independents. Zachariah, if you wish to curry favour with him, pander to his financial interests, but don't trust him. He presents himself as a pious Puritan, but he is untrustworthy when it comes to his business affairs. The only other person I can recommend is Nicholas's secretary, Mr William Ryves. Yet, he seems to have withdrawn since

Nicholas's death. He no longer calls, so I have to make time to visit him. He tried to stand up to Mr Heydon to prevent him from seizing the contents of Nicholas's private library. But to no avail because, as you know, a widow's assets become the property of her new husband.' Standing aside on the threshold, she concluded with a sigh, 'I think Mr Ryves has given up and I can understand how he feels. I am sure, however, if I ask, he will see you.'

'Yes, I would be grateful for any introductions you may be able to arrange. But for now, I will follow up on this Mr Brooke.' Stepping into the street, Zachariah turned and said, 'Oh, one last thing. Do you know where I can get a copy of that book on *aurum potabile?*'

Her face suddenly brightening, Jane replied, 'I know exactly where you can get a copy. If you wait just a moment.'

Jane soon returned carrying a cloth-covered parcel. Handing it over she said, 'Mr Heydon may have demanded I give him my key to the apothecary shop.' Grinning and holding up an iron key, she continued, 'But he didn't demand I hand over the spare key! Without his knowledge, I often gain entry with this, usually to retrieve ingredients and other items I may require. Rummaging in a cabinet, I came across a stack of newly printed books. Your mention of the name just now jogged my memory. I remembered those words were in their title.'

Quickly unwrapping the cloth, Zachariah cradled the leather-bound book. Opening to the title page, he read aloud: '*Mr Culpeper's Treatise of* Aurum Potabile. *Being a Description of the Three-Fold World: Elementary, Celestial, Intellectual. Containing the Knowledge Necessary to the Study of Hermetic Philosophy…'*

He paused, unsure of the meaning of the title. What is this three-fold world and how is it connected to Hermetic philosophy, he wondered? Something he needed to investigate further.

Tenderly laying her hand upon his, Jane said, 'Zachariah, don't dilly-dally. Be on your way. And please care for this book and return it as soon as you are able. I don't know if Mr Heydon has kept a record of his stock. As soon as Mr and Mrs Heydon return, I will send a message to you at the Dolphin Inn.'

Strolling across the cow paddock with the book held securely against his chest, Zachariah pondered over the conversation with Jane. And what of that outbuilding, what was its true function? To find out, he decided that at the first opportunity he would need to gain access to investigate its concealed mysteries.

***

Chapter Three

Nathaniel Brooke's Bookshop, Cornhill
Thursday, 1ˢᵗ May 1656, late morning

Entering the bookshop, Zachariah approached the man behind the counter and asked if he was the proprietor, Mr Nathaniel Brook.[44]

'No, I am the stationer. Mr Brooke has stepped out for a while, but I am expecting him to return soon. If you wait, I will enquire if he will see you, Mr…?'

'Mr Zachariah Jenkin.'

The stationer waited for his customer to elaborate, but Zachariah merely smiled and informed him that he would wait.

Zachariah explored the shelves lining the walls from floor to ceiling. He was nervous and needed something to occupy his mind. He had been rehearsing what he would say to the people he needed to talk with, the result being rushes of confidence then second thoughts that led to his nerves getting the better of him.

He was about to compose another mental introduction, when he spied a book by Nicholas Culpeper. Taking the volume from the shelf, Zachariah examined its title: *Culpeper's Last Legacy … Left and Bequeathed to his Dearest Wife, for the Public Good.*

Zachariah flicked through the pages, pausing to read pertinent phrases:

'This my last piece the reserve of all the rest, I had never thought to have published till now finding indisposition of body to be such as that I have no other way left to continue my own fame ...'[45]

Turning the page, he faltered. The printer seemed to have used too much ink, as the lettering was so smudged, the type was difficult to read. Lifting the book to his face, he adjusted its angle in order for the filtered sunlight to illuminate the page. He could just decipher the words: '... but by publishing these my last re... ma... nes... Ah remains!'

'I wonder what that means?' Zachariah muttered more loudly than he intended. Bending his head back to the page, he continued reading, '... which I have left to my doest, um... dearest wife... my legacy, being the choicest secrets which I locked up in my breast, and never made known—'[46]

'Mr Jenkin, I understand you desire to speak with me.'

Zachariah's concentration was suddenly broken by the intrusion. Feeling like a child caught with his finger in a pie, he spun about to be confronted by a man wearing an ingratiating seller's smile.

Disconcerted, Zachariah's carefully rehearsed and tactfully crafted introductions were suddenly forgotten. In a rush he said, 'Er... yes, I am Mr Jenkin. I would very much like to discuss with you the works of Mr Nicholas Culpeper.'

At the mention of Nicholas's name, Brooke's smile vanished, replaced by an unwelcoming stony, mask-like glare.

A moment of silence hung between them, as Zachariah scrutinised the bookseller. Tall and lithe, Brooke was dressed expensively in a close-fitting crimson silk shirt lined with gold braid. He appeared younger than Zachariah had imagined, possibly in his early thirties, but dressed like a dandy, as if he were trying to preserve his youth as long as possible. From his tawny, reddish skin and piercing, distrustful hazel eyes, Zachariah concluded he must have a choleric disposition.

'I am the person you seek,' Brooke said in a steely suspicious tone, as he looked about the shop as if searching for someone. 'Who sent you? Did you come alone?'

'Um… er… pardon, I don't know what you mean,' Zachariah said, also gazing about the shop in bewilderment.

'Was it that woman, Alice Heydon, who sent you or her mountebank husband?' Brooke snarled, advancing on Zachariah.

Fearing he was about to be struck, Zachariah held out the book to shield himself. Brooke reached out and wrenching it from his hands shouted, 'Why are you so interested in Mr Culpeper's publications?'

Standing so close, Zachariah could smell a stale odour of ale wafting from Brooke. It would seem that 'stepped out for a while' meant spending time in the local tavern.

Trying to salvage the situation caused by his impulsive statement, Zachariah replied to Brooke's allegations, 'Sir, I think you confuse me with someone else. I am Mr Zachariah Jenkin, an apothecary from Crawley in Sussex. Mr Culpeper and I were apprentices together and we became fast friends. I have only just been informed of the widow Culpeper's recent marriage to Mr John Heydon. I have not seen Nicholas's widow since well before his death, nor have I ever met her new husband.'

In the light of this hostile response, Zachariah decided to refrain from mentioning that Jane had recommended he speak to this man.

'I knew Nicholas for many years. He was both my friend and associate. But I cannot recall him ever speaking of you,' Brooke said. Looking haughtily down his nose, he added, 'And you still haven't answered my question. Why are you interested in this book?'

'Er… sadly Nicholas and I drifted apart during the early years of the war. He had left his master and I, having completed my apprenticeship and married, moved to a town south of London to establish my trade. I heard too late of his demise and so was unable to attend his funeral. While in London, I seek to buy a few of his more recent works, those published since his death to add to my small collection,' Zachariah rambled, his thoughts in confusion at this unhospitable welcome.

Gesturing towards the text Brooke was still grasping to his chest, Zachariah concluded, 'But it would appear I will need to be careful about which books to purchase.'

Instead of mollifying him, Brooke's face turned crimson. 'What do you mean? Who have you been talking to?' he spat. 'You can't trust anything that silly woman has been saying. The Stationers Company legitimately transferred the rights of this title to me. I have been publishing Nicholas's manuscripts for years. She hasn't a right to make those accusations. It's that Peter Cole you have to worry about. He is the one claiming to possess manuscripts written by Nicholas, but which I know are inferior works by other men's hands—'

'Sir… sir! You misunderstand me. I was reading the epistle

by Nicholas's widow when you approached. She claims that several books have been published under her deceased husband's name, but which are not his. I must emphasise, I have not seen or spoken with Mrs Cul— er… Heydon, nor any of her associates.'

'Hmff,' Brooke sniffed. Staggering, he toppled forward, off-balance, grasping at a shelf. Zachariah moved to support the man. He suspected Brooke's erratic behaviour was caused by taking too much ale so early in the day.

'Excuse me, I need to sit down,' Brooke said, wiping his hand across his brow.

Zachariah felt alarmed when Brooke began to retreat to the back of the shop. Though uninvited, he trailed behind.

Brooke entered a small workshop. Lined with bookshelves, the chamber smelled of freshly tooled leather. Brooke's awkward limbs collapsed unceremoniously into a chair. He braced his hands against a battered and ink-stained pine table stacked high with manuscripts and books.

'If you please, would you forgive my outburst?' Brooke said, fearing his inebriated manner may stain his reputation. 'It has been a busy morning as I have been entertaining demanding clients.' Gathering the papers together and neatly arranging them in a pile, he invited Zachariah to take a seat opposite. Apparently preoccupied with the papers before him and unable or unwilling to look Zachariah in the eye, Brooke eventually glanced up and said, 'I feel accosted and my reputation sullied by people whom once I called friends. I have registered at the Stationers Company manuscripts authored by Nicholas. I obtained the manuscripts during the months before his untimely demise. Yet recently his widow has accused me of compiling works by other authors and presenting them as her deceased husband's.'

Brooke pointed to the book he had deposited on the table and said, 'Mrs Heydon claims she did not authorise the publication of *Culpeper's Last Legacy*. She has also attested in various quarters that the only authentic manuscripts from her deceased husband's estate are held by her or Mr Cole.'

'Are you referring to the Mr Peter Cole who published the *Physical Directory* and *A Directory for Midwives*?'[47]

A look of contempt passed across Mr Brooke's face. 'You need to understand Mr Culpeper was first and foremost an astrologer and herbalist. He sold me most of his astrological manuscripts, which I subsequently registered and had published. Certainly, Mr Cole did commission Nicholas to translate the College's *Pharmacopeia* and published it under the title *A Physical Directory*. Once it had become successful, Nicholas's name became valuable. So valuable, I am grieved to say, that he and Mr Cole conspired to publish additional works that were not authored by Nicholas. I tried to counsel Nicholas, as I respected him both as an associate and a friend. But he disregarded my advice. The promise of wealth and prestige made him stoop so low as to agree to have his good name used to sell the inferior works of others. *A Directory for Midwives* is the most desperately deficient of them all and should never have seen the light…'[48]

Brooke paused, adjusting his collar as if it were suddenly strangling him. Unable to maintain eye contact with Zachariah, taking a deep breath, he stammered, 'You must understand, Mr Jenkin, I had considered Nicholas my friend. But he abused our friendship. For the good of our midwives,

I felt it my duty to expose his fraud in one of my most recent works, the *Complete Midwife's Practice*.[49] Even after his death, the conspiracy continues. Now his widow and her new husband use Nicholas's name to sell books authored by others. In collaboration with Mr Cole, they now accuse me of both publishing unauthorised books of Nicholas's authorship or ones not written by him.'

Zachariah felt uncomfortable. In his inebriated state, Brooke was revealing to a complete stranger so much of himself and his views of others. His near drunkenness could explain why his statements were so inconsistent. Putting his qualms aside, Zachariah resolved that while Brooke was in such an unguarded state, he may be able to glean some useful information.

Reaching for *Culpeper's Last Legacy*, which seemed to be causing Brooke so much angst, Zachariah began hesitantly, fearful of the man's response, 'You claim Nicholas's widow has condemned this book? Yet, her epistle has authorised you to publish the treatises contained herein. And what about the epistle supposedly written by Nicholas?'

Squirming as if troubled by worms, Brooke replied, 'Ah… I had tried to maintain my friendship with the widow Culpeper following the tragic death of her husband. This book was the fruit of our close ties, but now our friendship has broken down irrevocably and so her tune has changed to my detriment.' Gazing forlornly down at the desk, Brooke seemed to retreat into lost and regretful memories.

Zachariah waited, wondering how he was going to broach the subject that brought him here. As he was about to speak, Brooke interrupted him.

'So enough about me and my troubles. You say that you and Nicholas met when training for the apothecary trade and you are in London to reacquaint yourself with Mrs Heydon?' Brook said in a friendlier but enquiring tone.

Suspicious and confused at Brooke's inconsistent comments, Zachariah was guarded with his words. Deciding not to mention his patron unless it became necessary, he repeated his story about meeting Nicholas during the early years of their apothecary apprenticeship. Seeking to set Brooke at ease, Zachariah spoke of those days with affection. Repeating the comment he had made to Jane about how he thought Nicholas invited guests to his home in Isfield in the hope that his grandfather's wrath may be tempered in the company of strangers, Brooke smiled knowingly.

'Ah, the Reverend William Attersoll! Nicholas told me of their frequent clashes over theological matters.' Sighing wistfully, Brooke continued, 'I believe that if Nicholas's father had lived, young Nicholas would have gladly studied for the church and eventually become the rector of Ockley when his father had retired. Unfortunately, his grandfather's zealousness soured Nicholas's attitude towards the clerical life.'

Zachariah confirmed Brooke's assessment of Reverend Attersoll, and could well imagine Nicholas balking at the notion of following in his grandfather's footsteps.

'Nicholas told me that his grandfather was surprised that he agreed so readily to leave for university to study divinity,' Brooke continued. 'Obviously he didn't realise that Nicholas saw this as an opportunity to escape the smothering confines of the rectory. Attersoll must have been a sour old sot during his university days. Or he had just forgotten his own youthful exuberance, if he had ever expressed any!'

'Nicholas told me of his experiences at university', Zachariah said. 'I recall his tales of life in Cambridge, and how he spent more time in the taverns than at his studies. He thought he would find freedom in Cambridge, but became disillusioned by the dull lectures and the study of ancient Greek and Roman authors. His grandfather sent him there to study holy orders but he was more interested in medicine, and would often attend lectures on anatomy. I suppose that is why he eventually left without graduating.'

'Is that what he told you? I suppose, back then, the incident was too recent and painful to discuss. Actually, Nicholas left Cambridge following the death of his betrothed.'

'I was not aware that Nicholas had been betrothed prior to meeting his wife Alice!' Zachariah was intrigued.

'Prior to leaving for Cambridge, Nicholas had met a young heiress and they fell in love. He did not reveal her identity to me.[50] But from what he did say, her family were members of the local gentry who owned an estate close to his grandfather's rectory. This lady had more than two thousand pounds in personal estate from which she received five hundred pounds a year. Realising that her father would not agree to a marriage between his daughter and a gentleman of simple means who was destined for the church, they decided to elope.'

Brooke related how Nicholas had taken the funds his mother had given him to finance his studies in Cambridge and plotted to elope with his betrothed. 'He hoped that following the marriage their parents would be pacified. Packing her valuable jewels and accompanied by a sympathetic gentlewoman, she fled her family home and made her way to the rendezvous. Suddenly a violent storm arose! Claps of thunder, flames and flashes of lightning rained down on the two as they struggled across the fields in search of shelter. Then, as she fought against the wind and rain, there was a huge crack and a white-heat flash, and his betrothed immediately fell down dead.'

'How did Nicholas react to this tragic event?' Zachariah asked, feeling overwhelmed at this shocking tale.

Sombrely, Brooke related how Nicholas had also been caught in the storm. 'Through the darkness he could see a shapeless form in the distance. On investigating he came upon the gentlewoman companion wailing and moaning, drenched and huddled by the side of the road. Nicholas became frantic as it took several minutes to revive the woman. Eventually she was able to relate the tragic events. On learning the terrible fate of his betrothed, Nicholas fell to his knees and almost fainted away.'

Zachariah witnessed the sadness in Brooke countenance as if he was personally reliving the tragic episode.

'By chance, an acquaintance of the family found the pair prostrate on the side of the road,' he said wearily. 'He took them in his coach to the rectory in Isfield. Nicholas's mother joyfully greeted her unexpected guests, but on hearing of Nicholas's rash decision to elope and the tragic events, she fell into a fit of sickness, from which Nicholas confessed she would never fully recover.'

Brooke lapsed into silence. In a tone of abject resignation he continued, 'I recall the grief in Nicholas's voice as he related this sad episode to me. After all those years and even being married to Alice, it was obvious that the loss of his jewel whom he valued above all worldly considerations continued to cause him to fall so deeply into melancholy…'

Brooke's voice again trailed off. He glanced fleetingly at Zachariah. It was as if Brooke was wrestling with a decision. While Zachariah quietly waited for his host to speak, he became aware of an aroma, the delicate whiff of sweet vanilla tobacco.

'Ahhh, I suppose anyone who had experienced such a terrible series of events would begin to question their meaning,' Brooke sighed resignedly. 'Having recovered from the initial shock, our friend withdrew from the world, finding some solace in his home in Isfield, reading and walking the trails in solitude; seeking some kind of sign from God and wrestling with his conscience and his faith. Eventually, he decided that a life in the church was not for him. No longer finding meaning and direction in the Scriptures, he abandoned his university studies. His melancholic contemplations had revealed to him a new path: to pursue a life dedicated to the study of the occult mysteries as revealed to him by the philosophy of Hermes.'[51]

'Who… what? I don't understand.'

'Nicholas rejected the theology of his grandfather, finding it empty and without solace,' Brooke explained, pausing at Zachariah's shocked expression. 'Nicholas said he abandoned his university studies, because he was disillusioned with their blind reliance on the ancient Greek philosophers, Plato and Aristotle. So he turned to an even more ancient corpus written by Hermes Trismegistus and his followers, which has become the foundation of a new natural philosophy.'

'I still don't understand. Who is this Hermes Trismag…

this ancient philosopher?'

'I specialise in the publication of occult works that include astrology, alchemy and natural philosophy,' Brooke
began in a derisory tone, gazing condescendingly down at
Zachariah. 'My clients are men of letters, great scholars and
philosophers who dedicate their lives to the study of these
occult mysteries. Certainly, the common man purchases my
wares, seeking to glean the secrets that lay buried in their
pages, trying to decipher their meanings and grasping for
their truths, but invariably failing as they do not understand
this higher knowledge.'

A hot surge of humiliation and anger flushed across
Zachariah's features. Brooke's fearful response suggested that
Zachariah had not masked his displeasure. Taking advantage
of the moment, in a steely tone Zachariah demanded Brooke
answer his question.

Brooke proceeded to explain that Hermes Trismegistus
was a great sage and contemporary of Moses. He blended the
knowledge of the ancient Egyptians and Greeks to create a
collection of treatises called the *Corpus Hermeticum*.

'The philosophies of Hermes were thought to be lost following the destruction of Rome. But they were rediscovered
centuries later to become the foundation of a new natural
philosophy. Hermetic scholars and adepts employ the tools
of astrology, alchemy and medicine to discern the secrets of
nature, as revealed through the complex relationships between
the microcosmic body of man and the celestial macrocosm,
being God's Creation.'[52]

'Pardon,' Zachariah said, interrupting Brooke's lecture.
'Did you say alchemy? I am of the understanding that one

of Nicholas's treatises has recently been published on this subject in relation to a universal elixir. Am I to understand you are the publisher?'

For all his boasting of being a specialist in the publication of occult titles, Brooke's response was totally unexpected.

'That book is a fake and I refused to publish it,' he snapped. 'Mr Heydon approached me with a lucrative offer to publish this manuscript he claims was written by Nicholas, with the promise I could profit also from the sale of this elixir. But I understood Nicholas's employment of the alchemical arts, and they never included the making of a universal elixir.'

Curious, Zachariah asked, 'But what of the handbills advertising an elixir called *aurum potabile* made from a secret recipe of Nicholas's? I have seen this bill. You know it is dated only a few days before his death. Surely this proves that Nicholas had discovered the universal medicine.'

With a gleam in his eye, Brooke replied, 'Ah… so this elixir interests you, Mr Jenkin! You are not the first to make enquiries about its mysterious recipe.'

'I understand that under the direction of Nicholas's widow, a few of his associates are now making and selling an elixir at his old apothecary shop in Spitalfields.' Zachariah said, deflecting Brooke's question while trying to remain calm as to not betray that indeed this was what interested him.

'As I stated before, you cannot trust Mrs Culpeper. Or should I correct myself… Mrs *Heydon*,' he said, spitting her new husband's surname as if it were a bitter pill. 'While Nicholas lived she was merely his wife and the mother of his children. Now he is dead, a strange miracle has occurred: she is claiming she can cure all diseases. Truly, Mr Jenkin, she is not much unlike the… err… forgive my language… the Whore of Babylon, who with her curious golden potion sought the delusion of many of the poor and ignorant.'[53]

'Are you suggesting this elixir is really only a fraudulent concoction made by Mrs Heydon and her associates?' Zachariah asked, startled not only at Brooke's suggestion, but also his unseemly language.

Throwing back his head with a laugh, Brooke said, 'Mrs Heydon is but a poor silly woman! No, Mr Jenkin, she has two apple-squires. One calls himself a gentleman, yet he has no more wit but to defile his name by associating himself with the legendary stories that woman tells. The other conspirator, I know his name, but I durst reveal it. I have heard reports he began a practice of extracting goods out of people's houses by force, but fled when his crimes were discovered.'[54]

'I assume you are referring to Mr Heydon and either the Dr Harrington or Dr Freeman mentioned in the handbill?'

'They were never associates of Nicholas. Dr Harrington I know little of. Dr Freeman is Heydon's main co-conspirator, or should I say hired ruffian,' Brooke replied with an expression of disdain. 'Do you know when and under what circumstances this cockatrice Heydon came into the Culpeper's lives?' Brooke snarled.

'No, Mr Brooke, I know very little of Mr Heydon and do not recall Nicholas ever mentioning his name.'

'During the last months of Nicholas's illness, his wife convinced him to bring in a boarder to supplement their dwindling income. That boarder was Mr Heydon.' Leering, Brooke continued. 'It is my view the arrangement suited both Mrs Culpeper and Mr Heydon very well. He soon made himself very comfortable and accommodating to that young lady while her husband lay dying.'[55]

Zachariah felt his throat flush in embarrassment. His mind raced. Was Brooke insinuating that an intimate relationship had existed between Mrs Culpeper and Mr Heydon while Nicholas still lived? Jane had not mentioned this scandalous arrangement. Was she too frightened or ashamed to speak of it? Or was she protecting Alice for reasons of her own?

Brooke watched him so closely, Zachariah felt as if the man were peering into his soul. Zachariah flushed again and looked away, feeling certain Brooke knew he had understood his damning words.

'Mr Heydon introduced those two supposed physicians into Nicholas's life,' Brooke scoffed. 'They didn't even wait for Nicholas to die before they embarked on their fraudulent quest. It is they who are behind that advertisement and the subsequent publication, not Nicholas.'

Too embarrassed to discuss the allegation that Nicholas had been cuckolded, Zachariah quickly bought the subject back to the elusive elixir.

'So you believe Mr Heydon and his associates are exploiting Nicholas's good name for their own selfish ends?'

'Yes, Mr Jenkin, there is a conspiracy in Spitalfields hatched by this small congregation. One of these rare phoenixes claims himself an alchemist. As an apothecary, you should know alchemists cheat those fools whom they think will be snared with golden bait. To hoodwink the ignorant, they have been advertising a whole list of diseases for which they now claim a cure. Yet, even a blind man can see these are the impostures of mountebanks who delude and amuse the vulgar sort of people.'[56]

'You seem familiar with the schemes and conspiracies of these alchemical frauds, Mr Brooke. How so?'

'As I just said, my interest is in alchemical and astrological works. I have recently commissioned the publication of several alchemical texts by philosophers who know the true application of these Hermetic arts. Such esteemed scholars do not seek to empty the purses of the unwary. Yes, Mr Jenkin, I do know the difference between a true alchemical philosopher and those who seek to deceive the gullible with their golden piss-potions. Mrs Heydon and her conspirators advertise their elixir as true and philosophical. But their claims cannot stand alone. No! They need the testimonies of others to support their assertions.'

'I must confess, I have not had the occasion to familiarise myself with the making of these alchemical elixirs, nor read the works of the ancient philosophers,' Zachariah admitted. He was not about to admit that he had begun examining his borrowed copy of the *Treatise*.

'To be truthful, Mr Brooke, my Latin skills are poor. My knowledge of most of the works of the ancient authorities is sadly lacking. I would be interested if you could enlighten me on these philosophies.'

Seeming pleased to have a platform to demonstrate the breadth of his knowledge of the alchemical arts, Brooke proceeded in lecturing Zachariah.

'This elixir cannot be said to be the product of philosophy, as Mrs Heydon's conspirators claim.' Ignoring Zachariah's statement that he was unfamiliar with the works of the ancients, Brooke added, 'Such assertions, Mr Jenkin, are easily disproved simply by referring to the ancient physicians and their brethren, the philosophers.'[57]

Zachariah wondered if Brooke had slipped back into his derisory demeanour by again referring to his lack of a university education: The ability to read Latin fluently and familiarity with the ancient authorities separated the gentleman from the artisan, or the learned from the ignorant.

'If you look to the works of these esteemed authorities, you will see how many of them have exposed and condemned such golden elixirs as things wholly destructive and pernicious.[58] You will find the ancient physicians set down medicines which are far more agreeable to the temper of a man than gold.'

Turning to a bookshelf behind his chair, Brooke reached for a tattered well-thumbed volume and handed it to Zachariah. Glancing down at the fraying spine, all he could decipher was the name Pliny, as the remainder of the title was in Latin.

'Pliny, the great Roman natural philosopher, spoke of the dangers concerning the hurt and inconvenience the use of alchemical gold would cause,' Brooke lectured, 'for being mixed with sulphur, it is not agreeable to any sick person due to its smell and will harm the flesh of any who touch it. No metal can nourish the body for, if ingested, it clogs up the mouth and stomach, thus spoiling the appetite!'[59]

'Yet, what of its making, Mr Brooke? Do you know the ingredients these alchemists use to make these elixirs? I have often been called upon to make medicines to try to counteract their effects. Such dangerous concoctions had either loosened people's bowels or made them vomit. To counteract the elixirs, I need to know their ingredients and preparation.'

'Ah, Mr Jenkin, the mystery of their making should remain a secret, lest you are tempted to make the elixir yourself,' Brooke replied, wagging his finger in Zachariah's face.

Zachariah sighed glumly. Brooke may have provided him with the answers he was seeking. What would he tell Sir William? That Nicholas's elixir was nothing more than a mixture of dangerous ingredients rather than a cure-all?

Mr Brooke laughed. 'If you are so determined to find the secrets of *aurum potabile*, Mr Jenkin, why don't you purchase the treatise that silly confident woman claims was written by her husband that those swindlers have recently commissioned Cole to publish?'

'But you just said that the treatise is a fake!' Zachariah cried, frustrated at the contradictory and confusing discussion.

'I have seen a copy of the original manuscript Mrs Heydon purports to be the fruit of her dead husband's labours. And yes, I am of the opinion it was not written in Culpeper's hand. And since the manuscript is so notorious a fraud, I can only conclude, therefore, so is the recipe. I have written my own treatise unmasking these mountebanks and I hope my readers take heed of the imposture for no other reason but their own good.[60] But, Mr Jenkin, there isn't smoke without fire. So, as I said, don't completely dismiss Nicholas's interest in the alchemical arts all together.'

'What do you mean, Mr Brooke? Either Nicholas was the author of the treatise and the originator of the recipe or he was not,' Zachariah spluttered in confusion.

'Ah, Mr Jenkin, I think I have said too much,' Brooke replied smiling in such an enigmatic, supercilious manner that for an instant, in his frustration, Zachariah considered wiping it off with a well-directed punch.

Brooke must have seen the glint of anger in Zachariah's countenance. Rising from his chair Brooke said, 'I'm sorry, Mr Jenkin, I have nothing more to say on this matter. I do recommend you undertake enquiries into the veracity of Mrs and Mr Heydon's claims.'

Trying to smooth over troubled waters in case he required more information from Brooke as well as being intrigued by its contents, Zachariah purchased the copy of *Culpeper's Last Legacy*. Brooke's abrupt transformation from his sour demeanour suggested Zachariah's tactic was successful.

Escorting Zachariah to the street, Brooke said in a conciliatory tone, 'I suggest, Mr Jenkin, if you intend to approach Mr Heydon on this matter, you prepare yourself for such a meeting. Become familiar with Nicholas's works and especially of the contents of that book his new wife now claims contains the secrets of *aurum potabile*. I warn you, Sir, if Mr Heydon thinks he can befuddle you with his silky tongue and philosophical aphorisms, he will. And so you will also be drawn into his web of deceit and believe every tale he spins you.'

Pausing in front of the shop, Zachariah reflected on Brooke's comments. The bookseller claimed the treatise was not written by Nicholas. Yet, the style of language resembled that of Nicholas's other works. Could the author, whoever he may be, have drawn on Nicholas's mannerisms to hoodwink the unwary? Brooke seemed very familiar with alchemical works, and especially this elixir. Why? Was it a philosophical interest, as he so claimed?

Obviously he couldn't trust the word of this one man, especially considering his claims of a friendship between him and Nicholas were clearly contradictory. It would appear Jane was right. Brooke seemed more concerned with his personal profit and reputation than with the welfare of Nicholas's name and the fate of his works. Yet he would take Brooke's advice, for he did need more information before he could report back to Sir William.

Zachariah checked the address of another of Culpeper's publishers and one of Brooke's rivals, Mr Peter Cole. Only a few streets away, Zachariah decided to walk the distance.

***

Chapter Four

Peter Cole's Publishing House, Leadenhall
Thursday, 1st May 1656, early afternoon

'I should have taken a coach,' Zachariah mumbled as he trudged east up Cornhill Street on his way to Leadenhall. Cole's bookseller had told him his employer was at his printing shop further along the road. Only a short distance the boy had said. Not likely, Zachariah mused. The road was still wet from the morning drizzle. While the traffic was light, he feared being splashed with muddy water, or his shoes sinking into something he would prefer not to identify.

Eventually Zachariah spied a sign depicting a printing press hanging above the ground floor door of a substantial three-storeyed brick residence.

The bookshop was unattended. Hearing voices from a rear chamber, Zachariah approached and peered through the doorway entrance. Spying a man bent over a table littered with papers, to get his attention he cleared his throat and asked to speak to Mr Peter Cole.

Glancing up, the man said, 'I am he. What is your business?'

Identifying himself, Zachariah explained that he was making enquiries into Mr Culpeper's publications and that he was of the understanding that Mr Cole owned the rights to several of his current manuscripts.

'Are you planning to publish other titles?' Zachariah asked.

'Yes, you have been informed correctly. May I ask why your interest in Mr Culpeper's publications?'

Having already determined the subjects of the elixir *aurum potabile* and the book of the same name were sensitive issues, Zachariah revealed only enough to pique Cole's monetary interests without breaching any confidences.

'Specifically,' Zachariah concluded, 'if my investigations prove productive, Sir William will consider supporting ventures involving Mr Culpeper's publications.'

As Zachariah explained his business, Cole's morose face broke into a covetous grin. Zachariah concluded Jane's assessment of this man was correct. Evidently, Cole was quick to recognise financial possibilities, especially when it was he who would profit.

'You have come at an opportune time, Mr Jenkin. If you had come earlier, I would have had to decline your request for an interview. But you arrived just as I was completing a task, so I have time to speak with you.'

Strolling back to his worktable, he said over his shoulder, 'If you please, I will just finish here and then we can retire to my residence.'

While Cole was occupied, Zachariah assessed his host and his surroundings. Taller than average, Cole's well cut plain brown breeches and simple white shirt under his leather work apron were intended to suggest that, while wealthy and successful, he observed the regimental strictures expected of a committed Puritan. His neatly trimmed brown beard vainly masked a sickly, swarthy pallor and sunken cheeks. Deep lines around his mouth and eyes made him appear beleaguered. Zachariah deduced that Mr Cole was not a well man.[61]

Cole turned and looked directly into Zachariah's eyes, as if sensing he was being assessed. Embarrassed, Zachariah looked away and pretended to be interested in the staff preparing a printing press that dominated the chamber.

Eventually Cole returned and escorted his guest to a flight of stairs. Zachariah was surprised to find a well-appointed residence fit for a gentleman above the workshop. They entered a richly decorated wood-panelled library.

'These represent the many titles I have purchased and published,' Cole said as he gestured towards a row of book cabinets. 'I also have collected the best examples published both here in England and from the Continent. Here you will find most of Mr Culpeper's titles, even some published by rival printers.'

Gesturing towards a pair of ornately carved walnut cabinets, Mr Cole continued, 'Those books hold a special place in my collection. You will find many of Mr Culpeper's titles. He was, by far, my most successful author. I plan to publish them as part of a series I will call the *Rational Physician's Library*.'[62]

Directing Zachariah to a chair, Cole settled himself opposite behind a large writing desk. Smiling indulgently as if calculating what profits he could make out of Zachariah's patron, he said, 'Now, how can I be of assistance to you and Sir William?'

'I understand you commissioned Mr Culpeper to translate the College of Physicians' *Pharmocopoeia?*'

'You are correct. I first met Mr Culpeper back in the early '40s when we were involved in opposing the Royalist forces.

We supported the aims of the Levellers, especially their call for law reform and the establishment of free schools and hospitals.'

Gesturing towards a row of open book shelves, Cole continued, 'Those tracts represent the publications I offered to print for the dissenting brethren, sometimes to my own detriment, having had my printing press seized on occasion. I suppose Mr Culpeper saw in me the same zeal for change and reform as he felt. So we became firm friends.'

'I can well imagine him being attracted to a fellow sectarian,' Zachariah said, laughing softly. 'I recall he often abandoned his work to join some dissenting rabble passing by.'

'I gather you knew him back then, Mr Jenkin?'

'Sir William secured my services as he knew we were friends during our youth.'

Zachariah went on to clarify his association with Nicholas, again ensuring he only revealed enough to set Cole at ease. He decided to maintain an air of formality, as he didn't wish to appear too friendly and forward.

'It would appear you and Mr Culpeper met after I had left London to establish my business,' Zachariah began. 'During our apprenticeship, he introduced me to the sectarian groups who gathered in Coleman Street. Yet, to be truthful, while the sermons appeared to invigorate his reformist zeal, I usually did not understand their arguments.'

'Then I am surprised we hadn't met, Mr Jenkin. Like you, it was sermons such as those of the renowned Goodwin, that set me on a course that eventually led to me meeting Mr Culpeper.'[63] Hesitating, Cole enquired, 'did you know he didn't finish his apprenticeship?'

'Yes, while I had moved to Crawley in '43, during the early years we often met when I was in London. Sadly though, over time our close friendship waned. On the infrequent occasions we met, he spoke less and less of his life and especially his troubles.'

'It would appear my friendship with Mr Culpeper was establishing at the time yours was waning, Mr Jenkin. After he had left his master, he soon found himself with a young wife with prospects. But he quickly squandered her dowry and, later, his father all but disinherited him. He tried his hand as an astrologer, as well establishing an apothecary shop in Spitalfields. Unfortunately, he descended into financial difficulties. Did you know he was nearly killed in '43 during one of the battles?'[64]

'Yes, I knew about his involvement with the trained bands and the sad outcome. I understand he never recovered from his injuries?'

'That and his incessant taking of tobacco,' Cole replied. 'I heard him say tobacco was the greatest enemy to his health. He admitted he was too much accustomed to cease taking it.[65] It may be said the tobacco he took hastened his death. It certainly debilitated him, so much so he was forced to cease his astrological and apothecary practices.'

Zachariah smiled, recalling his friend's indulgence in tobacco. As he reminisced, he imagined he could detect that same sweet vanilla aroma here in Cole's library. He was about to ask if Cole indulged in the same tobacco mix when he was interrupted by a knock at the door.

An elderly man entered balancing a couple of glasses of white wine on a tray. Gesturing to Zachariah to help himself, Cole continued. 'If it had not been for his education and language skills, he would have descended into penury. Soon after he had sufficiently recovered from his wounds, he approached me seeking employment as a compositor at my printing shop. I quickly realised he could better serve me as a translator. So I set him the task of translating the College's *Pharmacopoeia*, the rights of which I had earlier registered with the Stationers Company.'[66]

'I understand you and Mr Culpeper both profited from that daring venture.'

'Yes, Mr Jenkin,' Cole replied sharply. 'We did profit. But I must emphasise our shared aims were not for financial gain, but to break the chains of ignorance that had so long bound the ordinary people of our nation. I need not tell you, Mr Jenkin, the College of Physicians monopolises medical knowledge by locking it away in a foreign tongue. Nicholas's skill of translating, coupled with my resources, broke this monopoly.'

'Not only the College, Mr Cole. I recall he used his publications as a vehicle to attack all the professions. I assume you encouraged him.'

'Like I said, I soon recognised his talent.'

Sipping his wine, Zachariah considered his host's comments, since Sir William had also requested he investigate Culpeper's political activities with the aim of discerning the motivations behind his actions.

'From my acquaintance with the blatant political themes contained within his prefaces, it would appear medical knowledge was not the only form of information he and you sought to disseminate, Mr Cole?' Zachariah prompted.

'It turned out we were of the same mind when it came to spreading knowledge amongst the English people. The Levellers' platform provided us with direction and purpose. For so long the English people had been crippled by the tyrannies of the Norman Yoke, whose benefactors claimed their positions were God-given, and therefore beyond challenge.'[67]

'Yet it was this challenge of the King and his laws that caused so much trepidation amongst the people,' Zachariah replied.

'But where do you think these tyrants obtained their powers?' Cole shot back. 'It was not God. It was William the Bastard who, centuries ago having conquered this nation, forced us into subjugation.' As he spoke, Cole's voice rose as his agitation increased. 'It was these foreign invaders who imposed their Norman laws on the English people, thus usurping God's divine plan for this nation. It was they, with their multiplicity of needless rules and their Latin language, who reduced us to slavery and ignorance. And King Charles, the professions and the established Church are their inheritors. So, Mr Jenkin, this is what set us about translating the *Pharmacopoeia*.'

'But why the *Pharmacopoeia* in particular?'

Instead of responding, Cole rose from his chair, turned and pointed to the dozens of volumes lining the walls. 'You see these tracts and books, Mr Jenkin? They are filled with sermons and speeches by learned men and sectarians who called for the overthrow of the Norman Yoke to prepare for the New Jerusalem. They proclaimed that ordinary men were Saints whose God-given task was to prepare this nation and themselves for Christ's Coming.[68] But while these texts say much, very little has been done to prepare His way. Many of these tracts were written by learned men for learned men and only really understood by men of such high stations. So it is a closed circle.' Standing before the bookcase, and with a sweep of his hand he said, 'Mr Culpeper and I knew how to spread these ideas throughout this nation and, most of all, how to prepare England in a pragmatic and simple way.'

Selecting a book, he returned to his desk and handed it across to Zachariah. 'Do you know the works of Comenius?'

Inspecting the title, *A Reformation of Schools*, Zachariah replied, 'No, Mr Cole, his works are unfamiliar to me.'

As if detecting an odour of ignorance, Cole sniffed, peering disdainfully down his nose. Zachariah, feeling humiliated, feared he was being assessed and found wanting.

Sighing, Cole said in derisory tone, 'I suppose not. What about Samuel Hartlib?'

Placing the unopened book on the table, Zachariah said, 'I have heard the name, but cannot recall in what context.' Actually, he had never heard of Hartlib, but wasn't going to confirm Cole's low opinion of his educational shortcomings.

Gesturing towards the book, Cole explained. 'Mr Hartlib and several notable associates were inspired by the works of the German educational reformer Johann Comenius. In 1642, he had Comenius's work *Prodrumus Pansophiæ* translated into English under the title *A Reformation of Schools*.[69] I was inspired by Comenius's theory of pansophic learning, or the teaching of useful and universal knowledge.'

'What does that mean?' Zachariah asked politely, hoping if he indulged his host they would eventually return to the subject that bought him to Cole's door.

'Comenius and Hartlib believed learning and educational methods require reforming. The traditional university scholastic method is atrophying, weighed down by centuries of empty rhetoric and semantic disputations derived from the authority of the ancient Greeks and Romans. If knowledge could not be affirmed by these ancients, it is considered invalid or superstitious nonsense.[70] Then Sir Francis Bacon came to prominence with his publication *Novum Organum*. Bacon developed the inductive method based on experimentation, observation and his radical interpretation of the source of reason, with the aim of expanding the realm of scholastic knowledge.'[71]

Zachariah decided not to enquire as to the identity of this Bacon. He assumed he was one of the many educational reformers to have emerged in England following the Reformation.

'If you and Mr Culpeper were of a like mind,' Cole continued, 'I would have thought you fully supported his desire to reform learning through the process of observation and experience. After all, he wrote extensively on these subjects in the books you claim to have read. His Dr Reason and Dr Experience became well known catchcries, so much so, his readers associated these terms with his works. And yes, Mr Jenkin, he was critical of the College for their scholasticism. And true, he did promote the skills of observation and experience, as well as providing reasons for his work. But his opposition was targeted at the scholars who, in their application of this new inductive method, monopolised the knowledge gained for the express purpose of lining their pockets. It was this misuse of knowledge that Comenius and

Hartlib sought to challenge. It was their ideas that inspired me and Mr Culpeper to act.'

'In what way?'

'While Mr Culpeper never directly referred to or quoted either Comenius or Hartlib, his commentaries suggest he supported their program for the universal teaching of useful knowledge. Hartlib acknowledged Mr Culpeper's contributions to these debates, and he even received a favourable mention in one of Hartlib's works.'[72]

'Please explain the relevance to Mr Culpeper's works of this educational reform platform,' Zachariah asked, rankled at Cole's pompous lecturing.

Cole rose from his chair and while browsing his bookshelves, continued his instruction. 'As Comenius has written, knowledge is not useful if it's only for the purpose of material profit. Rather the true profit from knowledge is that it reveals the glory of God.'

Considering this revelation, Zachariah asked, 'I understand your argument about applying Bacon's inductive method purely for material gain. But surely his method is the same as that which Mr Culpeper expounded.'

'They may seem similar, Mr Jenkin. But the aims are so different they are irreconcilable. Mr Bacon claimed his method of observation and experimentation would be an endless quest of progress and expansion of knowledge for the betterment of mankind. But!' Cole shouted, startling Zachariah, 'but Mr Jenkin, if the accumulation of knowledge is a never-ending quest, then the end of days will never come, because man will never be able to accumulate all the knowledge of Creation. And this is impossible, for as the Scriptures unequivocally say, Christ will return when mankind is ready. And I need not tell you the events plaguing England these dark days herald this glorious day.'

'End of days? Do you mean Judgement Day, as revealed in the Book of Revelation?'[73]

'Yes! It is the duty of mankind to prepare for Christ's Second Coming, Mr Jenkin. But before he comes, man must demonstrate to God that he is worthy. And by worthy, I mean man must raise himself up through education so that he may know the glory of God by understanding all there is to know of His Creation,' Cole said as he pointed at Zachariah as if he were making a personal comment as to his unworthiness.

Leaning back into his chair, Zachariah considered Cole's comments and especially his increasingly zealous manner.

Fearing they were wandering off the track, Zachariah sought to bring the subject back to Nicholas's publications. Later, however, he would realise that contained within Cole's ramblings was the essential key to understanding the true nature of *Culpeper's Treatise of* Aurum Potabile.

'If Mr Culpeper never actually mentioned the works of Comenius or Hartlib, what relevance do they have to his publications?'

'Mr Hartlib, inspired by the works of his associate Comenius, aimed to teach useful and universal knowledge to all people in all ways.[74] Through their education, the people of this nation can learn to improve their lives and with knowledge of medicine could cure themselves of disease. Thus prepared, they would become closer to God.' His voice raised in agitation and vigorously thrusting his finger at Zachariah as if giving a sermon from a pulpit, he continued,

'Mr Jenkin, it will not be until man has lifted himself up that he will receive Christ!'

Dropping his accusing hand to the table, Cole seemed to deflate back into his chair. Leaning over as if with great effort, he grasped his wineglass and holding it suspended at his lips, stared as if mesmerised into the depths of the golden liquid.

Awed by Cole's zealousness, Zachariah said quietly, 'I have not heard of these matters, Mr Cole. Has Mr Hartlib achieved his program for the reform of learning?'

Cole hesitated. Just as Zachariah thought he was not going to receive an answer, his host sighed despondently and said, 'His platform for the establishment of a Council for Learning was well received by the Parliament. Later, Cromwell also expressed an interest. Unfortunately, the Parliament has not provided funding. So thus far, Hartlib's plans have not been realised.[75] It would appear that with the Protectorate in the state it is now, I doubt we have time to prepare ourselves before this nation is forced to wear the yoke of kingship again. But I maintain my faith in Christ's Coming. If not now then in the near future, even if this nation is not ready.'

The two men sat in silence, each troubled by their personal thoughts. Considering Cole's supercilious and dismissive mannerisms, it appeared his host did not practice his lofty principles. Shifting uneasily, Zachariah also reflected on Cole's treasonous attitude towards the Protectorate. He was relieved they had not met in a tavern or other public place. And what does all this have to do with Nicholas's publications, Zachariah mused, feeling his annoyance rise.

Cole's dark mood suddenly evaporated. 'But all was not

lost, Mr Jenkin,' he said enthusiastically, 'Mr Culpeper and I realised the reforms Hartlib and others were advocating required a practical approach in order to disseminate knowledge to a great audience.'

Returning to the book cabinet, Cole opened the glass-paned doors. Gently caressing the shiny leather spines of the various sized tomes, his host explained, 'The success of Mr Culpeper's first translation and the response it received in the press and by the College made me realise his name and notoriety could serve a multiplicity of purposes. Firstly, and most importantly, a series of medicinal texts written or translated by Mr Culpeper would instruct this nation in the knowledge of physic and the skills required for self-treatment. I could also use the texts to promote titles written by our reformist brethren, thus spreading their ideas to a far wider audience than Hartlib and his publishers could ever achieve. With my backing, I set him the task of translating and compiling other medicinal works, while encouraging him to continue to insert political commentary in his prefaces.'[76]

'I am familiar with several of Mr Culpeper's medicinal works you published soon after his translation of the *Pharmacopoeia*, such as the *Treatise of the Rickets* and *Galen's Art of Physic*,' Zachariah said, hoping to impress his host with his knowledge of his friend's works. 'I am also aware he also published astrological-themed works, such as his *Semeotica Uranica* and *Catastrophe Magnatum*. Yet, if my memory serves me correctly, these texts were not published by you.'

A shadow of sour distaste brushed Cole's features. 'Mr Jenkin,' he began contemptuously, 'the subject matter of my publications reflects my personal tastes and those of my readers. I am not averse to controversy. I am the first to admit my authors generate much angst amongst the professions and the Church. But I draw the line at becoming a vehicle for charlatans who deceive this nation with their astrological and occult nonsense. I do not wish to have the reputation of my establishment tarnished by an unwise decision to publish astrological works by anyone, even Mr Culpeper, which could subsequently cause me embarrassment.'

Shocked at Cole's attitude and wishing to defend Nicholas, Zachariah replied, 'But Mr Culpeper was a learned and well-respected astrologer who employed his skills to help the poor. And what of his *English Physician*, you were the publisher were you not?'

'Oh, I respected Mr Culpeper's astrological knowledge,' said Cole. 'Yes, I published his *English Physician* since I recognised his ingenuity in applying astrological principles as a method to instruct his readers in the identification of herbs as well as their proper preparation and uses. His astrological medicine was applauded by his readers. And the commentaries he inserted in his successive prefaces that outraged the College were an added bonus. I also readily acknowledge the worthiness of many esteemed astrologers, such as William Lilly. Yet, you must admit, Mr Jenkin, the craft is open to abuses and such misuse is easily unmasked. Consider the debacle that occurred following the failure of Mr Culpeper's predictions published in his *Catastrophe Magnatum*.[77] I am sure you heard of this?'

Even in Crawley, Zachariah had heard of the event that had tarnished Culpeper's reputation. Years earlier, on Monday, 29th of March, 1652, to be precise, he and other astrologers had predicted that an eclipse of the sun would herald the era of the Fifth Monarchy, when Christ would return to reign.[78] Culpeper had published a tome on this very subject, entitled *Catastrophe Magnatum*, where he confidently predicted kings, magistrates and priests would either die or be imprisoned and the common people would then rise up and prepare for Judgement Day.[79] The astrologers had gathered at Southampton to witness the fall. But the great did not fall. The sun disappeared for several minutes, many people panicked, but then the sun reappeared to grace a clear blue sky.[80]

Zachariah cringed with the memory of the scathing attacks from the press:

> That Greenland cuckoo Culpeper begot of the sperm of a shot star and the Hippomanical piss of a wincing mare, him I charge ... that he meddles not with any stars, but such as he can cut out in paper ... or black patches.[81]

'I should think you would agree my decision not to publish was correct,' Cole asked, disturbing Zachariah's recollections. Savouring a sip of wine, he stared directly into Zachariah's eyes adding smugly, 'It was not my establishment that suffered, but that other publisher who deserved all he got.'

'I assume you are referring to Mr Nathaniel Brooke?'

'That man is an excellent example of why I do not publish astrological and occult themed books, Mr Jenkin,' Cole said, his hand jerking so violently drops of wine spilled over his hand and onto the table.

From Cole's reaction, Zachariah realised he must have hit a raw nerve. He grasped the opportunity to see where this line of questioning would lead.

Shifting in his chair as if making himself comfortable,

Zachariah made ready for an explosive response from his host. 'I understand there is some bad blood between you and Mr Brooke regarding the rights to Mr Culpeper's unpublished manuscripts?' he ventured.

Cole went rigid. Hands clenched, his mouth set in a line so sharp it could cut paper. Zachariah was about to mumble an apology for raising an obviously distressing subject when Cole broke his silence.

'I recall the last time I was in Mr Brooke's company. It must have been around Christmastide, a few weeks prior to Mr Culpeper's death. I was attending him at his home. I recall we were discussing the publication of some of his manuscripts. I was trying to convince him to accept my suggestion that we use the honorary title of doctor in future publications. After all, he was a great teacher of medicine and had incomparably more disciples in that art than the physicians from the College.'[82]

'Oh, I can imagine his response to your suggestion, Mr Cole,' Zachariah replied smiling, trying to lighten the mood. 'He was averse to presenting himself as a member of the professions, preferring to associate himself with the healers and unlicensed practitioners he sought to defend.'

'That may be all well and good, Mr Jenkin. But my aim was to legitimise his reputation as a learned practitioner. For years, I had been trying to persuade him to focus on translating and writing medicinal books rather than continue writing dubious astrological works. Whilst my clients expected political commentary, they also desired their authors to be learned. And who is more learned than an esteemed doctor? It was during this exchange when Brooke burst into the room, uninvited I may add. I suspect he had been standing behind the door listening to our conversation.'

Zachariah imagined how Brooke would have responded to Cole's tirade against the arts he specialised in publishing.

'I later learned the housekeeper had informed him that Mr Culpeper was unavailable. Brooke enquired as to the reason. She replied the master was discussing some matter with his publisher, Mr Cole. On hearing my name, Mr Brooke pushed past her and rushed up the stairs to Mr Culpeper's study. He must have stood at the door trying to eavesdrop on our discussion. I won't bore you with details of the subsequent heated exchange, but it involved Brooke ranting and raving about his rights to certain unpublished manuscripts, as well as telling Mr Culpeper not to listen to my 'uninformed' opinions on astrology and alchemy. The housekeeper eventually bundled Brooke out of the chamber. As she ushered him down the stairs, we could hear him shouting and making threats against me.'

Cole's recollection of the event and especially his description of Brooke's erratic behaviour reminded Zachariah of their encounter.

As he bent down to retrieve the satchel at his feet, Zachariah said, 'I must confess, Mr Cole, I visited Mr Brooke earlier today and purchased his latest publication *Culpeper's Last Legacy*.'

Offered the book across the table, Cole lifted his hands in a disdainful gesture saying, 'I do not need to inspect that book, Mr Jenkin. I already know its contents. I am pained to tell you it is an unauthorised publication.'

'Are you telling me it's a forgery?' Zachariah cried. Dis-

mayed at the thought he had wasted his money and been
made a fool by Brooke, he dropped the offending item on
the table in disgust.

'I would not go that far, Mr Jenkin. If my recollections
are accurate, it would appear the contents are a compilation
of scraps written by Mr Culpeper during the early days of
his practice when he was learning the art. As happens during
apprenticeships, people do make mistakes and later correct
themselves. Consequently, that book is damaging to Mr
Culpeper's reputation. Not just because it is an unauthorised
publication, but worse, it presents the author as a hypocrite,
as some of its contents are contradictory.'[83]

'Alice Heydon's statements in the epistle are therefore
also fake I presume?'

'Mr Brooke expected… no… I should say demanded of
Mr Culpeper's widow first choice of her deceased husband's
unpublished manuscripts. When she kindly sold the bulk
of his works to me, Brooke was outraged and threatened
retribution on both of us.'

Stabbing his finger viciously at the offending item, Cole
continued. 'That book is just one spawn of Brooke's venom.
He all but stole its contents. He then had the effrontery to
attack and ridicule the manuscripts I legitimately purchased
from Mrs Heydon and which she also authenticated. Mr
Brooke calls himself a friend of Mr Culpeper. But in attacking me and Mrs Culpeper, invariably he also besmirches his
reputation.'

Cole ceased his tirade. Bracing his hands against the edge
of the table, he breathed deeply trying to check his temper. In
a controlled and level tone, he continued, 'If… if I ever stoop

so low as to converse with that man again, I would advise him to pull down the sign of the angel above his shop and replace it with the devil, so that people may guess what commodities he sells.[84] So to answer your question, Mr Jenkin, any epistle attached to Brooke's publications, purportedly by Mrs Culpeper, is certainly counterfeit. My publications, however, are indisputable, as attested by Mrs Culpeper.'

'I suppose your guiding hand so soon after Mr Culpeper's death was a great comfort to his widow?' Zachariah asked.

'It was the least I could do for the poor woman,' Cole replied amiably, appearing relieved at the change in topic. 'While her husband's death was expected, as you may understand it left her vulnerable to exploitation. I need not mention by name to whom I refer? It was me she put her trust in. Through her graciousness, I secured sole rights to the manuscripts that will soon complete my venture with Mr Culpeper, the *Rational Physician's Library*.'

If Zachariah had not been forewarned by Jane of Cole's duplicity and his rapacious character, he could have succumbed to his host's persuasiveness. Trying to conceal his scepticism, he asked innocently, 'And your promotion of the elixir *aurum potabile* as well as the publication of Culpeper's manuscript of that same name will also ensure Mrs Culpeper's financial security for many years to come?'

The effect of Zachariah's words was dramatic. Cole's sanctimonious expression wavered, his eyes turning hard. Nervously hesitating, he replied, 'Er… can you explain your meaning, Mr Jenkin?'

'From what you have just told me regarding your position on not publishing titles on the occult arts, I am surprised you assisted Mrs Culpeper and her new husband, Mr John Heydon, in the promotion of the elixir *aurum potabile.*'

As if suddenly realising he could not fool his guest, Cole ceased his charitable pretence and replied, 'In business, Mr Jenkin, men sometimes are required to act in ways not always compatible with their principles and beliefs. Mrs Culpeper agreed to authenticate the manuscripts I wished to publish under her deceased husband's name if I agreed to promote the alchemical elixir her associates were making and selling. I must emphasise, it was purely a business agreement, Mr Jenkin.'

'And the publication of *Mr Culpeper's Treatise of* Aurum Potabile,' Zachariah persisted. 'It seems such a title would appear incongruous on your shelves, considering it would be the only one of its type in your collection.'

'You have been misinformed, Mr Jenkin,' Cole replied haughtily. 'Mr Heydon is the driving force behind this venture. It is he who has assumed control over Mr Culpeper's estate. It was he who tried to persuade me to publish the manuscript. However, I was able to convince him and Mrs Heydon that I was not the best choice of publisher, considering I am not a seller of occult and alchemical titles. I assume you have not actually seen a copy? For if you had, you would know I was not the publisher. Mrs Culpeper sold the title to a Mr Eversden and it is currently being sold at his shop in St Paul's Churchyard.'[85]

'Actually, Mr Cole, I have recently obtained a copy, but have not had the opportunity to read it.' Zachariah replied, choosing not to admit his mistaken assumption as to the publisher and especially from whence he obtained his copy.

'Have you read the book, Mr Cole? If so, in your opinion, do you think it a genuine product of Mr Culpeper's hand?'

Squirming, Cole appeared unable to look directly at Zachariah. Instead his gaze drifted to the window. Lowering his brow, he replied coldly, 'I have given you more time than I had planned, Mr Jenkin. It is late. I have tasks to complete before this day is over.'

'You have not answered my question, Mr Cole,' Zachariah pressed.

'Frankly, Mr Jenkin, I have not bothered purchasing the book. It will never grace my shelves. So I cannot, in truth, satisfy your curiosity. I have heard Mr Brooke has condemned it as a forgery. Yet, if you take his most recent behaviour into account, he may well have been motivated by spite, considering he was not approached to publish the book. I might add being the type of fiddle-faddle Brooke is famous for, he would have been best placed to sell such a title.'

Realising he had overstayed his welcome and Cole would not furnish him with any additional information, Zachariah made ready to leave.

The two men descended the stairs in silence. Pausing at the threshold, Zachariah was about to express his thanks to his host when Cole said, 'Mr Jenkin, if it is of any help, Mr Culpeper once said to me that while he held a high opinion of the alchemical arts in relation to their usefulness in the study of natural philosophy, he believed the best rules of medicine are those of Galen and Hippocrates.[86] I suspect, therefore, if he is the author of the manuscript, I doubt it was written for the purpose that Mr Heydon now claims.'

Before he could respond, Cole closed the door in Zachariah's face. Staring blankly at its painted surface, Zachariah reflected on Cole's enigmatic comment. Brooke had also made a similar statement. As he strolled down the muddy street trying to avoid the worst of the rotting food scraps thrown from kitchen windows, these words echoed in his head: If Mr Culpeper was the author of the manuscript now titled *Culpeper's Treatise of* Aurum Potabile, he never intended it to be used for the purpose it now served.

Where to now, Zachariah thought, as he gazed down at his lengthening shadow.

***

Chapter Five

Dolphin Inn, Aldgate
Friday, 2nd May 1656, morning

A woman's insistent shouting roused Zachariah from his wool-gathering. Picking at his breakfast of fish and bread, his mind wandered from planning his movements for the day to thinking about his family back in Crawley. His wife, Anna, would be rousing the children from their beds on this cold spring morning, while his apprentice prepared to open the shop for another day's trade.

He basked in the glow of the morning sun streaming through the adjacent window. Suddenly, a shadow fell across his table. Glancing up, he found the proprietor of the Dolphin Inn, Mrs Blackburne, glaring at him. A smile froze on his lips. He wondered what misdemeanour he had inadvertently committed.

Zachariah was about to ask when the proprietor hissed, 'Mr Jenkin, there is a *lady* here to see you.' Eyebrow rising questioningly, he noted Mrs Blackburne's disparaging emphasis of the word *lady*. It suggested she considered his visitor anything but.

'I do not allow my guests to invite single women to their chambers. This is a respectable establishment,' she said, flaring her nose in distaste. 'But the woman refuses to leave and demands to see you immediately. I have left her in my private parlour, away from my other guests.' Turning abruptly on her heel, she snapped, 'Please follow me.'

Annoyed at the interruption, but intrigued at the identity of this mysterious woman, Zachariah meekly followed the Dolphin Inn's formidable mistress from the dining hall. He could hear snickering and whispering from fellow guests speculating on the identity of this mysterious lady.

'I caution you,' Mrs Blackburne said as he followed her up the narrow, cramped stairs, 'she is ailing.'

Zachariah hesitated mid-step. Could someone have heard there was an apothecary staying at the Dolphin Inn, he wondered. While he often carried some medicaments in his pack, they were for personal use. If he were caught practising medicine in London, he could be prosecuted by the College.

Reaching the landing, Mrs Blackburne turned and told him not to dawdle. While she swept into her parlour, Zachariah lingered at the threshold peering into her private domain. Evidently she didn't quibble over her comforts, as indicated by the expensive furnishings. A selection of padded chairs and plain folding stools flanked a large circular table dominating the centre of the chamber. From the half-eaten food scattered across the central table, it was evident Zachariah wasn't the only one whose breakfast had been disturbed.

The morning sunlight streamed through a large bow window framed by a heavy green brocade curtain. Seated on a padded bench set into the nook was a figure almost completely enveloped in a heavy brown, woollen travelling cloak. The glare of sunlight prevented Zachariah from distinguishing the person's features.

At the sight of Zachariah, the figure jumped from the

bench and retreated behind the table. Her face now entirely visible, Zachariah recognised his mysterious guest. It was Nicholas's widow Alice.

It had been many years since he last seen Alice Culpeper. He guessed she must now be in her mid-thirties. While her complexion remained fair, her dark eyes were framed by deep frown lines. She appeared as petite as when Nicholas had married her. Black ringlets framing her oval face cascaded over narrow shoulders. If it were not for her overwhelming receding chin, she would have been thought winsome.

Zachariah advanced into the chamber intending to introduce himself, but paused on seeing a wisp of alarm flittering across her face. Taking a step back, she glanced nervously at Mrs Blackburne and then to Zachariah. They stared at each other for several seconds. Straightening her posture, she said angrily in a nasal tone, 'I have been informed you are making enquiries about my deceased husband, Mr Nicholas Culpeper.'

'Mrs—' Zachariah began. He was about to address Nicholas's widow by her new married name. He paused, deciding to allow her to believe he was unaware of her recent betrothal, especially considering Sir William Culpeper, who continued to support Alice following the death of his cousin, was unaware of this development.

'Mrs Culpeper,' Zachariah repeated smiling while holding out his hand in greeting, 'my name is Zachariah Jenkin. I was a dear friend of your deceased husband. I recall meeting you on several occasions many years ago.'

Her eyes widening in recognition, Alice replied testily, 'Oh yes, I recall you were an associate of my husband. What do you want?'

'Who told you I was here, Mrs Culpeper?' Zachariah replied, his smile frozen on his lips. He was unsure of himself. Who had told her of his whereabouts and his enquiries? Surely it wasn't Jane. She would have informed him of her mistress's return, so he would have had time to prepare for this meeting.

'If you must know, I arrived back in London late last night and called on my publisher, Mr Cole. You remember Mr Cole, do you not? He informed me you are making enquiries about my husband's publications on behalf of my deceased husband's relative, Sir William Culpeper.' Wringing her hands nervously, she added, 'I ask you again, what is your interest in Mr Culpeper's publications?'

Trying to set Alice at ease, Zachariah explained his relationship to Sir William. Telling a half-truth, he explained his patron had expressed concern at her current circumstances. But having no knowledge of her fate, he had instructed Zachariah to undertake discreet enquiries.

'I would have taken the opportunity to call upon you, even if Sir William had not asked this of me,' Zachariah continued delicately. 'Nicholas was a dear friend of mine who I sorely miss. I also have thought of your fate, now you are widowed.'

Zachariah was appalled at Brooke's account of Alice's conduct since Nicholas's demise. It was common knowledge that a widow's morals were suspect since they were no longer under the dominion of a male relative. Authors and playwrights portrayed them as harpies who, without even waiting for the corpse of their deceased husband to be buried, would snare vulnerable, wealthy young men into a marriage contract. According to Brooke, the widow Culpeper had not disappointed the playwrights. Yet now, as he stared at this nervous and vulnerable woman who seemed on the brink of hysteria, Zachariah could not imagine her using wiles to snare anyone.

Alice's defiance evaporated in response to Zachariah's conciliatory tone. Shoulders slumping, she appeared to shrink before him. Apparently, deciding to answer Zachariah's questions, she removed her travelling cloak and draped it across the back of a chair. Concealed beneath the cloak was a dark green silk dress, tastefully embroidered and lined with delicate lace. Zachariah was taken aback at the restraint of her attire. The only visible jewellery was a simple pearl necklace almost hidden beneath a fur stole covering her shoulders. Considering the reputation she seemed to have acquired, he was expecting her to be wearing the garishly coloured, excessive attire usually associated with women who didn't have the breeding to present themselves appropriately in public.

Mrs Blackburne hesitated as if unsure of the situation. Alice's initial belligerent manner and her barging into a public house unaccompanied by a servant, had suggested she was little better than a whore. But the timid woman now before her was not the harpy who had confronted her earlier. Now she carried herself as a well-spoken, cultured lady of high station.

As if reading her thoughts, Alice flashed a warm smile and said, 'I must apologise for my rash behaviour, Mrs…'

'Mrs Blackburne, my lady,' she replied deferentially, 'I am the mistress of this establishment.'

'Mrs Blackburne, I thank you for receiving me into your

private quarters. I left my servant in the carriage with my young daughter. I did not deem it appropriate to leave her unaccompanied in the courtyard. But I must speak with Mr Jenkin urgently. Again I apologise for any inconvenience I have caused you.'

Responding to Alice's gesture, the mistress of the Dolphin Inn bowed and with a wave of her hand dismissed any suggestion of a need for an apology. Inviting Alice to take a seat, she quickly cleared away the remains of her breakfast while asking if her distinguished guest required any refreshments.

'As I seem to have developed a cough during my travels, could you bring me honey mixed with boiled water to soothe my throat? And yes, if you have any pottage and bread so that I can break my fast.'

The Landlady smiled and turning towards the door she started, as if forgetting Zachariah was there. 'And you, Mr Jenkin?' she said, glaring at him.

Hesitating, Zachariah did not know how to proceed. He glanced towards Alice now seated demurely, her gloved hands folded on her lap. He wanted to speak to her in private, but now believed it not appropriate to be in a chamber with an unaccompanied lady, especially having reconsidered his opinion of her virtue.

'Mr Jenkin,' Alice began, indicating a seat across from her, 'would you please join me at my breakfast?' Addressing their host, Alice continued, 'Mrs Blackburne, Mr Jenkin was a dear friend of my now deceased husband. We need to discuss matters of a private nature. I can assure you, I am safe in his company.'

'I will fetch your daughter and servant and take them to

the kitchen,' Mrs Blackburne said. Glaring at Zachariah for a moment as if assessing his trustworthiness, she backed out of the chamber, gently closing the door behind her.

As soon as they were alone, Alice turned on Zachariah saying in a steely tone, 'Let us dispense with the pretence, Mr Jenkin. You address me as Mrs Culpeper. Yet, I understand you know I have recently married a gentleman by the name of Mr John Heydon.'

Zachariah felt a flush of embarrassment rise from his throat to his hairline. Unable to maintain eye contact, his gaze dropped to the table. Stammering he said, 'Er... yes, I recall it mentioned you were newly married. I felt it too forward of me to address you by your married name.' He realised he had to be tactful. Both of them understood the implications of Alice's recent remarriage, not simply because her rash actions had caused much comment amongst her deceased husband's associates and friends. Unaware of the marriage, Sir William continued to pay the small stipend he had provided Nicholas for many years. Evidently, Alice had either deemed it unnecessary to inform her deceased husband's patron of her changed circumstances. Or she was deceiving him.

Feeling Alice's gaze boring into him, he glanced up to see her lips pursed in anger. Sighing, she said softly, 'My husband is a learned man of independent means, Mr Jenkin. I need not justify to you my decision to remarry.'

'I am certain Sir William will be pleased to hear of your remarriage, Mrs... Heydon,' Zachariah replied tentatively. Hesitating, he decided to approach Alice with the same directness as she had displayed. 'Nevertheless, there is the issue of Sir William's patronage. I am sure you agree his support of you and your daughter is no longer required?'

Reaching for her cloak Alice replied tersely, 'Mr Jenkin, I am sure you will inform Sir William at the earliest opportunity of my good fortune. If that is all the information you require, I say good day to you.'

'Wait!' Zachariah cried. 'I have some more questions for you.'

'I really don't think we have anything further to discuss, especially now I am no longer under Sir William's patronage. After all,' Alice said sarcastically, 'my recent marriage has voided the contract Mr Culpeper had with his esteemed cousin.'

Fearing he was losing control of the situation, Zachariah blurted, 'Oh, Sir William has expressed interest in your new venture, the making and selling of that elixir, which your husband is making.'

Damn! Zachariah chastised himself. He had done the one thing Sir William had warned him against: revealing the extent of his interest in the elixir. He would have to proceed with greater caution to salvage the situation without alienating himself or Sir William from Alice and her new husband's affairs.

'I mean… I admit Sir William was unaware of your recent marriage to John Heydon. Nonetheless, he was aware of this gentleman's involvement in the promotion of Nicholas's recipe. Sir William requests I make enquiries on his behalf. You do understand, Mrs Heydon, if Sir William wishes to continue his patronage in another form, he needs to be assured it would be a mutually beneficial arrangement?

Yet, in truth, currently I am unable to provide him with an encouraging report, considering the information I have gleaned from others thus far.'

Placing her cloak back on the chair, Alice considered Zachariah as if she were weighing up his words. Securing a wealthy and titled patron would enable her husband to boast in his publications of his association with men of high station. Such a connection would not only legitimise their venture, but an esteemed patron's financial support would guarantee continued success.

Sensing her wavering, Zachariah said, 'I reiterate, Sir William has requested I make enquiries into Nicholas's recent publications as well as this elixir. Thus far, the only information I have acquired has been second-hand, and much of that unfavourable. Yet,' he said frowning, 'I know Sir William would be displeased with me if my reports were based on mere gossip. So, it would be of great assistance if you would furnish me with the information I require while countering any gossip I may have gleaned from others.'

Scrutinising Zachariah through hooded eyelids, Alice remained silent. She raised the crumpled kerchief to her nose and blew into it with an unladylike honk.

'Oh, where is that woman?' she said, glancing anxiously towards the door. 'Would you care to see if there is any ale in that jug over there?' she added waving her gloved hand in the direction of an ornate cabinet.

Tasting the vessel's contents, Zachariah identified it as a light wine. Pouring two glasses, he returned to the table. Smiling sweetly, she asked, 'So what do you want to know, Mr Jenkin?'

'As Mr Cole has evidently informed you, I have been making enquiries into the publication of Nicholas's manuscripts. I am especially interested in the recent title, *Aurum Potabile* and the elixir,' Zachariah explained.

While he summarised the discussions he had had with Cole, Alice either nodded in agreement or spoke only to clarify a point.

'What I don't understand,' he concluded, 'is that Mr Cole was not Nicholas's sole publisher. Yet, it would appear there has been some kind of estrangement between you and Mr Brooke.'

Alice's demeanour abruptly altered at the mention of the latter bookseller's name. In an instant, the demure, petite, well-bred young lady transformed into the vicious harpy Mrs Blackburne must have initially encountered.

'Anything that flouncing braggart has to say is false, Mr Jenkin,' she snarled. 'Certainly, he was one of my husband's publishers. But that didn't give him the right to assume that situation would continue once Mr Culpeper was deceased. Anyway, as Mr Heydon so wisely says, Mr Cole is a respected publisher of medicinal works, so he is best placed to uphold Mr Culpeper's reputation as a physician and gentleman.' Tilting her head and sniffing as if offended by a noxious odour, she added, 'Whereas Mr Brooke's contribution to the bookshops is restricted to cheap and dubious astrological tracts.'

A gentle knock interrupted Alice's tirade. Alice responded in a most demure voice as abruptly as she had turned sour.

Mrs Blackburne entered carrying a mug of steaming honeyed water. 'I have added a few stalks of flower-de-luce,' she said, glancing haughtily at Zachariah as if insinuating that herbal knowledge was not restricted to apothecaries.

Taking the hot mug between her hands, Alice smiled mischievously, replying, 'Thank you, Mrs Blackburne, it will ease my cough.'

While Mrs Blackburne fussed over her distinguished guest, she explained she had retrieved Alice's daughter and servant from the carriage and settled them in the kitchen, where they were currently breaking their fast. 'Your meal will be ready directly, madam,' she added as she left the chamber.

Once Mrs Blackburne had gone, Alice turned to Zachariah and said, 'Mr Jenkin, if it were not for Mr Cole, my family would have descended into poverty many years ago. During their long association, he paid handsomely for Mr Culpeper's toil. I understand, at the time of my husband's death, he had completed seventeen works for Mr Cole. My husband left me a further seventy-nine manuscripts, mostly of his own making.[87] These were his only assets, Mr Jenkin. So, in order to support myself and my young daughter, I did not hesitate in selling these manuscripts to Mr Cole. I am confident under his respected stewardship none of these books will have any disguises or forgeries. Unlike the tracts published illegally by that dandy, Nathaniel Brooke, I must add.'

Zachariah enquired if she considered her hostility towards Brooke was caused by his public condemnation of her, as well as his allegation that Mr Heydon had appropriated Nicholas's manuscripts for his own purposes. He insinuated that, while Sir William was not easily swayed by gossip and slander, he too would be perturbed at the rumours that Alice cuckolded her dying husband under his own roof.

'It may help your case, Mrs Heydon, if you explain the

sequence of events leading to your business arrangement and subsequent marriage to John Heydon,' Zachariah proposed.

A flush of crimson colouring her cheeks, Zachariah watched as she wrung her hands in frustration. Roughly pushing her chair away from the table, she strode to the window. Standing with her back to him, she gazed down to the street where the sounds of carts and shouts of pedlars drifted through the open window.

Almost in a whisper Alice began, 'Sometimes I wonder how I survived all those years with Mr Culpeper and the disappointments he brought down upon us all.'

'I beg your pardon?' Zachariah replied, feeling confused.

'People condemn me for marrying in haste after the demise of my husband. Yet, they are ignorant of the circumstances that forced me into this course of action.' Turning to face him, her chin lifted high in defiance, she continued: 'Mr Jenkin, as Mr Culpeper lay dying, I knew I would have to fend for myself. I no longer had my family to turn to. His disgraceful conduct ensured that!'

Grasping the edge of the heavy curtain, Alice made to examine the weave. Yet, her unfocused eyes indicated her mind was elsewhere. Resentfully, she added softly as if to herself, 'My father… my betrothal certainly didn't bring the rewards he had so hoped.'

Glancing away in embarrassment, Zachariah thought Alice must have been aware he knew of the circumstances leading to her betrothal to Nicholas. He cringed at the memories. While they were fast friends, he was often disturbed at Nicholas's guile. He knew only too well Nicholas had pursued the fifteen-year-old Alice Field solely for her family fortune. Social mores meant he would not have had an opportunity to court the young girl in person. Nicholas hinted he actually had not met her before he had approached her father, a wealthy London merchant.

'I suppose you are wondering as to the reason why I married Mr Culpeper,' Alice said, breaking into Zachariah's thoughts. Turning to face him, she continued, 'My father wished to arrange a good marriage. But he feared if he waited too long, the conflicts between the Royalists and Parliamentarians would make that impossible. So when Nicholas unexpectedly approached him, my papa saw it as an opportunity for our family to establish ties with a titled family—'[88]

'But Nicholas did not have a title,' Zachariah blurted, 'he was the son of a parson and an apothecary's apprentice.'

'Oh, my father was aware of his circumstances,' she replied dismissively. 'But the Culpepers are an ancient titled and distinguished family.' Her cold eyes boring into his, she added, 'Do you know, Mr Jenkin, it was as a consequence of Sir William's distinguished family, who had a long association with the royal court, which persuaded my father to accept his proposal of marriage?'

'No, I was not aware of that,' Zachariah lied, unable to maintain eye-contact.

In an accusing tone, she continued, 'I don't have to tell you, Mr Jenkin, my husband was very conceited. If he wanted something, he could present himself as a learned scholar and gentleman with prospects. At the time of our betrothal, Mr Jenkin, my father believed Nicholas would bring honour to his family and raise our status in society.'

It was true. Nicholas often exploited his distinguished name to gain access to men far above his station. Even penniless, Nicholas's birth into the gentry automatically conferred upon him privileges that money could never provide. In contrast, merchants who had grown wealthy through their own efforts could only achieve higher social status via marriage into the gentry.[89]

Embarrassed, eyes downcast, Zachariah fidgeted with a spoon.

Alice laughed sullenly. 'Honour,' she spat. 'It didn't take long for my family to discover the truth about my husband. You may recall that soon after our marriage, my husband abandoned his apprenticeship and so we were forced to move into a lowly residence outside the city walls. He promised it would only be temporary. He made many promises, Mr Jenkin. Invariably they all turned to dust. He promised that my dowry would enable him to establish an apothecary practice and we would prosper. What he didn't explain was the reason why we needed to live outside London's boundaries. Oh, the shame he brought down upon me and my family,' she said, bringing the kerchief to her face to hide her humiliation.

Zachariah didn't know what to say. Thankfully, the sound of Mrs Blackburne's voice beyond the closed door broke the awkward silence. Knocking gently, she entered carrying a cloth covered tray.

Returning to her chair, her face still flushed with anger, Alice ignored Zachariah. As if realising the tension, Mrs Blackburne silently distributed bowls of steaming, fragrant pottage. Placing a platter of bread and cheese between her two guests, she left them to their meal.

As Zachariah traced the meat floating on the surface of his gruel with his spoon he reflected on Alice's words. He recalled he was shocked when Nicholas announced he didn't require a licence to establish an apothecary trade. Gloating, he boasted he didn't need the authorisation of the Society of Apothecaries. 'After all,' he had said, puffing himself up like a peacock, 'I will be conducting my business outside of London's walls beyond the Society's jurisdiction.'

Nicholas had placed Zachariah in an awkward position. Out of friendship, he wanted to support Nicholas's enterprise. But Zachariah had only just completed his apprenticeship and so feared the wrath of the Society. Nicholas may have been beyond their jurisdiction, but to practise without a licence was not only illegal, it was also not the conduct of a gentleman. Zachariah knew his friend's arrogance would lead to disaster. So, when he had approached him requesting a partnership, Zachariah declined. He was thankful for his good sense because later, the Society had threatened prosecution of a fellow apothecary, Samuel Leadbetter, who had been foolish enough to take up with Nicholas.[90]

Many merchants had supported the political reform movements during the early years of the war, and so Nicholas's involvement would not have perturbed Alice's father. It was a different matter when he began to display behaviours considered scandalous by his learned gentlemanly peers. His abandonment of his apprenticeship was only the first betrayal. He was soon to offend the College of Physicians by openly practising medicine at his home in Spitalfields. His illicit practice of astrology only made matters worse, especially when he was accused of witchcraft.

Zachariah sighed dejectedly, recalling his friend's foolishness. Nicholas could have joined the ranks of the professions by becoming a parson, a favoured choice for second sons from the higher gentry.[91] The church would have provided him with a comfortable parsonage and enough income to live modestly, if not well. Yet, he rejected the opportunity and the social benefits it would offer. He could have become a respected apothecary, a trade considered suitable for the sons of the lower gentry, but the Society was not good enough for him. His stubbornness and pride had led to his fall.

While Alice probably did not have any say in the matter of her betrothal, it was she who suffered as a consequence of Nicholas's rebellious conduct. Honour! Alice had said. Zachariah could imagine how the radical actions of her wayward husband had reflected badly on her. After all, a woman's honour was dependent on her husband's. If he fell, so did she.

'Nicholas meant well,' Alice said as she mopped up the last of her broth with a piece of bread. 'He was a man of conviction and stood by his principles, even when they were damaging to his reputation and his pocket. He was free-hearted and generous. If a patient could not pay, he would donate his services. He was careless with his purse, claiming his mind was so preoccupied with higher mysteries, he would not stoop to such worldly trifles…'[92]

She paused, a shadow of grief and loss descending upon her. With a strangled sob, she added, 'he was a better physician to others than he was to himself or his family.'

Sensing her distress, Zachariah reached out to comfort her, but Alice pulled back. Zachariah froze, fearing he had already compromised her reputation simply by them being unchaperoned. To be seen trying to console her might be misinterpreted.

Sighing, Alice's shoulders slumped as if she were burdened by a great weight. 'While Nicholas practised his physic on the poor for little return, he could not save his own children,' she whispered, her voice ragged with controlled emotion. 'During our fourteen years of marriage, I bore seven children. Only my fourth, Mary, has survived.'[93] Her features brightening, she glanced up at Zachariah and said, 'She is a true picture of her father, with her dark locks.'

Sighing again with frustration she said, 'My husband's disrespectful and rebellious conduct caused me to become estranged from my papa. Father became enraged when he realised his hoped-for patronage had evaporated as a consequence of Nicholas betraying his position as a gentleman.'

Eyes flashing, straightening her spine, she added proudly, 'Be that as it may, Mr Jenkin, I stood by my husband. I tried to be a dutiful wife. I never encroached on his prerogative nor disturbed him in his studies. I managed the household while my husband was busy with his books and his patients. I was only fifteen when I married,' she cried, her voice rising with emotion. 'Yet it was I who fought to maintain our honour while my husband reduced us to penury with his lofty thoughts and vain, unrealised promises.'[94]

Evidently Mr Field had wiped his hands of his disappointing and wayward soninlaw, Zachariah thought as he gazed at Alice with pity and newfound respect. While it was her father who had arranged the betrothal, it was apparent he also blamed his daughter for his thwarted plans to rise in society. Now she was estranged from her family and left to fend for herself. Possibly, he mused, her father had also heard rumours of her dalliance.

Alice poured herself another glass of wine. 'You asked the circumstances in which Mr Heydon came into my life, did you not?' Choosing a seat adjacent to the window she continued, 'Just before Mr Culpeper's health had failed completely, he all but abandoned me by relocating to his house in Berkshire.[95] He claimed living so close to London was not conducive to his health. I was left alone in Spitalfields to care for the household. He was too ill to write, my dowry all but spent, what choice did I have? I had chambers to spare, so I let a couple out to boarders. It was my good fortune when Mr Heydon approached me seeking accommodation.'

Glancing towards the window, she spoke slowly as if choosing her words carefully, 'I offered Mr Heydon the rental of one of my spare chambers because he told me he was well versed in philosophy and had travelled much.' Smiling faintly to herself, she added, 'I thought he would be a good companion for my husband and provide some assistance to his work.'

Zachariah was quickly forming the opinion that Alice had woven these tales so often as a means to defend or justify herself, that she now believed them to be true. He had not met the man in question, yet Brooke's account suggested Alice was beguiled by Heydon's charms. He was confident that Nicholas would never have been persuaded by such a peacock.

'So did they establish a working relationship?' Zachariah asked innocently, trying to keep his tone neutral as not to betray his doubt.

Blushing, Alice's gaze dropped to the floor. 'Er… when my husband returned, his health was failing. He wished to secret himself in his study with his secretary, Mr William Ryves. I… understand… Mr Heydon met him on a few occasions. He later told me he had approached my husband with a proposal to make the elixir. But, inexplicably, Mr Culpeper declined.'

Wringing her hands in frustration and gazing imploringly at Zachariah, she wailed, 'Oh, Mr Jenkin, my husband could be so unreasonable! I did not understand then. I still do not understand! If my husband had in his possession a recipe that cured all ills, why didn't he use it on himself? And why did he refuse Mr Heydon's generous offer to finance and oversee its making?' Falling back into the chair in despair, she whispered, 'I just don't know.'

Try as she might, Alice's pleadings did not ring true. If Nicholas had refused Mr Heydon the recipe, why then did she so readily agree to hand it over so soon after his death? Zachariah's mind drifted to the handbills and tracts promoting the elixir that she and Heydon had recently printed.

'Er, I recall reading one of your epistles, Mrs Heydon,' Zachariah began nervously, knowing he needed to discover the truth, but fearful of Alice's reaction when confronted. 'From my recollection, you claim a learned friend had persuaded you to publish one of your husband's manuscripts containing references to the elixir *aurum potabile*. I recall you called it a rare golden liquor, or cordial, and universal medicine.[96] Didn't you also claim the discovery of the recipe was the result of collaboration between your husband and a Dr Freeman? And that Nicholas had left the recipe and manuscript to you, so you could realise his wish to make and sell it?'[97]

While he spoke, Alice rose from her chair and turned to face the window. Even though he could no longer see her features, Zachariah knew she was angry. Grasping the edge of the brocade curtain again, she wrung it so tightly it threatened to fall. Her rigid posture suggested she was trying to control her temper.

He suspected Alice was quite aware that he was subtly goading her, because the likelihood that she had actually written any of the epistles or commentaries signed in her name was very slight indeed. Certainly, as the daughter of a wealthy merchant she may have been tutored in the art of reading, as all she required was a book and a patient tutor. Yet, writing was another matter. As writing implements—inks, pens and paper—were expensive commodities, usually only sons learned to write. Possibly, she could manage to sign her name, but the question of Alice's ability to write these epistles, write anything at all, hung in the air.

Finally, she turned and faced him. Flushed, eyes ablaze, she said in a steely, strained tone, 'Mr Jenkin, Mr Heydon was a pillar of strength to me when my husband died. His kind offer of support was gratefully accepted. He did not ask anything in return. Not like Mr Brooke and, I must confess, Mr Cole, who proffered sympathy. But I knew they coveted my husband's manuscripts. Mr Heydon was sympathetic to my plight. While my husband left many unpublished manuscripts, what would become of me once I had sold them all? My dowry was gone. I had a child and household

to maintain. Mr Heydon, being a learned gentleman, was of
the opinion my husband was not in his right mind during
those last weeks. He assured me the best course of action was
to hand over the remaining manuscripts to Mr Cole, who
would ensure they were published. Even though my husband
refused to take the elixir himself, Mr Heydon convinced me
it was my duty to release his secret, so that it could relieve
people's suffering. After all, Mr Heydon reminded me my
husband dedicated his life to teaching the poor and sick how
to treat themselves. If he had been in his right mind at the
end, he would have wished this for me and for the people
of England.'

Zachariah pondered Alice's claims, concluding she had
lost touch with reality and now lived in a fantasy world. Yet
the discrepancies between her accounts and the contents of
these tracts could not be ignored or argued away. What of
the handbills posted around London so soon after Nicholas's
funeral advertising the elixir, yet claiming they were drafted
by Nicholas a year before his death? Was Alice aware of the
contents of these handbills, had she seen them pasted on the
walls around the town, or was she preferring to ignore them?

He was about to broach these delicate questions when
there was a commotion in the hallway. The door bursting
open, a small figure tumbled into the parlour. It was a girl of
about ten, her dark woollen dress decorated with embroidered
coloured thread. While examining the young visitor, Zachariah rose from his chair. Aware she was being watched, the
girl began to smooth out her dress. Looking up in defiance,
her eyes met Zachariah's and held his gaze.

He instantly recognised Nicholas's countenance in the

child's expression. Mary indeed, Zachariah thought. Nicholas's sole surviving issue. He glanced in her mother's direction, seeking an introduction.

Alice's composure returned as she introduced Mary to Zachariah.

Mary only nodded at Zachariah. Turning to her mother, she whined, 'Mama, when can we leave? I am tired, I want to get home. We have been away for so long, Mama.' Stamping her foot in defiance, she shouted, 'I want to leave now!'

Breathless, Mrs Blackburne appeared and hovered at the door, uncertain if she should enter. Making her apologies, she explained Mary had suddenly rushed from the kitchen seeking out her mother.

Headstrong as her father, Zachariah thought as he gazed down at this firebrand, wondering if Nicholas had been so wilful. Realising they could no longer continue their conversation, Zachariah addressed Alice, 'I have kept you from your daughter long enough. I hope you understand I need to discuss this matter with Mr Heydon. Could a meeting be arranged?'

Alice wavered, appearing uncertain how to respond. Zachariah felt Alice's reaction to her daughter's sudden intrusion was more relief than annoyance. After all, the distraction had saved her from answering further difficult and possibly incriminating questions.

'I will consult with my husband. But I am sure he would be agreeable to Sir William's proposal,' Alice said, smiling stiffly.

Allowing Mrs Blackburne to assist with her cloak, she continued, 'I cannot recall if I mentioned that Mr Heydon had sent me ahead. He is still in Cambridge, but I expect him to return to London by tomorrow evening. When he returns, I will raise these matters. I expect he will send a servant to the Dolphin Inn with a response.' Taking her daughter's hand, she bid Zachariah a good day as Mrs Blackburne escorted her from the parlour.

* * *

Chapter Six

Heydon's Residence
Saturday, 3rd May 1656, mid-morning

Zachariah decided to visit Nicholas's house, hoping he could find out more about the mysterious outbuilding before Mr Heydon returned to London that evening. On arrival, he knocked on both the shop and residence doors, only to discover no-one was home. Wandering to the rear, he made his way to the outbuilding and climbed up to the window where the shutter was askew. His nose pressed to the glass, he was so preoccupied he didn't hear the sound of approaching footsteps.

He started as something rough was thrust over his head. Struggling, he would have fallen from the chopping block if a pair of rough hands hand not grasped him around the waist and dragged him to the ground. As he thrashed about in terror, his attacker bound his hands. Dragging Zachariah to his feet, he pushed him forward. Realising resistance was futile, Zachariah allowed himself to be manhandled.

He sensed he was being led into a chamber. Forcing Zachariah to sit, the rough hands readjusted the bindings, securing his arms to the back of a chair. He couldn't move. The sack was dragged off his face so harshly it scraped his nose, causing his eyes to water. His eyes adjusting to the gloom, the almost overpowering stench of burnt sulphur suggested he was inside the laboratory building.

'Who are you?' a voice barked from a darkened corner of the chamber.

Zachariah was incensed. How dare this rogue manhandle him! Rebelling and refusing to co-operate, he remained silent.

'I repeat. Who are you? If you do not explain yourself, I cannot promise what your fate will be,' the voice threatened.

Zachariah couldn't help himself, he was so infuriated. 'Sir,' he began forcefully, 'my name is Mr Zachariah Jenkin. I am an apothecary from Crawley in Sussex.'

'I have never heard of you. Why are you trespassing on private land?'

As he was about to answer, he heard a woman's scream. Turning his head, he recognised Alice Culpeper standing on the threshold, her hands raised to her face, eyes blazing in shock.

'Oh, oh! Mr Heydon...'

Rushing from his corner, the man grabbed Alice's arm and bundled her out of the chamber.

Wailing hysterically, Zachariah heard her say, 'He is here representing Mr Culpeper's patron, Sir William Culpeper. I met with him yesterday, but forgot to inform you of his offer! He wishes to speak with you about financing the elixir. You have to let him go!'

Voices now indistinct, he could not catch the remainder of the heated discussion between Alice and this man, who Zachariah assumed must be the elusive Mr Heydon.

Re-entering the chamber, the man approached him, fawning. 'Mr Jenkin, I am so, so sorry for this misunderstanding,' he said, wringing his hands.

Addressing someone standing behind him, Heydon snarled, 'Hurry up and untie this poor man.'

Turning his head, Zachariah saw a man dressed in restrained plain attire typical of a devout Puritan, yet incongruent with his rough, hostile expression. Seeing him brandishing a knife, Zachariah tried to jerk out of the way, fearing he was to be stabbed.

'Don't frighten him,' the younger gentleman hissed. 'Here, let me do it,' he said, grabbing the knife. Walking behind the chair, Zachariah felt the bindings cut from his wrists. Pulling his arms forward, he began to massage his bruised and grazed flesh. Holding the offending bindings in soft scholastic hands, the man stood back far enough for Zachariah to study his features. He understood why Alice had become infatuated with this man.

Zachariah estimated Heydon was in his late twenties. Tall and lean, his straight, casual bearing projected an aura of arrogant or conceited confidence. His ruddy, clear, oval face, dominated by a haughty roman nose was framed by long, dark, flaxen brown hair curling over his shoulders.[98] His attire was that of a prosperous gentleman. Too extravagant for Zachariah's tastes, Heydon wore expensively cut tight crimson breeches and a white silk shirt edged with oversized ruffled cuffs. Glittering silver buttons decorated his embroidered silk waistcoat.

'Please, Mr Jenkin, accept my heartfelt apologies for this misunderstanding,' Heydon said with a smile Zachariah immediately found ingratiating and sycophantic. 'We have not been formally introduced, but I am Mr John Heydon.' Offering his hand, Zachariah noticed Heydon's fingernails were manicured, but stained with a grey substance that had eaten deep into his flesh.

Helping Zachariah to his feet, Heydon suggested they retire to his parlour. Offering his guest a comfortable padded chair, Heydon called for refreshments. Zachariah noticed Heydon's associate leaning against the windowsill. Staring momentarily at Zachariah in an overtly hostile manner, he then turned away and peered into the street.

Zachariah's discomfort was briefly alleviated when Jane entered carrying a tray. Pouring the wine, she totally ignored her master's guest. He played along, not even glancing in her direction.

'Please excuse me, I need to attend to an urgent matter,' Heydon said as he followed Jane. Even though closing the door behind him, Zachariah heard him tell Jane they must not be disturbed for any reason.

'Mr Jenkin,' Heydon said cordially, sweeping back into the room. Gracefully extending his hand towards the window, he continued. 'I haven't had the opportunity to introduce my esteemed associate, the physician and scholar Dr William Freeman. Please doctor, join us at the table.'

Dr Freeman sauntered arrogantly to the table, all the while scowling. Zachariah recognised his name: Dr Freeman was mentioned in Alice's handbills as the man responsible for selling the elixir.

Heydon settled into an elaborately embroidered and carved chair, almost a throne, Zachariah mused.

Heydon smiled, yet his humour didn't reach his cold unblinking eyes. Reaching for his glass, all the while watching Zachariah intently, he took a sip. Gesturing, he encouraged

Zachariah to indulge. Tasting his wine, Zachariah nodded in appreciation.

Satisfied his guest was settled, Heydon said, 'Mr Jenkin, let me explain this unfortunate incident. I hope you can appreciate there are many rogues in London ever ready to rob you blind.' Heydon squirmed in his seat. 'Er… please Mr Jenkin, put yourself in my place. I arrived home after a long journey only to find someone trespassing on my property and appearing to be trying to break into my laboratory. What should I think but to assume he seeks to steal this cordial from me? I did what any resourceful man would do to protect his investment…' Pausing, it seemed as if he were seeking some acknowledgement from Zachariah.

Zachariah gazed back impassively, as he considered that the only rogues who had intruded onto Nicholas's property were seated before him.

Heydon smiled and said, 'My dear wife, Alice, has just explained the true purpose behind your enquiries. Again, Mr Jenkin,' he cried, wringing his hands in distress, 'if I had known, I would never have acted so rashly. Please accept my apologies.'

Seeking to ingratiate himself with his host, whom Zachariah surmised would readily respond to such an advance, Zachariah returned his host's smile. 'Mr Heydon,' he said smoothly, 'under the circumstances, I accept your apologies. I understand your desire to protect your investment.'

Taking a deep breath, Zachariah boldly broached the subject that had bought him to London. 'I assume that Alice has informed you that I have been charged by my patron, Sir William Culpeper, to make enquiries into this elixir you speak of. I have been instructed to assess the veracity of this cordial.'

Zachariah paused. Taking a sip of his wine, he observed Heydon lean towards him, waiting expectantly.

Not wishing to disappoint and knowing exactly what his host wanted to hear, Zachariah continued his baiting. 'Mr Heydon, I must emphasise I am undertaking these enquiries on behalf of Sir William. I am to make a report of my findings and conclusions. If they are favourable, Sir William will consider extending his patronage to you in the form of financial assistance. In return, he seeks to share in the profits from the sale of this elixir.'

Holding up his hand in response to Heydon's attempt to interrupt, Zachariah continued. 'The report must include my opinion of your character. And sadly, to date, it will not be favourable, no matter what apologies and explanations you may extend.'

Heydon appeared mortified. 'Oh Mr Jenkin, how can I rectify my rash conduct? What can I do to dissuade you of your lowly opinion of me?' he cried in an overly theatrical manner.

'Well, firstly, you can begin by telling me why Mr Culpeper's widow has entrusted her deceased husband's secrets to you.'

'Ah, where to begin,' Heydon said, settling himself into his chair, his distress instantly transforming into smugness. As if relishing the opportunity to play centre stage, he launched into an elaborate biography.

His father, Mr Francis Heydon, was a London gentleman who ensured his son received a comprehensive Classical Greek and Latin education. Yet, having supported the Royalists meant that young John was unable to attend university as his family were forced to flee to the Continent.[99]

'I then travelled extensively throughout Spain and Italy, and as far east as Arabia and Persia,' he continued. 'While in the mysterious East, I studied the philosophies of the ancients and kept a journal of my discoveries.'[100]

Heydon proceeded to tell a tale of mystery, intrigue, adventure and his involvement with a secret society, the Rosicrucians.[101] If he had known, Zachariah could have read similar accounts in translated versions of three treatises originally published in Germany several years earlier: the *Fama Fraternitatis* and *Confessio Fraternitatis*, and *The Chemical Wedding*.[102] The pillars of the Rosicrucian movement, these books inflamed the imaginations of European and English scholars and gentlemen. The original German authors drew upon various contemporary intellectual traditions circulating in Europe, including Hermetic philosophy and Paracelsian alchemical theories and practices.[103]

Heydon told how he had followed in the footsteps of the founder of the Rosicrucian fraternity, Dr Christian Rosenkreuz, a German scholar, philosopher and doctor. 'Dr Rosenkreuz desired to travel to the East to gather wisdom,' Heydon explained. 'During his journey, he became acquainted with the wise men of Arabia and beheld what great wonders they wrought. Bargaining with the Arabians, he obtained their alchemical secrets, which he then translated into Latin.[104] It was in Arabia where he learned physic and philosophy, how to raise the dead, as well as the secrets of the alchemical arts. After three years of travelling and learning, he arrived in Egypt where he discovered the secrets of *aurum potabile*.

'You may know it by its common names, Mr Jenkin, the philosopher's stone or the elixir of life, an alchemical potion that cures all ailments and extends one's life,'[105] Heydon said, smiling indulgently.

Witnessing Zachariah start at the mention of the elixir, Heydon gestured excitedly. 'Yes, Mr Jenkin, it was Dr Rosenkreuz who first discovered the recipe for this wondrous elixir.' Sighing, he added, 'Sadly, the members of the Rosicrucian fraternity, who continue Dr Rosenkreuz's great works, conceal their secrets from the likes of ordinary men.'

Pausing, he glanced at his associate, who continued hovering menacingly. Addressing him, Heydon said, 'Sir, could you leave us? I trust you have matters to attend to in the laboratory.' His scowl deepening, Dr Freeman struggled from his chair. Without taking his leave, the doctor strode arrogantly from the parlour, slamming the door behind him.

Satisfied Freeman was out of earshot, Heydon whispered, 'I have been graced with the knowledge of this elixir, but have taken an oath to conceal the Rosicrucian's alchemical secrets. Yet I am able to break that oath if I deem that person worthy of these arcane secrets.[106] Hence in a gesture of goodwill, and in respect for your esteemed patron, I will reveal some of my most treasured secrets.'

Rising from his chair, Heydon gestured Zachariah to follow him. 'Let us retire next door to my library, Mr Jenkin.'

***

The men hurried the few short paces to the apothecary shop adjacent to the residence.

Zachariah knew they were to retire to his deceased friend's

domain, the study where Nicholas had spent much of his life writing and translating. He cringed, recalling Jane's comment that this chamber was where his friend had breathed his last. As he climbed the stairs, he remembered a chamber bathed in the glow of afternoon sunlight streaming through the tall wide window; of books and manuscripts, and astrological paraphernalia scattered over tables, as well as charts gracing the whitewashed walls.

Following Heydon into the chamber, he stared forlornly about because all that remained of his deceased friend was his old oak desk and worn padded chair. The chamber now reflected its new master's personality: table surfaces free of papers, books stacked neatly on shelves. It was a lifeless, sterile place.

Zachariah paused in his despondent assessment. Trying to conceal a satisfied smile, he realised Heydon hadn't been entirely successful in his seizure of Nicholas's domain because lingering in the air was the distinct aroma of sweet vanilla tobacco.

Taking Nicholas's favourite chair, grasping the arms in a gesture of ownership or possession, Heydon addressed his guest.

'Ah, Mr Jenkin, I understand you were absent during the final difficult year of Mr Culpeper's life, the very period when I had the good fortune of being welcomed into his household. By then, he had become secretive and protective of his works, fearing others would steal his labours. I came across his original alchemical manuscript and immediately recognised its significance. Yet, try as I might to convince him to reveal his wisdom to his readers, he refused to publish, fearing ridicule and condemnation. But that is the nature of these works, Mr Jenkin.'

'In what way?'

Pointing a long slender finger to a stack of books on the table between them, Heydon said, 'These books represent the finest works on the mysteries of alchemy. Eugenius Philalethes and Robertus de Fluctibus are not the author's real names, they are pseudonyms, Mr Jenkin. They spend their lives studying the alchemical mysteries, yet most are reluctant to reveal their true identities. These are dangerous times for alchemical adepts, Mr Jenkin.'

Whilst a popular pursuit amongst scholars and adepts on the Continent and patronised by European aristocracy, the practice of alchemy had become discredited during the reign of Queen Elizabeth and had never recovered. The English Queen jailed a European alchemist who failed to turn base metals into gold, and so forbade her subjects to practice the art.[107] Subsequently, alchemical practitioners became the butt of mirth and ridicule and were a popular theme for satirical plays and poetry.[108] Mocking the vocabulary of alchemical texts, audiences associated the practitioners with fakery and avarice, thus driving them further underground.

'The charlatans of old damaged the esteemed reputation of alchemical scholars and practitioners,' Heydon explained. 'Furthermore, in these present times, political radicals such as the Fifth Monarchists have borrowed the alchemical mysteries to articulate their causes. Have you heard of Mary Rand?'

Zachariah replied he was acquainted with the doctrines of the radical sectarian group who played a central role in the revolution. But Rand was a name not familiar.

'Mary Rand has recently predicted an alchemical adept will soon discover the philosopher's stone, or *aurum potabile*,' Heydon said.[109] 'The Monarchists claim this discovery will herald the coming reign of Christ and bring peace to the Commonwealth. Nonetheless, other self-interested men try to discredit or quash this notion by condemning the alchemical arts. So, not only are we beset by ridicule of what others claim we cannot do, we are now attacked for what people claim we can!'

'Yet I cannot find anything in Mr Culpeper's publications that threatens rebellion or discord through alchemical means. He condemned the fakery of alchemists and advised against the use of alchemical medicines,' Zachariah said defensively.

Leaning forward, Heydon shot back, 'You are mistaken. Mr Culpeper did discuss alchemical and Hermetic wisdom. However, he concealed these themes from the eyes of the unlearned by using allegorical and symbolic language.'

Zachariah stared blankly, confused at Heydon's comments.

Leaning back in his chair, Heydon selected a book from a shelf behind him and offered it to Zachariah. 'Have you not seen Mr Culpeper's most recent publication, his *Treatise of* Aurum Potabile?'

Not wishing to reveal from whence he had obtained his copy, Zachariah replied that he had recently purchased one from a bookseller in London, but not had an opportunity to study it in any detail.

'Most adepts write with such a wary and well-sensed skill. They fill their pages with riddles drawn out of the midst of deep occult knowledge and secret learning. Such skills of concealment make it impossible for any but the wisest to approach or come near the subject matter,' Heydon explained.[110]

Brandishing the volume at his host, Zachariah asked, 'So, Mr Heydon, what are the secrets contained within this book that Nicholas feared being revealed?'

Testing Zachariah's patience by smiling in his now familiar ingratiatingly indulgent manner, Heydon quietly said, 'Mr Culpeper was first and foremost an alchemist, Mr Jenkin, a purveyor of Paracelsian chemical medicines. From his research into these deep alchemical mysteries, he discovered the secrets of the universal elixir!'

'Sir,' Zachariah snorted, his tone betraying anger, 'whilst I have only briefly studied the text, I could not find any recipe for the making of an elixir. Mr Culpeper all but admits such in the conclusion.' Gently placing the book down on the table, he added confidently, 'From my reading, this work seems to represent Mr Culpeper's scholastic study of the creation and operation of the natural world.'

'But don't you see, Mr Jenkin, that is what Mr Culpeper intended,' Heydon snapped impatiently. 'His study of the operation of the whole world is a symbolic study of the anatomy of man. For it is only with this knowledge that the universal elixir can be discovered.'

Reaching for the book, Heydon turned to the final page. 'If you recall, Mr Culpeper stated that his treatise was theoretical and so was never intended to reveal the secrets of the making of *aurum potabile*. Why you may ask? Because wisdom needs to be gained before the practice can commence. By practice, Mr Culpeper was referring to the transformation of matter through alchemical processes.'

If Heydon's assertions were accurate, then Nicholas would have been one amongst the majority of alchemical scholars who restricted themselves to the philosophical dimensions of the art. Known as esoteric or textual alchemists, they spent their lives reading the works of earlier alchemists. Sometimes they compiled their own alchemical treatises, using the secretive and symbolic language of the adepts. Such works were often merely collections of passages copied verbatim from earlier works and cobbled together with little or no original contributions by the people who claimed to be the authors.

A minority of alchemical scholars delved into the actual practice of the art. They were either wealthy enough to afford the expensive equipment necessary for experimentation, or they secured patrons with promises of riches. Practical alchemists sought to discover the elusive transmuting agent for turning metal into gold, or creating the elusive medicinal elixir, *aurum potabile*.[111]

Speaking reverently and placing his hand on his breast as if to give a solemn oath, Heydon concluded, 'As I stated before, it was I with my breadth of knowledge into the alchemical mysteries who discerned the secrets hidden within Mr Culpeper's manuscript. With the assistance of my esteemed and learned associates, I am now making the universal elixir. I have undertaken this quest not for personal gain, but for the betterment of mankind. And that is all I have done.'

Rising from his chair, Heydon said, 'Please, let me show you the wonderful work my associates and I are achieving.'

Leading Zachariah down the stairs and through the rear workroom, they made their way through the garden plots to Heydon's alchemical laboratory.

Inspecting the brick edifice, Zachariah wondered why Heydon had the structure specially built, considering he already had Nicholas's fully equipped apothecary workshop. Stepping into the chamber, the answer was immediately obvious.

Wrinkling his nose at the acrid pungent fumes, Zachariah's attention was drawn to wisps of grey smoke leaking from a strange contraption that dominated the chamber. A large sealed egg-shaped glass vessel filled with bubbling steaming liquid sat precariously on a waist-high, barrel-shaped metal container. Attached to the barrel's curved side was a row of flues, and the thick grey smoke seeped from an unsealed joint on the largest of these. From the rear of the contraption light grey steam spouted from three smaller flues. Sets of tongs and other foundry tools hung from hooks screwed into the bare ceiling beams. Nuggets of coal and cuts of wood were scattered on the bare clay floor and stacked in untidy piles.

Wearing a tattered and blackened leather apron, a man busily worked a large set of bellows. He was blowing air into a charcoal-filled receptacle at the base of the barrel. Even though his grimy face was hidden behind strings of damp unruly hair, Zachariah recognised the worker as Dr Freeman.

While Heydon and Freeman engaged in a lively and animated discussion, Zachariah examined the chamber. Glass, ceramic and earthenware vessels were stacked on shelves that lined the walls. They appeared similar to those in his apothecary shop, yet instead of dried plant materials, these vessels contained unfamiliar powders, oils and chemicals of varying hues. A selection of burners, funnels, bottles and flasks were neatly arranged along a large trestle table.

Nailed to the whitewashed brick walls was a selection of parchments. Some were covered with a myriad of unfamiliar symbols, others depicted the zodiac and planetary systems. Most intriguing were the illustrations of fantastic creatures: winged serpents and dragons; a figure half-man, half-woman; an old, decrepit, crippled man watering a gnarled and twisted ancient tree.

'Those represent the secret cryptic language of the alchemists, Mr Jenkin,' Heydon said close to Zachariah's ear, causing him to flinch. Heydon grasped his guest's arm and drew him to the furnace. 'I have conferred with my associate, Dr Freeman. He agrees we should reveal the secret processes involved in the making of the elixir, so you can write an accurate and favourable report to Sir William.'

Glancing towards Dr Freeman, his characteristic scowl now an expression of barely concealed rage, Zachariah doubted he had agreed to anything.

'Before you,' Heydon said loudly, pointing towards the egg-shaped container, 'is the Hermetic Vessel, or Philosopher's Egg, where the transmutations occur. Yet, not all men are able to perform these processes. No,' he exclaimed, placing his hand over his breast, 'one needs to be pious and pure of heart. To prepare, I must perform secret rituals over several days. Then I calculate an astrological chart to determine the best time to proceed.'

Gesturing to Zachariah to follow, Heydon moved to a stained wooden bench. Setting a marble mortar before him, from his pocket Heydon drew out a small, intricately cut, opaque glass vial with a brass lid. Withdrawing a speck of yellow dust with a pair of silver tweezers, he held it up to

Zachariah's face. As if awed he whispered, 'Gold, Mr Jenkin! The golden seed. The son of the philosopher's stone, it transforms base metals into gold.'[112]

Dropping the precious grain into the mortar, Heydon reached for a flask of what appeared to be plain water. Removing the stopper, he poured a small amount into the vessel. 'I dissolve this pure fine gold into a solution of Aqua Regis; a yellow liquor made according to the alchemist's art. I then add four ounces of salt and distil them together.' Pouring a drop of viscous liquid into the solution, Heydon narrated his actions, 'Now I add a drop of oil of tartar. As you can see, as soon as it touches the solution, it changes from its natural yellow hue to become clear and white. That indicates the gold has sunk to the bottom of the vessel.'[113]

Gazing up from his task at Zachariah's enthralled expression, Heydon frowned as he pushed the mortar to one side. Sighing, he said, 'I regret I cannot show you the remainder of the process, as I have to wait till the morrow to complete the transmutations. However, what I can reveal is this.' Heydon unlocked a reinforced door of a stout oak cabinet.

With both hands, he gently lifted out a large clear glass bottle containing dirty yellow liquid. Holding it up to a window to allow sunlight to illuminate the contents, he explained: 'This, Mr Jenkin, is the most precious liquor. For when it's transmuted, it becomes the most treasured of liquors, *aurum potabile.*'

Offering Zachariah the vial of gold dust he said, 'It is for this reason, Mr Jenkin, that a poor and impoverished scholar such as I require the financial support of a wealthy patron…'

'But why can't you make your own gold?' Zachariah

asked perplexed, as he closely examined the vial's decorative moulding.

Snatching the vial from Zachariah and slipping it back into his pocket, Heydon replied, 'Once transmuted, the gold loses its power. Gold made from gold cannot be used as a seed. The elixir contains only the spirit of gold. It is not gold in itself and so cannot transmute other metals. Consequently, Mr Jenkin, in order to make *aurum potabile*, I require a constant source of gold seed.'[114]

Guiding Zachariah to the polished oak table on the other side of the chamber, Heydon invited his guest to take a seat while he poured a couple of glasses of light wine from a glazed earthenware jug.

'Mr Jenkin, would it be possible for me to meet with Sir William in person?'

Taking a moment to consider, Zachariah replied, 'If my report is favourable, such a meeting could be arranged. In the meantime, my patron has charged me with negotiating a preliminary contract with you. If Sir William agrees to the terms, certainly he will invite you to his estate to formalise the arrangements. So, to begin, Mr Heydon, what do you propose?'

'An initial payment of three hundred pounds from your worthy patron, a man of high esteem and standing,' Heydon replied, unsuccessfully concealing an expression of naked avarice.

Blanching at the outrageous amount, Zachariah exclaimed, 'For three hundred pounds my patron could buy the recipe outright and secure my services to make it! And by patronage, I doubt Sir William means supporting you or your lifestyle.'

Smiling enigmatically, Heydon smoothly replied, 'Ah… Sir William may be able to purchase a recipe. But it won't be Mr Culpeper's. Even with a recipe, Mr Jenkin, you lack both the alchemical knowledge and skills to succeed.'

Facing each other in a silent standoff, Zachariah considered Heydon's proposal. Concluding he had nothing more to offer, he let it be known the interview was at an end. Rising from his chair he said, 'Thank you, Mr Heydon, for demonstrating the making of the elixir. I will present your offer to Sir William for his consideration. If he agrees, I will contact you again.'

Standing abruptly, causing his chair to clatter to the floor, Heydon asked in alarm, almost pleadingly, 'So, do you believe Sir William will agree to my proposal?'

'That I cannot answer,' Zachariah stated. Turning to the door he added, 'I have stayed here long enough. The earlier I can leave for Sussex, the sooner you will receive a reply.'

Heydon ordered Dr Freeman to go into the street and hail a hackney coach.

'Please, don't bother yourself,' Zachariah said, 'as it is a fine day, I will walk back to the Inn.'

Making his goodbyes and requesting Heydon extend his regards to his wife, Zachariah turned towards London with his thoughts on the report he was to prepare that evening for his patron, Sir William Culpeper.

* * *

Chapter Seven

William Ryves Residence, Southwark
Sunday, 4th May 1656, mid-afternoon

On his return to the Dolphin Inn that previous evening, Mrs Blackburne had presented Zachariah with a note from Nicholas's secretary, Mr William Ryves:

> *Sir,*
> *Mr Culpeper's housekeeper, Miss Jane Wilson, has requested we meet to discuss matters concerning the publication titled Culpeper's Treatise of Aurum Potabile. I will be waiting for you at noon under the arch at Saint Saviours in Southwark.*
> *Mr William Ryves.*

The traffic crossing London Bridge was frustratingly slow, having to weave between the food-sellers who had set up stalls along its length. Finally, the cab reached the great stone gate leading into Southwark. Noon was long past and so there wasn't anyone at the church to meet him. After several attempts at seeking directions, he finally located the address. The half-timbered building with its warped grey beams and peeling plaster walls was not a salubrious abode. Glancing about, Zachariah saw the entire district was dilapidated with cramped and dingy wooden houses leaning into the street, blocking out the sun. A miasma of odours and damp seeping from the Thames penetrated into these dank and darkened lanes. Disconcerted, his mood worsened when he knocked on the shabby entrance door.

The door opening wide enough on rusting, resisting hinges, a face stared out. Glaring up at him was a flustered middle-aged woman, with long greasy wisps of mousy brown hair partially obscuring her pock-marked and deeply lined features. Speaking through the narrow space, she said impatiently, 'Yeh, who do ya want?'

Shocked at this hostile welcome, Zachariah stuttered, 'Er… I understand Mr William Ryves lives here. Is—'

Cutting him off, the woman turned and shouted in a booming voice, 'Ryves, there's someone 'ere to see ya.'

Stepping forward, the door slammed shut in his face, the cracked, rough panel only an inch from his nose. He heard the woman yell again.

Eventually the door opened again, this time by a tall, youngish, muscular man. Zachariah was surprised. He was expecting a pale bookish scholar, but this man's ruddy clear complexion suggested a robust and healthy constitution. His modest but well-tailored dark brown linen attire was incongruous in his squalid surroundings. Clutched in his large square hand was a clay pipe wafting wisps of sweet-smelling vanilla smoke.

Before Zachariah could introduce himself, the man gruffly said, 'Mr Jenkin? I was expecting you at noon.'

Zachariah confirmed that yes, indeed he was Mr Jenkin. Profusely apologising for his lateness, he added nervously, 'It would appear from your note that Miss Wilson has spoken with you?'

'Yes, yes, Miss Wilson came to see me. She was agitated and implored me to meet with you,' Ryves explained. 'As she may have explained, I am displeased with the current goings on in Mr Culpeper's house. But I am unable to intervene. The least I can do for my deceased employer, though, is to try to counter any misinformation you will have been fed during your investigations.'

'Do you mean my interview with Mr Heydon?'

Ryves's brow clouded.

'I met with the gentleman yesterday,' Zachariah continued, deciding not to mention the manner in which they had met.

'Ah, you had better come in then, Mr Jenkin. I am sure your meeting was interesting, if not misinformative,' Ryves said sarcastically as he stood aside, allowing his guest to step into a narrow, dark passage.

Climbing three flights of rickety narrow stairs, Ryves led his guest into a large attic room. 'Most people don't like living higher than the third floor because of the stairs,' he said. 'I prefer the attic, for while the roof may be low, the rooms are spacious. Also, the noise and stench from the street and the river are less up here. So, I can think and write without being disturbed.'

Curious, Zachariah examined his surroundings. The ceiling was pitched low, making much of the large chamber inaccessible to a tall man. The water-stained ceiling had wadding stuffed into chinks where the cracked plaster was falling away from the rafters. Through an open narrow dormer window sunlight cast across the floor.

There were books everywhere. Instead of expensive glass-fronted cabinets or neat shelves, Ryves's library consisted of stacks of books, broadsheets, pamphlets and loose paper scattered on the floor, tables, and in storage cases turned on their side and thrust up under the eaves. Zachariah thought it would only take a stray spark from an overturned candle and the chambers would quickly be engulfed in flames.

Clearing pots of ink, pens and paper from a large battered table, Mr Ryves gestured Zachariah to take a seat on the only chair not covered with books.

Taking a cloth covered package he had concealed beneath his coat, Zachariah placed it on the desk. Ryves glanced at it but didn't enquire of its contents.

'Wine?' Ryves said, proffering a glazed earthenware jug.

Feeling parched from his arduous journey across the bridge, Zachariah readily accepted.

Sighing heavily, Ryves said wistfully, 'Mr Jenkin, I remember the stories Mr Culpeper told of his youthful escapades, usually during the times we shared a pipe after a long day of writing and revision. He spoke of you with deep affection and respect.'

'It grieves me that our lives parted when I left to establish my apothecary trade in Crawley,' Zachariah said. 'But I was comforted when Jane told me of your dedicated service to Nicholas and that you served his interests even after his death.'

'Ah, Jane speaks too kindly of me,' Ryves replied, mirroring Zachariah's intimate reference to Miss Wilson's Christian name.

Seeking to put his host at ease, Zachariah began his questioning by asking how he came to meet Nicholas.

'While employed as a stationer's apprentice, Mr Cole sent me to serve as Nicholas's secretary back in '47. He had commissioned Nicholas to translate the College's *Pharmacopoeia*. Sadly, even then, he was sickly and needed assistance to transcribe his notes.' Sighing, Ryves added, 'What had begun as a short contract ended in a deep friendship that lasted 'til his dying day.'

Zachariah frowned, nodding his head in sympathy, but chose not to speak, hoping Ryves would continue un-prompted.

Taking a sip of wine, Ryves hesitated as if choosing his words carefully. 'He was a great and learned scholar and a gentleman. It may be discreetly affirmed that nature was wholly unveiled to him. He must have received the benedic-tion of celestial illumination considering that he, at such a youthful age, possessed superlative judgement and impec-cable reason. He became well known and his works were admired by men not only throughout England, but also in foreign places. As for myself, I gratefully confess that during those few years as his secretary, I received more knowledge and light from him than from all the other conversations I have had or books I've read.'[115]

'It would seem you have sought to emulate him in other ways, Mr Ryves,' Zachariah said gesturing towards his pipe.

Grinning, Ryves replied that yes, he had taken a liking to his employer's choice of tobacco and had made up his own stash from Nicholas's personal recipe.

Relating how Zachariah had detected this distinct aroma these past few days, Ryves dubious expression suggested he thought Zachariah was imagining things.

Seeking to get their discussion back on track, Zachariah said, 'I understand you now also practise astrology?'

'Nicholas inspired me to search out knowledge in all its forms. Long ago I abandoned my apprenticeship and became his full-time secretary as well as his student. He became my mentor and teacher, Mr Jenkin. So yes, I now practise astrology.' Smiling boyishly, he added, 'And, with the assistance and collaboration of other great and learned scholars, I continue his work by practising physic on the poor.'

Easing himself from his chair, Ryves strode towards a red-brick chimney stack that penetrated the floor and reached through the ceiling. For the first time, Zachariah noticed that built into a niche adjacent to the stack was a small bookshelf. Unlike the rest of his collection scattered chaotically throughout the chamber with no apparent rhyme or reason for their classification, a dozen or so leather-bound books of various sizes stood alongside a collection of smaller booklets neatly arranged on two sturdy shelves. Even at a distance, Zachariah recognised some of the volumes as Nicholas's publications.

'These are my most valued possessions,' Ryves explained, his fingers gently caressing their spines. 'His personal copies of the works he authored and his translations.'[116] Randomly selecting several books from the shelves, he added, 'He was well-skilled, not only in translation, but also correcting the defects of earlier scholars who wrote on astrology, surgery and physic, as well as other arts and philosophies.'[117]

Removing the book he had brought from its protective cloth, Zachariah asked, 'What of this most recent work enthusiastically promoted by Mr John Heydon, *Culpeper's Treatise of* Aurum Potabile?'

Ryves reeled back, as if the book was some devilish harpy. 'That… that *gentle… man* Heydon,' he spat, as if the honorific was a bitter pill, 'is full of puff and bragging. His claims of a mysterious elixir are a fantasy and the work of a deceiving, money-grabbing babbler. Nicholas never intended his manuscript to be read or employed as Heydon now claims. He decried the use of chemical medicines during his life and so would never have created a universal elixir, especially one made using chemical processes.'

'So, you can confirm this text is derived from a manuscript written by Nicholas?'

His eyes darting from the book to Zachariah and then back again, Ryves paused as if trying to avoid voicing an expletive. With slow deliberation, he spoke quietly as if speaking to an idiot, 'I acknowledge that Nicholas was a student of the Hermetic arts and wrote a manuscript that was the product of his many years of study into the mysteries of God's Creation'. Drawing himself up and speaking in crescendo, he added, 'However, I categorically refute those claims of Heydon and his gaggle of thieving, lying quacks who profit from Nicholas's good name. And that includes his whor— his widow, Alice. Or should I say *Mrs* Heydon.'

Ryves collapsed back into his chair. Lapsing into silence, strong emotions playing across his face, his gaze bored into the book resting on the table before him. Sighing deeply, he continued, 'The original manuscript served as a reference for Nicholas's personal study. It especially assisted him in the writing of his herbal and astrological medical texts. I say to you, Mr Jenkin, the manuscript Mr Heydon stole for his own devious purposes was for Nicholas one of the foundations of his collection of works he called his whole model of physic.'

'Whole model of physic?' Zachariah repeated. 'I have come across references to this in a few of his works, but had not considered its significance.'

Retrieving a book from the shelf, Ryves handed it to Zachariah. Well used, the brown leather cover was scratched and worn, its pages dog-eared and stained. Opening the book, Zachariah recognised it as a copy of the first edition of the controversial *Pharmacopoeia*. Its margins were filled with annotations in two writing styles. The older hand he recognised as Nicholas's. The later additions he assumed were Ryves's.

Ryves repeated Nicholas's allegation that physicians kept their fellow countrymen and women in ignorance by writing in a language only known to the university-educated elites. Nicholas told his readers that in order to counter this monopoly on medicinal knowledge, he planned to write a series of books in the English tongue, which he intended to call his *Whole Model of Physic*.[118] Imploring his readers to diligently learn from his books, he asked them to instruct their fellow countrymen, especially the unlearned, in the knowledge of herbs and medicines.[119]

Bending over his guest's shoulder, Ryves turned the pages back to the preface while summarising its contents. 'As part of their training, Italian doctors are expected to volunteer their time to treat the poor of their nation. Yet here in England the physicians may never actually touch a patient during all their years of training. English physicians consider such menial tasks only fit for lowly surgeons who spend their days bleeding or draining boils. The people of London believe the service the College provides is the way it is everywhere. So they think not to complain.'[120]

Zachariah certainly well understood the situation in

England, for the story was a sad annoyance to many members of the Society of Apothecaries. The closest London came to a regulated medical service was the College of Physicians. Established in 1518, the College served as a regulatory body that licensed and supervised medical practitioners, as well as prosecuted unlicensed empirics and physicians. It also controlled the activities of the apothecaries, restricting them to the making of medicines. Surgeons were also forbidden to operate independently of College physicians. [121]

From its founding, the College monopolised medical practice within the city walls of London. Not even fully qualified physicians who had studied and received their degrees from renowned European universities could legally practice in London if they had not obtained a license from the College. Consequently, by the mid-seventeenth century, for every ten thousand London inhabitants, there was only one College physician to call upon.[122] Yet the College was not stretched to its limits, since licensed physicians only treated people who could pay their exorbitant fees—the poor, therefore, were left to fend for themselves.

Following the breakdown of authority during the Civil War and the execution of their greatest patron, the King, the College lost many of its monopolising powers. Apothecaries and surgeons took advantage of the disruptions to become the loudest opponents of the regulated medical system.

Reading and participating in the arguments for and against the reform of medicine, Zachariah had also witnessed many of the conflicts arising from these debates. The breakdown in censorship led to a plethora of medical publications written in English, often by non-medically educated authors.

The practice of medicine subsequently spread further than the traditional wise woman, as scholars, tradesmen, and gentlewomen dabbled in the art, even though their only qualification was the ability to read.

'I appreciate your loyalty, Mr Ryves. I also sympathised with Nicholas's aims and believe his motives were true. Yet…' he paused, fearful of Ryves's reaction to his next statement. 'Yet the bookshops are filled with medical and herbal texts enticing the unwary reader into trying to make and administer their own cheap medicines. You must realise the dangers present when people who have too little knowledge in these matters try to treat themselves?'

'Mr Jenkin,' Ryves replied, 'you must realise Nicholas well knew the dangers inherent in self-treatment. But you cannot equate him with mountebanks or the cheap books badly translated by scholars untrained in the art of medicine.'

Thumbing through the pages of the *Physical Directory*, Ryves continued, 'You can see Nicholas dedicated his translation to "the kind gentlewomen who freely bestow your pains, brains and cost to your poor wounded and diseased neighbours."[123] He told them he was already planning to publish a simple system of his own devising for the purpose of instructing his readers in the diagnosis of disease, as well as the making of safe herbal remedies.'

'Yet dozens of scholars have published medicinal titles, even though their only exposure to medical training is via the books they read,' Zachariah repeated. 'So, what separates Nicholas's collection from these? What is so unique about his whole model of physic?'

As if deflecting the question, Ryves selected another book

saying, 'You are familiar with Nicholas's *English Physician*
are you not?'

'Er… yes. It is one of my most valued possessions. I refer
to it often.'

'You are aware the contents are derived from an earlier
herbal written in 1640 by John Parkinson?' Ryves asked,
placing the large, heavy tome into Zachariah's outstretched
hands.[124]

Zachariah nodded. While he had never actually read
Parkinson's comprehensive herbal himself, mainly because of
its exorbitant cost, he had seen the Society of Apothecaries'
copy stored safely in a locked, glass-fronted cabinet.

'Nicholas made Parkinson's herbal his own,' Ryves explained. 'Instead of classifying the herbs under their Latin
names, he organised each specimen alphabetically, according
to their common English names. Nicholas also only included
plants readily found in English gardens or meadows. By removing the expensive woodcuts and irrelevant information,
Nicholas made his book affordable to most people at only
three pence a copy.'[125]

Pointing to a passage, Ryves said, 'Take note of the information Nicholas included in his descriptions. They differ
somewhat from the Latin original because, while Parkinson
provided excellent descriptions of plants, he didn't offer any
reasons as to why herbs cured ailments. Nicholas corrected
this failing by including reasons as to why particular herbs
were effective against specific diseases.'

Taking the book from Zachariah, he turned back to the
preface. Selecting a passage, he read:

'I knew well enough that the whole world and everything

in it was formed of a composition of contrary elements, and
in such a harmony as must needs show the wisdom and
power of a great God, I knew as well this creation, though
thus composed of contraries was one united body, and man
is an epitome of it. I knew those various affections in man
in respect of sickness and health were caused naturally by
the various operations of the macrocosm; and I could not
be ignorant, that as the cause is, so must the cure be, and
therefore he that would know the reason for the operation
of herbs must look as high as the stars.'[126]

'That, Mr Jenkin', Ryves stated confidently, 'is the foundation of Mr Culpeper's *English Physician*.'

Zachariah glanced up at Ryves, his expression suggesting
he didn't understand.

'Put simply, Nicholas attributed every herb to its appropriate planet! He employed astrological principles to
guide his readers in the best way to use Galenic therapies.'

Zachariah remained silent, reluctant to challenge Ryves's
assertion. Most practitioners, be they a local wise woman or
a university-trained physician, employed astrology as part of
their medical practice. After all, it was common knowledge
that the humours were regulated by the motions of the planets. So, the casting of a rudimentary chart assisted in diagnosis
and treatment. If one was unskilled in the art of astrology,
practitioners only had to refer to the cheap almanacs and
ephemerides sold on any street corner.[127] Thus, Zachariah
was bemused by his assertions that Nicholas's medical system
was unique simply because he drew upon astrology.

As if aware of his guest's cynicism, Ryves offered haughtily, 'Nicholas's medical application of astrology differed to
that commonly employed by Galenic practitioners. No, Mr

Jenkin! Inspired by Paracelsus, Nicholas revived and simplified the arts of the Hermetic philosophers who understood that astrology is the foundation on which everything rests.'

Zachariah affirmed that he found the astrological directions in Nicholas's *English Physician* unusual. But as he usually referred to the text as a guide to locating particular herbs in the English countryside, he never sought to delve too deeply into the text's astrological information. He confessed shamefacedly, 'While I possess some knowledge of Galenic astrology, to be honest, I do not really understand Nicholas's application of the art.'

Smiling knowingly, Ryves retrieved another large book and a small almanac from the shelves. Resuming his seat, he said, 'If you care to read this book, you will learn how to apply the astrological elements contained within the *English Physician*.'

Opening *Culpeper's Astrological Judgement of Diseases*, Zachariah flicked through the pages, pausing to read snatches of narrative. His eye catching an unfamiliar term, he drew Ryves's attention to the passage:

> 'I have given you here all my prognostications from the decumbiture of the sick party … The decumbiture is the safest and surest ground for you to build your judgement upon.'[128]

Glancing up from the page, Zachariah said, 'Decumbiture? I have not heard of this method before.'

'The title refers to a system of casting charts where a practitioner would calculate a prognosis from the time and place a sick person first retreated to their bed,' Ryves explained.[129] 'However, it is not the method of calculation that characterises Nicholas's astrological system. It was his blending of the

Galenic doctrine of contraries with the Hermetic principle of sympathetic medicine.'

'I recall reading references to this sympathetic medicine in Nicholas's other texts. So how does it work?' Zachariah was most curious.

As if anticipating such a question, Ryves quickly replied, 'If a customer came to you complaining of a headache, how would you diagnose his condition?'

Smiling, Zachariah responded confidently, 'I would suggest their ailment was caused by excessive heat and dryness of the humours. I would recommend they eat waterlilies or lettuce because being cool and moist, these foods would rebalance the affected humours.'[130]

'But why do they rebalance the humours according to Galen?' Ryves prompted.

'While contraries will cure contraries, then cool foods cure a hot constitution. Conversely, hot food cures or rebalances a cold constitution,' Zachariah asserted.

'Be that as it may, inspired by the Hermetic astrologers, Nicholas recognised the celestial realm played a greater role in medicine than Galen ever envisioned.'

'How so?'

Referring back to Nicholas's *English Physician*, Ryves explained, 'Remember I said Nicholas sought the unarguable reason for things was to be found in God's Creation, and so to find it, one needed to look as high as the stars? Nicholas acknowledged that nature was created with contrary elements, hence Galen's practice of treating disease with contraries. However, Nicholas also saw a harmony in this process,' Ryves said as he searched the text.

Pausing at a page, Ryves quoted:

'Though Creation is composed of contraries, it is one united body, because man is an epitome or mirror of Creation. So the various afflictions man suffers is naturally caused by the operations of the macrocosm, or the planets.'[131]

'Therefore, additional to the principle of contraries or antipathy, Nicholas's Hermetic medical astrology was based on the principle of sympathy and correspondences, where like cures like, for as the cause is, so must the cure be.'[132]

'But this is totally opposite to our Galenic tradition! How can this work? It would negate and render the principle of contraries ineffective,' Zachariah cried, feeling shocked at such an unconventional approach.

'Oh, it not only worked, Mr Jenkin, Nicholas successfully blended the two systems into one.'

Reaching for the small almanac, Ryves said, 'At the very end of his *Ephemeris for the Year 1651*, Nicholas explains all.' Turning to the back page, he read:

'Courteous reader, if you ever intended to study physic … be well skilled in this foregoing discourse, for here's enough for you to whet your wits upon. Sympathy and antipathy are the two hinges upon which the whole body of physic turns.'[133]

Gesturing to the volumes scattered across the table, Ryves said, 'These books contain the keys to Nicholas's Hermetic astrological medicine.'

'So, how does this system operate?'

Ryves explained how each part of a man's body and all diseases were assigned a specific planet. 'Take the example of your customer's headache. The head is ruled by the moon, while the headache is under the dominion of Aries.[134] God, in His wisdom, created herbs and animals also under the dominion of the planets. He provided clues as to which planet a herb or animal was assigned by stamping a corresponding image on their surface. These stamps also signify the diseases or ailments the herb will cure.'[135]

Recognising Zachariah's expression of bemusement, Ryves said, 'The kernel of a walnut cures headaches because its surface looks just like that of the brain.[136] Thus God had marked the kernel with His stamp for the wise to recognise their medicinal uses.'

While the discussion on Nicholas's application of Hermetic astrology was interesting, Zachariah was impatient to discuss the matter of the text that had brought him to Ryves's door.

'Please, Mr Ryves, can you explain the connection between Nicholas's astrological medicine and this manuscript now published under the title *Mr Culpeper's Treatise of* Aurum Potabile?'

Ryves snapped, 'Mr Jenkin, please do not persist in referring to the manuscript under that title. Nicholas's manuscript was untitled. Its published title is a pure invention by Mr Heydon, who exploited the few references Nicholas had made on the subject of *aurum potabile* in his manuscript.'

'So, why is this book, or should I say Nicholas's original manuscript, so important to his whole model of physic?'

'Have you actually studied this book closely, Mr Jenkin?' Ryves asked reaching over to refill their mugs.

Squirming in his chair, feeling somewhat sheepish, Zachariah replied, 'I have attempted to study it. But frankly, I found it rather confusing. Mr Heydon's attempts to explain its alchemical significance, and especially the secrets hidden within its pages, confound me even more.'

Ryves scowled disapprovingly at Zachariah. 'Forget everything that trickster has told you. His greed has blinded him to the true nature of the subject!'

Ryves gingerly picked up the book as if it were tainted. 'I must confess, I have had an opportunity to read enough of this unauthorised publication to know that, although the preface is a complete fiction, the chapters are essentially the same as those Nicholas had originally written. While he had tried to apply a more scholastic style to this work, he could not resist occasionally making sarcastic quips. I recognise his turns of phrase and the homely proverbs he so frequently used in his other works.'[137]

'Yet Mr Brookes claims the text is a complete fabrication on the part of Mr Heydon, and that he inserted those proverbs into the text to deceive people into believing Nicholas was indeed the author,' Zachariah said.

Ryves frowned. Hesitating, a pained expression crossed his face as he admitted that he had also heard rumours of Heydon telling his associates that while he was promoting the text as Nicholas Culpeper's, it was he who was the original author.[138] Ryves cynically suggested that Heydon, understanding the book market considerably, knew if he had published the text under his own name, it probably would not have sold very well. After all, Heydon was an unknown author. In contrast, the name Culpeper guaranteed good sales.

'I fear Mr Brooke may have heard of Heydon's bragging,' Ryves continued. 'Nonetheless, I thought I had succeeded in persuading him that Nicholas was indeed the author.'

Ryves proceeded to explain how a brief perusal of Heydon's alchemical books was enough to discern he was unskilled in the arts of tact and subtleties. The prefaces of his publications usually contain several dedications to patrons, as well as recommendations from associates. He could not resist liberally employing alchemical and philosophical language to confuse and mystify his readers. If Heydon had sought to deceive Nicholas's dedicated readers by drawing on his familiar and often used words and phrases, he would have been quite blatant. Instead, a reader would have to persist and be very familiar with Nicholas's style in order to recognise the text as his.

'You must remember,' Ryves continued, 'unlike his other publications where he addressed his readers most intimately, when writing that manuscript Nicholas was writing primarily for himself, firstly as a reference text that would inform his later writings, but also as a personal interest. I believe that if he did plan to publish, he would have redrafted the manuscript to suit his reader's tastes, and certainly the book would not have included the words *aurum potabile* in its title.'

Seeming to collect his thoughts, Ryves absent-mindedly browsed the pages.

'Do you recall I mentioned the main theme of the original manuscript was Nicholas's interpretation of the creation of the microcosm and macrocosm according to Hermetic principles?' Ryves asked. Not waiting for a response, he added, 'The foundation of his whole model of physic was also derived from the wisdom of the ancient philosopher Hermes Trismegistus.'

'Nicholas mentioned this learned scholar in his texts, I recall,' Zachariah said. 'But I do not recall he ever explained the nature of the philosophy in any of his books… or those I have read,' he clarified. 'Certainly, I do not remember him outlining its significance, nor the key role that you now suggest the Hermetic doctrines played in his medical system.'

Frustrated with the aimless direction of their discussion, Zachariah turned his attention to his host, saying abruptly, 'Why did Nicholas refrain from explaining the principles of Hermetic philosophy to his readers? Was he reluctant to acknowledge the depth of his commitment to the philosophies of this Hermes Trismegistus? If so, why?'

'Nicholas made no secret of his knowledge of the Hermetic arts,' Ryves replied sharply. 'But as he tried not to confuse the common folk with the complexities of Galen, so too was he reluctant to delve into the complexities of the arts associated with Hermetic philosophy. It was the exploitation of these arts by tricksters of Mr Heydon's ilk that dissuaded him from writing extensively on the subject, and especially revealing the depth of his commitment to the philosophy. Whilst Nicholas drew upon Hermetic doctrines and occasionally named his sources, he refrained from delving into the complexities of these occult philosophies.[139] Yet the key to the understanding of Nicholas's astrological method of physic is contained within this volume, as well as his other works.'

Without asking leave, Zachariah strolled over to the shelf and selected a book that had attracted his attention. 'Other books you say, Mr Ryves? Books such as this,' he said, pointing to the spine embossed with the title: *A New Method of*

Physick.[140] Taking the volume from the shelf, Zachariah saw it was less scuffed than the other books in the collection, as if it were either new or rarely handled.

Rising frustration and anger evident in his voice, Ryves replied testily, 'Mr Jenkin, the manuscript we have been discussing was not the only text from Nicholas's private library he would have preferred not to have been published in the state it was handed to the printers. That book you have selected was the first of these.'

Taking the tome from Zachariah, Ryves explained it was the last of Culpeper's works to be released for publication just prior to his untimely death. Yet, ironically, Simeon Partlicius's original Latin work *Medici Systematis Harmonici* may have been the first text Nicholas had translated, having done so in 1642.[141] 'It was this text,' Ryves explained, 'that contributed to his understanding of how the philosophies of Hermes could be practically and philosophically applied to the study of medicine and natural philosophy.[142]

'I recall transcribing the preface, Mr Jenkin,' Ryves continued with a tremor in his voice. 'It was one of the last tasks I completed before he died. Nicholas sought to explain to his readers he would have preferred to have drafted a version suitable for their use. Yet since he no longer possessed the strength to revise the manuscript, they would have to make do with a translation he had made for his own reference purposes many years earlier.'[143]

Placing the book gently on the table, Ryves sighed and said, 'So you see, Mr Jenkin, this book, as it was published by Mr Cole under the title *A New Method of Physick*, was also not in the form Nicholas would have preferred.'

'I assume you refer to the chapters on the uses of alchemy and chemical medicines?' Zachariah asked. 'After all, it was rather hypocritical of Nicholas to condemn the College for their use of these dangerous medicines while lauding those same therapies in his *New Method*.'

From Ryves's frustrated expression, Zachariah feared his comments were trying his patience. Holding his breath, he suspected Ryves was about to cut their discussion short.

Succumbing to his angry frustration, Ryves said, 'You are not listening, Mr Jenkin! I repeat, Nicholas was inspired by Partlicius's medical system, especially his blending of Hermetic astrology with the principles of natural philosophy and physic. If he had had the strength and time, he would have omitted the chapters that discussed the relationships between alchemy and physic. I remind you that he frequently explained to his readers that alchemy and chemical medicines were dangerous and so best not be used. Nevertheless, he believed his readers would benefit from Partlicius's wisdom, especially the importance astrology and natural philosophy had for the art of physic.'

Seemingly satisfied Zachariah now understood his persuasive argument, Ryves continued. 'Partlicius was inspired by the works of Paracelsus, who had revived the wisdom of the Hermetic philosophers. Paracelsus believed observation and experience of the natural world held the key to understanding God's Creation. Consequently, the knowledge of natural philosophy makes an able physician.'[144]

Before Zachariah had an opportunity to respond, Ryves pushed his chair away from the table and rushed to the bookshelf. Grabbing several books, he deposited them on the table with such force a cloud of dust rose up causing Zachariah to sneeze.

Pushing the pile to one side, Ryves turned his attention back to *A New Method of Physick*. Consulting its contents page, he opened the book to a section titled, *Of Virtual Anatomy, or the Harmony Between the Macrocosm and Microcosm*.

'This section holds the key to Nicholas's system, Ryves said enthusiastically. Here,' he said pointing to the passage:

'All things that are above are to be found in things below, or if you would have it a little plainer … there is analogy and harmony between the universal world and the body of man. Paracelsus and most other Hermetical Philosophers teach that man possesses a double body, one natural, elementary, visible and tangible, which was first made of the slime of the Earth. The other body is invisible, insensible and deduced from the celestial influences of the stars. Through virtual anatomy the student of medicine will learn the virtues of remedies, not from Galen, but from the Book of nature, via a process of Analogical comparisons.'[145]

Grinning triumphantly, Ryves exclaimed, 'So, Mr Jenkin, the key to understanding God's macrocosm is through the medicinal study of His microcosm, or the anatomy of man. And to discern the secrets hidden in God's Creation, both the physician and the Hermetic philosopher must seek out the signs God has stamped on all things in Creation. Suffice to say, the additional research Nicholas undertook is laid down in the manuscript Heydon would later steal away and deceptively retitle. Thus, in spite of Heydon's meddling, bragging and deceptions, if you read the main body of the *Treatise*, you will see it represents Nicholas's exploration of

the alchemical structure and operation of Creation from a
Hermetic perspective.'

'How so?'

As he flicked through the pages of the *Treatise*, Ryves
explained that the text was not only a detailed examination
of the creation of the Celestial macrocosm and Terrestrial
microcosm, the processes involved mirrored that of the
gestation of the microcosmic human foetus.

Ryves took another book from the pile, which Zachariah
saw was Nicholas's *Directory for Midwives*,[146] and placed it
next to the *Treatise*. 'The chapters that examine the creation of
the elements in the *Treatise* resemble Nicholas's description
of the generation of man,' Ryves said as he searched the text.
'Here,' he said, pointing to a passage in the *Treatise*. 'Nicholas
explains that each of the four elements of air, water, fire and
earth are seeds, while the rays from the sun, moon and stars
are the sperm. The planet Earth itself, as distinct from the
element earth, acts as a womb or matrix[147] that gestates the
seeds and the sperm to produce matter.'[148]

Turning back to the *Directory*, Ryves said, 'Now compare
that with Nicholas's description of the formation of the child
in the womb. Nicholas explains that in the act of copulation,
the woman supplies her seed and the man his sperm to make
conception.'[149]

Before Zachariah had time to read the passage, Ryves
closed the book and drew another from the pile. 'Nicholas
explains himself better in his *Anatomy of the Body of Man*.[150]
Ah, here it is,' he said pointing to a sentence. 'Nicholas advised
his readers that, "the knowledge of a man's self was the first
step to virtue."[151] Do you know what he meant by this?'

Zachariah blankly stared.

'He explains his meaning further down the page,' Ryves said:

> '… the knowledge of a man's self, being of all natural knowledge, is the most profound and most to be desired. For he that knows himself thoroughly cannot but know the world in its entirety, because he is an epitome of it.'[152]

Glancing up from the page, he continued, 'Nicholas was trying to explain why he had translated this particular book. Originally written in Latin by Veslingus, the text examines the anatomy of man. So, do you now understand the connection between Nicholas choosing to publish the *Directory for Midwives* and this text?'

'Er… if I read these books and understood their contents, I would come to understand the world?'

'Yes, Zachariah! And what is the world, or should I say, who made the world?'

'God!' Zachariah replied eagerly, suddenly comprehending Ryves's meaning. 'So the reason why people should study anatomy,' Zachariah offered, 'is because as man is a mirror, or epitome of the world, and the world is a reflection of God, then man will also understand not only all His works, but understand God Himself!'

'Yes, Zachariah! As you now realise,' Ryves continued, 'Nicholas published specific works such as the *Directory of Midwives*, as well as his *Anatomy of the Body of Man* and *A New Method of Physick* specifically because they examined the microcosm of man. And as man is the microcosm of the Celestial macrocosm, through his study of medicine as well as Hermetic and natural philosophy, Nicholas's goal was to understand God's Creation.'

'If I understand you correctly, then,' Zachariah said, hoping he finally grasped Ryves's meaning, 'Partlicius's original work was the catalyst that led to Nicholas studying Hermetic alchemy and natural philosophy, and these in turn motivated him to write and translate medicinal, anatomical and philosophical themed works?'

'Yes, Mr Jenkin! Yes!' Ryves cried excitedly. 'Also, you will discover clues of the authenticity of the ideas expressed in the original manuscript in other texts of Nicholas's authorship.' Gesturing towards the other books scattered in a disorderly fashion across the table, he continued, 'There are many parallels between the content of the *Treatise* and Nicholas's other works. Nicholas knew that the operation of the cosmic macrocosm could be discerned by observing the microcosm of the human body. You allege, Mr Jenkin, that Nicholas concealed his Hermetic studies from his readers. Well, I say he often employed Hermetic concepts in his other works. If you care to read the prefaces of many of his early works, you will see that he frequently mentions the Hermetic medical principles such as the operation of sympathy and antipathy, as well as the harmonies of Creation.[153] But students of physic cannot just rely on the printed word. In order for them to succeed in their studies, they must also labour to know themselves, because within them lies the secret that reveals the unity between them and God. That secret is not only encapsulated in his whole model of physic, it is also the foundation of his manuscript now printed under that dubious and misleading title *Mr Culpeper's Treatise of Aurum Potabile!*[154]

Closing the books, Ryves sighed. 'I have spent far too long discussing these matters. I fear I may not have answered your questions in the manner you may have hoped. Yet I have nothing more to say to you on Mr Heydon's claims, only that *aurum potabile* was never a medicinal cure-all. Rather, Mr Jenkin, it is much, much more. Nicholas's original manuscript encompassed a far deeper and more profound motivation and aspiration that I cannot… no, will not explain. I will not say any more because I would be betraying Nicholas's most private confidences.'

Before Zachariah could ask for clarification of these cryptic and cutting comments, Ryves gestured that their discussion was at an end. Ushering Zachariah from his chamber, while thrusting the volume *Aurum Potabile* into his hands, Ryves said, 'Good day to you, Mr Jenkin. If you wish to learn more about that book, you will have to glean your answers from elsewhere.'

As he made his way back to London Bridge, Zachariah considered what had just transpired. Ryves's enigmatic comments had raised even more questions that he feared would never be adequately answered, as he was Zachariah's last resort.

Zachariah felt confused. Everyone he had spoken to thus far had made contradictory statements. Brooke had said the *Treatise* was a forgery, yet Ryves confidently stated the main text was written by Nicholas. Heydon's account of a mysterious secret society and dubious alchemical demonstrations confirmed Zachariah's opinion that he was little better than a mountebank who exploited Nicholas's good name for his personal profit. But then, Ryves's comment that he should not dismiss the importance of the *Treatise* because of Heydon's devious misuse had only compounded Zachariah's confusion. Feeling dejected and defeated, he wandered down the lane searching for a hackney coach to take him back across the river. As he walked, he began to rehearse the letter he planned to write to his patron informing him he had failed in his task to discover the authenticity of the elixir *aurum potabile*.

***

Chapter Eight

Zachariah's Chamber, Dolphin Inn
Monday, 5th May 1656, early morning

There must have been thousands of them! Zachariah watched as line upon line of men crested the hill. Noblemen in smocks and leather aprons carrying hammers and cudgels; peasants festooned in muddied silken finery; tradesmen shouting, brandishing picks and hoes, all cavorting in the dance of death towards a blood-red horizon.

Beyond in the valley, he heard the deafening sounds of cannon and gunfire and screams of anguish. Stumbling down the hill, Zachariah stumbled disorientated as he picked his way through a field littered with dismembered and mangled bodies. He felt as if he was struggling in a sea of treacle, each step an effort, his breathing laboured under the acrid odour of gunpowder. The ground shifting under him, he dropped to his knees. Bare branches became tangled soil-caked roots, reaching out to grasp him in their fibrous clutches.

He felt the world was turning upside-down.

In the distance, he spied a man leaning against the trunk of a gnarled old tree, its branches stripped of leaves. Drawn by an invisible thread, Zachariah was speedily propelled towards this pitiful figure. One amongst thousands, but one he recognised.

It was his friend, Nicholas Culpeper.

Dressed in dark brown woollen breaches and a linen shirt spattered with blood, his left hand pressed to his side trying to stop his life essence ebbing away, Nicholas gazed up at Zachariah, grief and pain etched in his features.

Lifting his other hand, Zachariah thought Nicholas was reaching for him, but realised he was pointing to something beyond. Zachariah turned to witness a horrific panorama of war and conflict spread before him: mile upon mile of death, misery and destruction.

Struggling to speak, Nicholas gasped, 'Look what they have done, Zachariah! My Saints who promised to bring peace to this nation. Now they bring only war and betrayal.'

The fighting men paused mid-stroke and stared at the prophetic speaker.

'They know not what they would have,' Nicholas screamed in frustration, 'their thoughts are in chaos, dancing up and down from one thing to another without any order, they begin without order and end without issue.[155] The Saints have succumbed to the worst earthly base temptations and flout God's laws. They draw maps of their own desires and cut out such a kind of life as pleases them, and by their own thoughts put themselves into another condition other than what God has ordained for them.'[156]

Rising to his feet, Nicholas made to pursue the soldiers, only to collapse in Zachariah's arms. Struggling, Nicholas called out to the dishevelled men. At the sounds of his pleas, they turned to face him, their hands outstretched as if wishing to capture his every word.

'You… you,' Nicholas cried, pointing accusingly as if

addressing the rabble as one man. 'You who call yourself Saints and defenders of this nation, you seek signs of election, but you have succumbed to the temptations of power and violence. Yet to be saved, you must endure suffering, and not be partakers of the punishments of this world. You must keep yourself unspotted from the world.[157] Ah, soldiers, what shall I say to you? Look to yourselves. This I entreat you and I beseech you. Act fairly, make not war. Let reason rule you, mind the general good. Do violence to no man.[158] Then and only then will Christ come to herald the Fifth Monarchy and peace will reign for a thousand years.'

Coughing, Nicholas leant against his friend's breast. Burying his face in his hands, he whispered, 'Oh, Zachariah, the world has been rent asunder, the great chain of being is shattered. Men now call virtue vice and vice virtue. They call good evil and evil good.[159] It is a mad world where subjects would be kings and what nobles would be, neither they nor I can say.'[160]

Zachariah woke at the sound of a loud crash. His arms restricted of movement, he feared he was being attacked. Pausing, he calmed his rising panic. Realisation dawned. He wasn't being restrained. He was alone in his chamber. He recalled he had retired to bed for the evening to study the *Treatise* by lamplight. The fiend was his blanket now tangled about his body.

The lantern burnt out, the chamber was now cast in a feeble silvery glow as beams of moonlight streamed through gaps in the shuttered window. Freeing his hands, he groped around in the semi-darkness. Reaching down, he happened upon the book on the floor. Realising it had caused the thumping sound, he placed it on the side table.

Settling into his pillow, Zachariah recalled the nightmare. Why had he dreamt this? While he and Nicholas had joined their fellow apprentices in their street protestations, he himself had never partaken in the armed conflicts that had later erupted into civil war. He wondered if the dream was caused by his recent enquiries into Nicholas's life.

And what of Nicholas bewailing the fate of the Saints and the Fifth Monarchy? Even though isolated from the main fighting, like many of his countrymen, he had kept abreast of the battles via the printed broadsheets and newspapers. He had also read and easily recalled many of the commentaries Nicholas had inserted into his books and ephemerides on this very topic. Thus, to Zachariah's dismay, he well understood some of Nicholas's apocalyptic words.

In the darkness, he listened to the night sounds of distant snoring, catches of voices and a dog howling in the courtyard. His thoughts returned to the nightmare. The sectarians who had risen up against the tyranny of the Royalists held so much promise back then in the early '40s. Those heady days when he and Nicholas were drawn to the revolutionary sermons preached on the streets of London. So many promises. So many betrayals.

Zachariah wrinkled his nose, his musings disturbed. Tobacco, that sweet vanilla tobacco again, the same aroma he had encountered these past few days. This time the odour was distinct, even overpowering. It was as if the smoker was actually in the room with him. With that stray thought, a surge of panic gripped him as he sensed he was not alone. Agitated and confused, he struggled to a sitting position. In the darkest corner of his chamber, he spied a small glowing red light. His breath catching in terror, straining his eyes in the dim moonlight, Zachariah discerned a seated figure.

'Who… who are you? Wha… what do you want?' Zachariah shouted, fearing for his life. Reaching across to the bedside table, he grabbed the *Treatise* ready to brandish it as a weapon.

The shadowy indistinct figure remained silently motionless. Zachariah took a deep breath, trying to calm himself. The figure shifted, causing a moonbeam to cast its silvery radiance across its features. Wavy dark hair framed an oval face dominated by a long, classically Greek nose. But for a thin well-groomed moustache, his clean-shaven face revealed a familiar dimpled chin. His clothing lost in the gloom, Zachariah instinctively knew it would be a dark brown woollen jerkin covering a crisp white shirt and collar. Clamped in his mouth and held by a refined scholastic hand was a worn clay pipe wafting lazy tendrils of grey smoke.

Terror rising and trembling all over, Zachariah recognised the apparition seated before him. It was his dead friend, Nicholas Culpeper!

'Nic… Nicholas! How…? Why…? How is it you are here? Am I dreaming? Are you real?' he cried.

The figure laughed. Taking the pipe from his mouth, Nicholas said in his familiar husky voice, 'Zachariah, my friend, why ask these questions? I care for my friends and so my soul was drawn to you, the seeker of my secrets.'[161]

Zachariah was speechless. His mouth opening and closing, he couldn't form any words.

'You seem surprised, my friend,' Nicholas said. 'Do you

doubt that which your eyes perceive? I assure you; I am no demon sent to tempt or deceive you. I am he, your friend Nicholas. I have returned to the elementary world to enlighten you. Do not fear. Feel privileged, Zachariah. Most men seeking to commune with the ghostly realm require the use of a scrying crystal. I possessed one once, it belonged to John Dee, the great Hermetic philosopher, alchemist and consultant to Queen Elizabeth.[162] But you don't need to conjure me, because as you are in such dire need of my counsel, I came unbidden.'

Pausing, Nicholas settled back into his chair and smiled enigmatically. Just as Zachariah was beginning to regain his composure, Nicholas's serene expression suddenly transformed. Lunging forward he bellowed, 'And cease brandishing that book. It offends me so.'

Coming to his senses, Zachariah glanced at the book he was readying to throw. The spell broken, he gently placed *Culpeper's Treatise* in his lap and hoped that when he glanced up the spectre would have vanished. Blinking, he stared again only to discover the figure remained, its face illuminated by moonlight.

Not knowing how much time he had before Nicholas returned back to whence he came, Zachariah came straight to the point. 'You… you say you visit me in my dreams to reveal all. So, are Mr Heydon's claims correct? Did you practise alchemy and happen upon the secret recipe for the universal cure-all, *aurum potabile*? Does the manuscript contain the secrets of its making? Why did you conceal the manuscript from the scrutiny of your reading public?'

At the mention of Heydon's name, Nicholas's visage

changed from an ethereal serenity to naked contempt. Scowling, he spat, 'Disregard everything that mountebank told you. All that man stands for I reject, and all his claims are false.'

Nicholas paused, his voice trailing into silence. Raising his pipe to his mouth, he absentmindedly chewed the stem. Zachariah recognised this familiar gesture. His spectral guest had sunk deep in thought, contemplating mysteries beyond the terrestrial realm. Squirming, Nicholas furtively glanced at Zachariah, then looked away.

* * *

The light in the room intensified, forcing Zachariah to shield his eyes. Feeling the bed shift from underneath him, he cried out as he tried to grasp the mattress. Instead of clutching cloth, his hands grasped wooden arm rests. Eyes flying open, he gasped. He was no longer in his chamber at the Dolphin Inn.

Zachariah recognised his new surroundings. He was seated in a familiar chair in Nicholas's study in Spitalfields! Not John Heydon's lifeless, dull and sterile chamber, but the light-filled domain of his memories. They had been transported not only in space, but also in time.

Relishing memories now made manifest, Zachariah gazed about in wonderment. Streaming through tall leadlight windows, golden sunlight bathed the chamber in a warm ethereal glow. Zachariah chuckled at the incongruity of this serene image combined with the characteristic chaotic disorder of Nicholas's study. It was as he remembered all those years ago: books, manuscripts and papers strewn over every surface.

Now seated in the same chair Heydon had recently

commandeered was the man Zachariah remembered from their youth. Gone was the careworn, lined face he had seen at their last meeting.

'Ah… this is more to my liking,' the spectre said, his hands gliding in an encompassing gesture. 'I feel more at ease surrounded by my books and manuscripts instead of cooped up in your cold, dank chamber. Here I can best explain how I came to write that manuscript that interests you so much.'

'So you *did* write the manuscript Heydon has recently published?' Zachariah asked eagerly.

'Patience, Zachariah! All will be revealed in good time.'

Settling back into his chair, hands clasped with his chin resting on his forefingers, Nicholas appeared the picture of scholastic contemplation. Gazing absently at the table before him, he whispered, 'Where to begin, where to begin?'

Zachariah waited, a sense of anticipation rising in his chest.

'Many years ago I experienced a series of events that I knew were signs from God. As He has stamped His sign on every creature and it is the task of men of wisdom to discern their meaning, I therefore saw my life's work laid out before me,' Nicholas said emphatically, gazing into Zachariah's eyes as if seeking a challenge.

From the depths of his inner being, his clear authoritative voice filling the room, Nicholas continued, 'The great Jehovah, the Lord Jesus Christ, and the Holy Angels have conferred upon me divine illumination that I shall now reveal to you!'[163]

Zachariah leaned forward in anticipation, words forming on his lips. With his open palm, Nicholas gestured him to be silent as he began his tale.

Initially, Nicholas had thought his destiny would be that of his father and grandfather: to enter university in preparation for becoming a pastor. 'But my heart was not in it, Zachariah. As my dear friend Brooke told you, I abandoned my studies following the loss of my dear jewel in that dreadful storm…'

'I beg your pardon?' Zachariah interrupted. 'What do you know of my conversations with Brooke?'

'I have been your invisible companion these past few days as you have searched for the secrets of *aurum potabile*.'

Zachariah now realised the significance of those stray whiffs of sweet vanilla tobacco that had followed wherever he went.

'Brooke inferred I had experienced a profound spiritual crisis, but not even he knew the depths to which I descended after my jewel was smitten,' Nicholas sighed. He cringed as he relived the onslaught of his grandfather's wrath following the incident. As if the eighteen-year-old Nicholas had been a child, Reverend Attersoll had railed against him, brandishing the Bible as he battered the message into his grandson's head.[164]

'God expects unconditional obedience! God knows in advance who will be saved and who will be damned,' Attersoll had shouted, 'and your wilful conduct that has led to the death of an innocent child proves you are forever damned!'

Voice trembling, Nicholas said, 'My grandfather's severe Puritan zeal offered neither solace nor answers to heal my wretched soul. One day, while locked in the grips of a black melancholy, I sought refuge in his library. It was there, by chance, I happened upon Thomas Tymme's, the *Practice of Chemical and Hermetical Physic.* Browsing through its pages, I spied a passage that changed my life. I can recall it even now', he said:

> 'Plato said that philosophy is the imitating of God … that we may be able to know God more and more, until we behold Him face to face in the kingdom of heaven. So that the scope of philosophy is to seek to glorify God and His wonderful works: to teach a man how to live well and to be charitably affected in helping our neighbour.'[165]

Raising his arms is if praising the Lord, a radiance enveloping his visage, Nicholas said, 'God had shown me the way, Zachariah! He had shown me the path I should follow. I should seek out the key to all knowledge, which alone must let me into the secret chambers of wisdom.'[166]

Nicholas told how he readily accepted his grandfather's decision to secure him an apothecary apprenticeship. He was surprised that his wilful grandson had so readily agreed.

'Ryves explained to you the reasons why I studied physic and astrology, did he not? To reiterate, I became a scholar and practitioner of medicine because it enabled me to understand the operation of the terrestrial microcosm, which is man. But,' he added insistently, 'unlike those armchair scholars of Heydon's ilk, it was not riches I sought. Rather, I shared my skills and knowledge of physic with my countrymen, so they were best able to treat themselves.'

'But what does all this have to do with the manuscript and elixir *aurum potabile?*'

'Everything, Zachariah, Everything!'

***

Rising effortlessly from his chair as if suspended by an invisible thread, Nicholas entered his book closet and rummaged about the shelves. Zachariah recalled this small chamber contained the author's most treasured manuscripts.

Returning, Nicholas gently placed two old tattered books on the table. Gesturing to his guest to open the worn calfskin covers, Zachariah was surprised to see they were not printed. Rather, the stained, frayed, yellowed pages were covered in Nicholas's distinctive handwriting characterised by his bold, confident strokes and flourishes.[167] Nicholas had been proud of his handwriting: it marked him as a gentleman and learned scholar.

Writing came easily to Nicholas, Zachariah pondered as he examined the neat lines. Unlike his, which after all these years, remained stilted and clumsy as if he were a boy still grappling with his letters on a writing slate.

Gently turning the pages, Zachariah saw the script was in draft form: words, sentences, even whole paragraphs written over, scribbled on or crossed out. Small cramped commentaries and annotations filled the narrow margins. Arrows and tiny illustrations of pointing hands highlighted important sentences and paragraphs. Carefully executed symbols dotted the margins, their meanings known only to the author.

'Those are my most treasured works,' Nicholas said as he watched Zachariah slowly turn the pages. 'That is my translation of Simeon Partlicius's *Medici Systematis Harmonici*. The second manuscript is my own work, the one Heydon stole and published under that ludicrous title, the name of which I refuse to speak.[168] It represents the culmination of my years of studying the mysteries of God's Creation; a task

I had commenced during my translation of Partlicius's work, and which had also been my inspiration.'

Gesturing emphatically towards the *Treatise*, Nicholas explained that the Hermetic philosophers realised that a medium, or a key, must exist that united the terrestrial microcosm with the celestial macrocosm.

'So they resolved to spend their wits to discover this key that would unite the planets with the body of man, and it was through divine illumination that God revealed all.' An expression of amused smugness playing across his features, Nicholas asked, 'And do you know what the key to Creation is, the key that establishes a direct communication between the self and the Divine, the third principle or medium that unites the microcosm with the macrocosm?'

Mesmerised, Zachariah shook his head.

'Do I have to remind you of the doctrine of the Holy Trinity, Zachariah?' Nicholas said. 'As there is a trinity in unity in the Godhead and a unity in trinity, so must there also be a trinity to be found in all God's works.[169] So, too, does Hermes teach us that the three Arts of astrology, natural philosophy and religion are the tools with which the philosopher can discern the three unities, or the trinity of the intellectual, celestial and elementary worlds.[170] Now do you understand the significance of the divine number three?'

Zachariah understood the nature of the Trinity. He could hardly recall a sermon or a religious tract where the Trinity was not mentioned. It was a fundamental tenet of faith central to Calvinist Puritan doctrines. Theologians, clergymen, even the laity would spend hours contemplating the meaning of the Trinity and its significance not only to one's religious life, but most importantly to the fate of one's soul.

One of the few non-medicinal themed texts Zachariah owned was Lewis Bayly's *The Practice of Piety*, which examined the nature of the Trinity. He recalled a passage from the book summarising the essential nature of the doctrine:

> 'First, In knowing the essence of God … The diverse manner of being therein, which are three persons – Father, Son, and Holy Ghost … As the Father is God, begetting God the Son; the Son is God, begotten of God the Father, and the Holy Ghost is God, proceeding from God the Father and God the Son.'[171]

Zachariah informed Nicholas that he didn't need instruction in Puritan doctrine and could not see the relevance of the Holy Trinity to their discussion.

Nicholas sighed with exasperation. 'To refresh your memory, the Celestial refers to the macrocosmic realm of the planets and stars. The terrestrial realm encompasses the minerals that makes up the Earth, as well as the flesh of man, the animals and plants. Yet, as the Scriptures prove, there must be a third principle, because the number three is a most powerful number, a number of perfection, and there must be a unity in that trinity. All creatures and all minerals consist of three principles, sulphur, mercury and salt, which are reflected in the body of man, who is made of three essences, spirit, soul and body.[172] So, if there is a trinity in the elementary realm, there must also be a third principle in Creation, and what do you suppose that is?'

Not able to think of an informed response, Zachariah chose to remain silent.

'I have already given you the key, Zachariah, so pay attention,' Nicholas snapped. 'I said the third principle is the intellectual! It manifests in many guises and has had many names over the centuries since the time of Hermes Trismegistus, who was the first philosopher to recognise its secrets. It is the elixir of elixirs, the quintessence; it is the philosopher's stone!' Smiling triumphantly, his face radiating as if conferring onto Zachariah divine knowledge, Nicholas said, 'The third principle, therefore, is *aurum potabile!*'

Startled, Zachariah seized on Nicholas's words believing he had betrayed himself. 'So, Heydon was right?' Zachariah shouted triumphantly, 'the *Treatise* contains the secrets for making a universal elixir!'

Nicholas didn't respond to Zachariah's supposition. Calmly and silently, he stared back, as if refusing to be baited.

Zachariah felt cynical, assuming that Nicholas's silence was caused by him trying to rehearse a persuasive argument to defend his hypocritical and confusing contradictions.

'Zachariah, I watched as you studied that text in your chamber at the Dolphin Inn, so I know you are familiar with its contents,' Nicholas said smoothly as he gestured to the *Treatise*. 'Did I include a recipe or instruction for the making of a universal elixir, as Heydon now claims and you are so ready to believe?'

Zachariah stared resentfully, feeling his anger rising in response to Nicholas's provocative manner.

'It seems you are unable to answer,' Nicholas said, smiling indulgently. 'To put it as plainly as I am able, no, I did not include a recipe for the making of *aurum potabile* simply because it is not the universal elixir Heydon seeks.'

His voice rising in volume as if sharing an ecstatic revelation, Nicholas repeated, '*Aurum potabile* is not a thing or an object to be grasped and coveted, rather it is the third principle, the intellectual realm, or the realm of knowledge, which enables man to communicate with and understand God and all His works!'[173]

Before Zachariah could respond, Nicholas continued in a derisory tone. 'Heydon and avaricious men such as he will never discern the secrets of *aurum potabile*, because their motive is to covet riches; they spend their days sweating over their alchemical furnaces, vainly seeking to transform base metals into gold, or distil elixirs from cow's piss.'

Sighing resignedly, he continued, 'Zachariah, why do you think the ancient philosophers wrote in riddles? It is because God instructed them to write in such a way as to conceal these mysteries from unworthy wretches who account this world as their heaven, riches to be their God and thereby gain their godliness.[174] Only those philosophers whom God has graced with divine illumination will ever discern the secrets of nature and Creation. All I can say is that had it not been for Divine providence instructing me in a special way, I would never have attained such wisdom for myself.[175] It was these divinely inspired revelations that set me on the path to seeking the signs He had placed in Creation.'

'Now you speak in riddles,' Zachariah shot back, annoyed at Nicholas's circular logic. 'You say that the third principle is *aurum potabile* and that this is knowledge or the intellectual realm, but that the Trinity is the key to this knowledge. So please explain yourself.'

Without answering directly, Nicholas proceeded to explain that his *Treatise* held the explanations to all of Zachariah's questions, a response that only further annoyed him.

Nicholas materialised next to Zachariah, who watched in amazement the pages of the book turn unaided as Nicholas described the structure of his *Treatise*. Flicking back and forth, Nicholas quickly read out the titles of chapters and subsections, explaining that the subject matter of the entire manuscript was a systematic examination of the various manifestations of the Trinity in the elementary, celestial and intellectual worlds.

'Being blinded by avarice, Heydon could not see that he held the key to wisdom in his hands; it was as plain as the nose on his face. You claim I wrote in riddles, but with a little knowledge you can see I wrote plainly and clearly. For those with the eyes to see or the wisdom to discern, my *Treatise* is an examination of the process of Creation from an alchemical perspective. By employing the art of philosophical alchemy and being graced by sparks of divine illumination, the *Treatise* unravels the mysteries contained within the Trinity and in so doing reveals the divine secrets of Creation.'

***

Zachariah sighed and shook his head to dispel the cobwebs clogging his senses. Thus far, Nicholas had denied that *aurum potabile* was the universal cure-all Heydon and his associates were selling. Certainly, there wasn't a recipe for the making of such in the *Treatise*, as Heydon claimed. Yet, after denying the absence of a recipe, Nicholas was now asserting that the *Treatise* was an alchemical text!

'If the study of medicine leads to the understanding of man, what art do you think directly reveals the secrets of

God's macrocosmic Creation?' Nicholas said, breaking into Zachariah's thoughts.

Without waiting for a reply, Nicholas explained how God had revealed to Paracelsus that Creation was an alchemical process performed by Him.

'Paracelsus taught that besides natural philosophy and astrology, alchemy is the art the ancient Hermetic philosophers also employed to discern the secrets of Creation. It is the fountain of sound philosophy, the key to wisdom and the mark all wise men shoot at.[176] Yet consider this, if God creates with alchemy, so too can He destroy. Thus, the Hermetic philosophers turned to the study of the alchemical Creation in their quest to discern when God would return to establish His Fifth Monarchy, or if you have forgotten, the second coming of His Son, Christ!'

'So Heydon was correct when he claimed you practised alchemy?'

Scowling furiously, Nicholas shot back, 'Never! I only ever employed alchemy in a philosophical way. Never did I seek to ape those puffers who vainly sought to make gold out of horse dung.'[177]

Confused at Nicholas's vehement denials, Zachariah asked for clarification.

Nicholas recounted his early years when he embarked on his quest to learn and apply the principles of alchemical and natural philosophy. While England was disintegrating into chaos following the disastrous war with Scotland and the subsequent conflicts between the King and Parliament, Nicholas was busy translating his copy of Partlicius's *Medici Systematis Harmonici*. Having mastered the occult arts of astrology and the Cabbala[178] and from the knowledge gained from this translation, he embarked on the study of the signs revealed by motions of the planets. These calculations became the foundation for his later publication *Catastrophe Magnatum*.[179]

'As you may read in my *Catastrophe Magnatum*, the stars revealed that a great eclipse would herald the coming of Christ in March 1652—'

'You refer to Black Monday,' Zachariah cut in derisively. 'Well, we all know what happened on that date, or should I say what didn't happen!'

Nicholas glanced indignantly at Zachariah, obviously angry at being reminded of his humiliation. Regaining his composure, he said, 'Please be patient, I am trying to explain why these predictions did not come to pass.'

Speaking calmly and seemingly trying to control his temper, Nicholas spoke of the terror he had felt when his calculations revealed that Armageddon was imminent and when Christ would return.

Quoting from his *Catastrophe Magnatum*, Nicholas said,

'You shall hear of wars and rumours of wars; nations shall rise against nation ... there shall be famine and pestilence, and earthquakes; ... men shall be lovers of their own selves, covetous, boasters, blasphemers, unholy, despisers of those that are good, high-minded lovers of pleasure more than lovers of God.'[180]

Nicholas was only one of many voices who speculated on the imminent return of Christ. Books and pamphlets flooded the London markets, warning that God had chosen England as the site of His Fifth Monarchy, but that the nation and the people had to ready themselves for His arrival. Most prophets and doomsayers were drawing on millenarian predictions and prophecies derived from earlier translations and interpretations of the Books of *Daniel* and *Revelations*.[181]

'Thus, my motive for writing the *Treatise* and later the publication of my *Catastrophe Magnatum* was to assist the people of this nation to prepare themselves for this momentous event. My intention was to increase their knowledge of themselves and of God's Creation, but most of all to reveal the signs in the heavens that would herald the Fifth Monarchy.'[182]

'One moment,' Zachariah said vehemently, realising there were discrepancies and inconsistencies in Nicholas's tale. 'Black Monday was a disaster; Christ did not come and all you achieved was condemnation and a severe blow to your reputation.'

As if unable to offer an explanation, Nicholas remained silent.

Incensed at the contradictory arguments, Zachariah continued his resentful tirade. 'Furthermore, you claim you drafted this *Treatise* with the aim of helping the English people prepare themselves. Pray tell me, if you never intended to publish the manuscript, then how could the *Treatise* have helped if no-one could obtain it?'

Shaking his head in frustration, Nicholas explained that as God had revealed the path he was to follow, he was also restrained as to the extent to which he could share such illuminations with his readers. Only Hermetic luminaries were deserving of divine wisdom and as such their writings remained private and were rarely published during their lifetimes. Nicholas had heard rumours of Hermetic scholars writing on creationist topics, but who had also refrained from publicly revealing their contents.[183]

'That doesn't answer my question,' Zachariah said, his confusion mounting. If he was hoping to be enlightened, thus far his bewilderment was only increasing. 'Again, why draft such an important manuscript, one that holds the secrets to Creation and the meaning of the Holy Trinity, if you never intended to share these revelations with the people of this nation?'

'Of all people, Zachariah, you should be able to answer your own question,' Nicholas shouted angrily as he gestured towards his books scattered across the table. 'Even in the company of the author, you find it difficult to grasp the meanings and secrets contained between their covers. Thus, consider my readers! Your difficulties confirm my position that this draft that Heydon has published will be beyond the common man's understanding.'

Pausing, Nicholas looked away as he said, 'Hence, my decision not to publish my *Treatise*.'

Zachariah noticed his hesitancy. It seemed Nicholas was not being entirely truthful, or maybe didn't entirely believe his own justifications.

***

Silence once again descended, the only sounds being the faint hubbub of Londoners going about their daily chores.

'Oh, Zachariah,' Nicholas said, his voice trembling with emotion. 'I tried, I tried…' Rousing himself, Nicholas gazed towards the window, a faint rosy-yellow glow of the late afternoon sun tinging his features. 'My time with you is coming to an end, but I need to share the reasons why I wrote the *Treatise*.'

Sitting forward in anticipation, Zachariah held his breath waiting for Nicholas to speak. Finally, after all these days of futile searching, Nicholas was going to reveal the secrets behind his *Treatise of* Aurum Potabile.

Turning back to Zachariah and staring directly into his eyes, Nicholas said, 'Do you know why I dedicated my life to writing and translating medicinal and astrological texts as well as offering my medicinal skills to heal the sick in body and mind? Why I railed against the monopoly of the College of Physicians and condemned the practice of keeping the people of this nation in a state of ignorance? Hence why I advocated the reform of learning, as well as the institutions of the Church and of the Law? Also, why I supported the Parliamentarians and followed the Saints into the battlefield?'

Zachariah didn't answer. Instead he sighed deeply, thinking Nicholas was wandering off track again.

'I undertook all these tasks because when I embarked on my journey, the world was in chaos. Recall the dream I sent you this night, Zachariah. It revealed the rulers of this nation were as fit to govern as a sow is to fiddle, and would make as good harmony of the Commonwealth as the crying of a hog would amongst a consort of musicians.[184] Witnessing the Parliamentarian troops and their fall from grace, their fighting and squabbling, and their ineffective wars showed me that violence and conflict would never herald Christ's Coming. Rather through Christ I realised that the path to Salvation was not war, but through repentance and the peaceful preparation of the self. Hence, I sought to prepare the people of this nation for the Coming of Christ, because He would not come if their bodies were diseased or their minds in a state of chaos and ignorance. My aim was to help people treat themselves and their ailments, and in so doing I sought to increase their knowledge of themselves. And as their bodies are a microcosm of the celestial macrocosm, through this self-knowledge they would also be enlightened as to the nature and meaning of God's Creation.[185] Hence, my astrological and medicinal publications sought to teach people how to order themselves and their nation, rather than succumb to violence and disorder. By studiously reading the Scriptures and studying natural philosophy, the knowledge gained would restore perfect balance to the world and make it and mankind ready for the Coming of Christ!'[186]

Gesturing again to his many publications scattered across the table and gracing his book cabinets, he continued, 'In these books, Zachariah, I encourage people to undertake their tasks with care and diligence, because by their good works and charity towards others in their allotted time, the Lord would reward them with salvation.[187] I asked them to look diligently into themselves and know themselves very well, because there they may find the unity between themselves and their God, and then they may know what shall be in this world and in the world to come.'[188]

His eyes ablaze with an inner light, Nicholas spoke as if he were preaching a sermon to his flock. 'To attain knowledge of the Trinity, of the philosopher's stone, or of *aurum potabile* brings much joy to a man. Indeed, it is the joy of life because those who have been graced with such insights know they are amongst God's Elect. So, at the allotted time they will rise from the Earth and be united with Christ.'[189]

Bemused, Zachariah mulled over Nicholas's words. While it remained unspoken and unacknowledged, he realised that Nicholas was confessing to the motives that drove him to translate and write his medicinal texts, as well as instructing his readers on the mysteries of natural philosophy and astrology. If Nicholas had been entirely honest, he would have acknowledged that he well knew that such publications would be best-sellers. Books that provided instruction on self-improvement sold because the theologians instructed people that their desire to better themselves was a sign that God may have chosen them to be amongst His Elect. Zachariah recalled the very popular theological works of William Perkins, who had written that God's Elect were graced with qualities that encouraged and enabled them to accumulate knowledge necessary for them to prepare for Christ's Coming.[190]

Reflecting back on his own life, Zachariah acknowledged that one of the reasons why he had dedicated his life to the apothecary trade was as an act of public duty to ease the suffering of others, trusting that his charitable actions were a sign he was of the Elect.

Disturbing Zachariah's thoughts, Nicholas decried resentfully, 'You accuse me of withholding the wisdom contained within my *Treatise* from the people of this nation!' His voice rising in pitch, his face flushed crimson, Nicholas railed, 'On the contrary! If you care to study many of my works you will see that I indeed reveal its secrets. But,' he spat, 'I well understood my readers were like children who must learn to walk before they run!'[191] Thus I refrained from employing the complex terms and concepts commonly found in Paracelsian and Hermetic texts. Nor did I use the incomprehensible alchemical language of those puffers and mountebanks of the likes of Heydon.'

A copy of his translation of the College's *Pharmacopoeia* materialised before Zachariah and the pages turned unaided. Stabbing his finger at a passage, Nicholas said, 'You accuse me of withholding my knowledge of the Trinity? So read the opening paragraph in my introduction to this work. There I discuss in detail the nature of the threefold world and the significance of the Trinity to the process of Creation.'[192]

Slumping back into his chair, Nicholas said resignedly, 'But you are right, Zachariah, I withheld too much until it was too late. As the dream I sent to you this night reveals, the people did not prepare themselves, Christ did not come and so the world has descended into chaos and war. Yet I dared not write all that was revealed to me because I had received these sparks of knowledge directly from God, and so it was forbidden for me to reveal all.[193] But, because of the events of Black Monday and Christ not coming, I realised I must act and seek to share the wisdom God had conferred upon me. By the end of '53, I knew my life was ebbing away and so I had little time to rewrite and prepare my earlier translation of Partlicius's text, which held the keys to Salvation.'

Gesturing to one of the small booklets on the table, Nicholas continued, 'I did, however, manage to outline much of my philosophy and include it in the *Ephemeris* I was drafting for the year 1654, so again my readers were alerted to the importance of understanding the significance of the Trinity and the role such insights would play in heralding the Fifth

Monarchy, whenever that day would come.'[194]

Vehemently pointing his finger at Zachariah to emphasise every word, he added, 'I warned them! I warned them! I wrote that Christ will come in such a way as you little expect Him to come. He shall come as Jesus, a Saviour, as Christ.'[195] Defeated, he whispered sorrowfully, 'But I fear it is far too late, far too late.'

* * *

Eyes downcast and absentmindedly fingering a quill pen, Nicholas sighed, 'To speak truthfully, Zachariah, my studies were not in vain even if the people did not heed my warnings, because it wasn't just this nation and the English people I sought to help prepare for Christ's Coming.'

Rising effortlessly from his chair, he glided to the window and gazed towards the western horizon, watching the sun begin its descent behind a scattering of buildings. His back to Zachariah, Nicholas spoke of his childhood and adolescence when his grandfather railed against his unruly behaviour, calling him a heathen and threatening him with damnation. His voice trembling with barely controlled emotion, Nicholas once again recalled those days after the death of his beloved 'jewel'. Overwhelmed with melancholy, Nicholas explained how in a vulnerable state, he believed his grandfather's assertions that those tragic events were proof that he was damned.

'I was tormented with memories and nightmares of that fateful day; dreams of damnation and burning hell; my waking hours spent reflecting on my life and my actions, asking myself if there was any small sign, anything that may reveal that God was working through me.'

Turning from the window, Zachariah saw Nicholas's face was distorted with emotion and zeal.

'My grandfather was wrong, he was wrong!' Nicholas shouted. 'Remember I said to you that during my darkest hour God had shown me the way when I happened upon that book on Hermetic philosophy? I realised that God had graced me with a craving for knowledge of His natural world and of useful herbs that healed the sick. Experiencing a divine spark of insight, I realised that if I shared what I knew and dedicated my life to the public good, to helping the sick and ignorant, to unlocking knowledge chained in the Latin tongue, that I too would receive my rewards, not in this life, but at the time of the Resurrection of Christ!'[196]

Slumping back into his chair, his melancholic disposition returned, settling around him like a well-worn coat. 'Yet I feared dedicating my life to the public good wasn't enough, Zachariah,' he sighed deeply. 'My grandfather's condemnations haunted me all my life. Not one day would pass where I didn't search my conscience and question my motives. My sins were great; I caused the death of an innocent through my wilful thoughtlessness and selfish actions.'

Gesturing towards the *Treatise*, he said, 'You are right, Zachariah. That manuscript was of little use to my readers because, truth be told, I didn't embark on the study of the elementary, celestial and intellectual realms for them.'

Zachariah flinched as Nicholas crashed his palm against the *Treatise* shouting, 'No! I didn't do it for them! I did it for myself! I had to demonstrate to God that I was indeed worthy of His forgiveness, to receive His grace and so be counted amongst His Elect.'

Silence descended as both men contemplated the implications of these fateful words. Zachariah roused himself, witnessing the figure before him slowly losing substance. Is it a trick of the light? Or is he fading, Zachariah thought as it appeared Nicholas was struggling to maintain contact with the elementary world.

'Zachariah,' Nicholas spoke softly, 'I dedicated my life to the exploration of the elementary microcosm and the corresponding celestial macrocosm to gain knowledge of myself as well as the structure and process of Creation. The journey's end for the student of Hermetic philosophy is to reach the intellectual world through divine illumination, which is highest in degree, and happy, yea, thrice happy is he who attains it.[197] Have I attained it, you wonder? Will I be rewarded with God's divine grace and sit beside Christ and live forevermore as a subject in His Fifth Monarchy? I cannot reveal these answers, because they are divine mysteries beyond the ken of the living.'

The spectre's substance dissolving into the ether, his voice trailing into nothingness, Zachariah strained to catch his deceased friend's parting words: 'Remember, Zachariah, *aurum potabile* is not an elixir; nor is it a golden stone made in an alchemist's furnace as Heydon so believes. No! *Aurum potabile* is a product of the intellectual realm. It is divine illumination! It is knowledge! It is the key to the Holy Trinity, the understanding of which will open the door to everlasting life!'

***

It is strange for a cock to be crowing in the evening, Zachariah thought as he struggled from his reverie. Opening his eyes, he saw he was no longer in Nicholas's chamber, but in his bed at the Dolphin Inn. It was mid-morning and the sun's rays streamed through the gaps in the shuttered window.

As he raised himself from his pillow, something fell to the floor with a thud. It was his borrowed copy of *Culpeper's Treatise of* Aurum Potabile. Shaking his head to dispel the traces of his dream, the events of the previous evening slowly returned. Was it all a dream, he wondered? Was he dreaming he had been dreaming? Was he awake now?

Pulling back the bedcovers, he struggled to his feet. Making his way to the washstand, he glanced at the chair in the corner of the room. Changing direction, he stood before it and gazed down. Was it all just a dream?

With a deep sigh of resignation, Zachariah turned and paused, his foot frozen in mid-step. 'That aroma!' he cried. 'It smells like vanilla spiced tobacco…'

* * *

Chapter Nine: Epilogue

Bethlem Hospital Graveyard
Wednesday, 6ᵗʰ May 1656, mid-morning

Seated on a rough wooden bench, Zachariah leaned against the stone boundary wall of the Bethlem Cemetery in which Nicholas Culpeper's mortal remains now lay. Face upturned, he soaked up the warmth of the morning sun as he waited for Jane, who was going to guide him to Nicholas's grave. He reflected on the events since his meeting with Sir William, now nearly a month ago. He felt somewhat melancholy and conflicted because he had also become enthused at the idea that possibly Nicholas had stumbled upon a recipe for some type of universal elixir. If that had been so and Sir William had secured some rights to the cordial, Zachariah would also have profited. Yet, being a professional apothecary, he maintained a degree of doubt, because such magical cures were always unmasked as being duplicitous, peddled by mountebanks whose motive was pure greed. He shuddered at the thought of his reputation being sullied if he were to become entangled in a scheme that would later prove fraudulent.

'Penny for your thoughts,' a soft, motherly voice spoke.

Zachariah smiled as he opened his eyes and gazed up

at the familiar figure standing before him. A large wicker carry basket looped over her arm, Jane was dressed in what appeared to be her Sunday best. Whilst well-cut and spotlessly clean, her plain russet-brown petticoat and waistcoat marked out her station in life, that of a servant. Zachariah admired the effort she had taken to line the borders of her white linen apron and bonnet with delicate lace.

'Oh, I was just thinking on the events of the past month,' Zachariah replied as he rose from his seat.

As they strolled along the narrow laneway to the cemetery gate, they avoided discussing the subject that had brought Zachariah to London. He pointed out some chickweed sheltering in the dank, shadowy corner of an adjacent building and the spleenwort and nightshade lining the narrow muddy path. They laughed as they squabbled over the names of herbs and their uses.

Upon reaching the gate, they paused as Zachariah gazed across a weed-infested field pockmarked with mounds and damp hollows under which the dead now lay. They picked their way gingerly between ornate headstones and simple wooden plaques, as well as graves marked out only by field stones or old brick borders.

'Here we are,' Jane said as she paused in front of a grey slate headstone.

Zachariah was surprised. Considering Alice's claims of financial distress at the time of her husband's death, he was expecting, at best, a simple wooden marker incised with a few lines of text. Yet, this was a substantial headstone worthy of a gentleman.

Carved into the arched top, trumpets and cherubs surrounded a radiant crown, representing the Last Judgement. Squatting on his haunches, Zachariah read the epitaph. From the crudeness of the text it was apparent that, while the carver was skilled at decoration, he was not so accomplished when it came to his letters, as some words were so crudely carved as to be all but indecipherable:

> 'Here lies Nick Culpeper, for want of a breast,
> To drink of a sack, was sacked by Death,
> The planets, signs and stars in the [illegible].
> To see their Prophet closed in the sad urn.
> Fortune did favour him, though he were wise,
> And did supply his wants, even from the Skies.
> Yet envious Death, 'cause Nick's skill often did save,
> Struck him a blow soon sent him to his grave.
> Where rest in Patience, and Patients rest content,
> Nick's life like ours, alas a thing but lent,
> When payable we know not, nor how soon,
> Nick's here eclipsed, and changed like the [illegible].'[198]

Glancing up at Jane questioningly, she explained that while Nicholas had left enough funds to cover the cost of his burial, friends and associates also helped.[199]

Snorting, she added resentfully, 'Heydon forbade Alice from contributing. If he had had his way, Nicholas would have been fortunate to have had a wooden plaque laid on his grave.'

'Oh, well, don't you worry about them anymore, Jane,' Zachariah said in an exasperated tone as he stood and grasped her roughened hand affectionately. 'This headstone is witness to the respect and friendship Nicholas enjoyed in life; a treasured gift Heydon will never receive in this life or the next.'

Changing the melancholic subject, Zachariah commented on the wildflowers growing in profusion around the grave. Jane explained that after the gravediggers had covered Nicholas's coffin, she had sprinkled flower seeds over the freshly turned soil. 'As you can see, the marigolds are in bloom, but it's a little too early in the season for the poppy.'

Her mood transforming and smiling radiantly, she added, 'Zachariah, come back here in mid-summer and this field is an explosion of colour when the meadow flowers and wild herbs have burst into bloom.' Laughing she added, 'Certainly, Nicholas couldn't have chosen a better place.'

Gently grasping his arm, Jane led him to the stone boundary wall well away from the graves where the wild grasses were thick underfoot. Taking a blanket from her basket and kneeling down, she unpacked a simple lunch of fresh bread and cheese and two glazed clay bottles of beer.

They ate in silence, each lost in their own thoughts as they gazed across the field at people strolling amongst the gravestones.

'Your suspicions were correct, Jane,' Zachariah said, disturbing their reverie. 'Heydon is little more than a deceitful mountebank and his elixir a product of his duplicitous overexcited imagination.'

Her interest aroused, she looked on questioningly as Zachariah began searching in his leather satchel. Drawing out a stiff leather-bound folder, he handed it over. Inside was a letter addressed to Sir William.

'Please, you read it,' she said handing it back to him.

'I spent all yesterday afternoon trying to write this letter,' he began. Smiling, he added, 'I am glad Sir William is paying for the stationery as I shudder to think of the cost of the expensive paper I wasted on drafts.'

My good Sir,

I regret to inform you that my interview with Mr Heydon has confirmed my suspicions that he and his claims about Nicholas Culpeper discovering the secrets of a universal elixir, aurum potabile, are fraudulent. His associate Dr Freeman is an uncouth ruffian who I am confident is no doctor of medicine.

Mr Heydon permitted me to observe him making the so-called elixir in an effort to persuade me of its efficacy. However, from my observations as a skilled apothecary, I have determined it is little more than flavoured, coloured water with some odious chemical ingredients added.

I can confirm that the book Heydon has published, titled Mr Culpeper's Treatise of Aurum Potabile *was written by Nicholas, but not for the purpose Heydon now claims.*

While Nicholas does employ the term 'aurum potabile', through a careful reading of the text it becomes evident that it refers to the knowledge gained through a dedicated study of natural philosophy.

Thus, contrary to Mr Heydon's claims, aurum potabile was never a universal cure-all.

I fear Mr Heydon will seek to establish contact in the hope that he can persuade you to contribute your good name and finance his ventures. However, it is my opinion, sir, that any future association with Mr Heydon will be detrimental to both your interests and Nicholas's memory.

The task you set me has not been entirely in vain. During my investigations, I had the pleasure of speaking with Nicholas's closest friends and associates. I am pleased to confirm that Nicholas is held at the highest esteem. They confirmed his life-long dedication to helping the poor and the sick of this nation through his medicinal publications, and his calls for the reform of educational institutions, as well as the London medical services.

Mr Culpeper's reputation as a skilled and knowledgeable medical author is demonstrated by the many reprints of his works. Therefore, I am confident that as long as his publications remain in print, the people of this nation will remember him with kindness and acknowledge the contributions he made to the practice of medicine in our age.

I will be returning home shortly. If you wish further clarification, please send word and I will attend to you at your convenience.

Your most obliging servant,
Mr Zachariah Jenkin.

Sighing, Zachariah rested the folder in his lap and gazed into the distance. Aware he was being scrutinised, finally his attention returned to Jane. As if he were the young man she had known all those years ago, he felt his neck flush in embarrassment and found it difficult to hold her gaze.

'Yes, there was more, much more, but I did not know how to explain,' he mumbled. He feared even Jane would think him mad if he confessed that Nicholas had come to him in a dream and had revealed the secrets behind his writing of the *Treatise*. On reflection, he doubted it himself.

His attempts at drafting the letter to Sir William were frequently interrupted by his attention wandering to that dream. Had Nicholas actually come to him, or was it just a fantasy? Was it merely his thoughts ordering and clarifying themselves in a dream state? After all, he had spent weeks reading and studying many of Nicholas's publications. Following the advice and directions of Brooke, Cole and Ryves, he had compared, contrasted and studied Nicholas's commentaries and discussions. Did the outcome of such intense study prompt the revelations that came to him during his dreams?

Certainly, anyone who had approached the *Treatise* with an open mind and compared its contents with Nicholas's earlier publications may have come to similar conclusions–that the original manuscript evidently was one of the first texts he had drafted through his own efforts, rather than merely translating, compiling or adding to the works of other authors.

However, what of the spectre's claims about the motivations behind not only the drafting of the *Treatise*, but also his life-long dedication to the study of medicine, astrology and natural philosophy? Worrying if one was amongst God's Elect preoccupied the minds of most people and influenced their actions. Yet, for all the sermons from the pulpit, such contemplations were highly personal, a communication only between oneself and God. Zachariah felt he could not betray his friend and reveal the revelations as to the ultimate function of his *Treatise*.

Zachariah remained conflicted and confused. In his parting words, Nicholas claimed the motive behind his writing of the *Treatise* was to try to ensure his place beside Christ on Judgement Day. But, if God had already chosen those who were to receive His grace, how could the writing of a text, even one that celebrated the wonders of God's Creation, persuade Him to change His mind? It was inexplicable. Zachariah concluded that the doubts and torments Nicholas had endured throughout his life drove him to seek redemption through his studies, his charitable works and his attempts to prepare himself and the nation for the

Christ's Fifth Monarchy. Zachariah was confident that of all people seeking redemption through good works and charity, Nicholas would succeed.

He tried to explain the contents of the *Treatise* to Jane, while omitting the more intricate details related to the Holy Trinity and its relationship to Culpeper's desire to seek or affirm his election. He felt reluctant to discuss such intimate and private details even with Jane.

Smiling and holding up her palm and gesturing for him to cease, Jane said, 'All this is confusing, Zachariah. Really all I needed to know was if this 'orrum potabal' is the magical medicine Heydon claims it to be. Your letter to Sir William confirms that it is not.' Reaching over and affectionately grasping his hand, she continued kindly, 'Your confirmation of Nicholas's good character is a comfort to me, even though we both know he was rather self-involved and some of his motives were not as charitable as others may think them to be.'

Smiling, Zachariah agreed.

'Well, now my task is at an end, I will be returning home soon,' he said as he inserted the folder back into his satchel. Gazing at Jane, he was about to speak, but her expression of sadness checked his words.

Glancing away, blinking furiously, Jane began to gather up the remnants of their meal, when Zachariah reached out and gently grasped her hand.

'Jane,' he said kindly, 'I have thought of this since the day I came searching for Mrs Cul— Heydon and instead found you. Witnessing your distress and experiencing Heydon's wrath myself, I realised you could not stay in that unwelcoming place. So please consider returning to Crawley with me.'

'Oh, Zachariah, that is a kind offer, but I cannot be a burden to you—'

'Never a burden, dear Jane,' Zachariah interrupted her refusal. 'Even though my task has proven futile and Sir William will not be profiting from any elixir, he promised to pay the full amount for my services whatever the outcome. I plan to use the money to expand my shop and so I will need an extra pair of hands to assist me. And I cannot think of anyone better!'

Before she could voice any further objections, Zachariah added, 'My family is growing, and my wife has no relatives close by who can assist her with the household. I am confident she will welcome you into our home.'

'Then, yes, Zachariah, I will accept your kind offer,' Jane said, smiling broadly. 'Truth be told, I believe my days are numbered in the Heydon household.'

Returning Jane's radiant smile, he asked how long it would take before she was ready to leave. Having only a few personal possessions, a few changes of clothes, some books and items from the apothecary shop, Jane replied that she would be ready by the morrow.

Strolling back along the boundary wall, they discussed their plans for departing London the next day. At the threshold of the gate, Zachariah turned and gazed once more at the headstones scattered in a field of flowers and herbs.

'Yes, Jane, you are right, this is a good place where Nicholas can rest in peace until he is called to Christ on Judgement Day.'

THE END

We can eafily defcribe to you what a Philofopher ought' to be that intends thefe ftudies, He ought to be guided by heavenly Principles in all his wayes, to love and fear God above all : God is all in all to them, and all their ftudy is to know the wonderfull works of God in the Book of the Scripture, and Book of the Creatures, to admire at his glory and excellency, and to doe good to their Neighbours for Gods fake. Thefe be the Principles that move them to work, and not to grow great and rich in this world. In fhort, they are guided by heavenly and not by earthly Principles ...

Figure 3: Extract from *Mr Culpeper's Treatise of* Aurum Potabile, 1656, pp. 185-186.

End notes: Contingencies, Life Choices
and Power-Relationships

It is not enough to rationalise Culpeper's marginalisation and subsequent erasure from the seventeenth century reform debates by assuming that the esoteric elements of his works damaged his credibility. Hartlib's reform proposals appear to be a mismatch of rational Baconian new philosophy, and metaphysical and millenarian superstition. Yet, as Young (1998) argues, members of the Hartlib Circle were considered important and influential men of their time; their ideas were taken seriously by their peers and, subsequently, by twentieth century historians researching the reform of learning during the Interregnum.

Skinner's (2002, p. 60) comment that 'the special danger with intellectual biography is that of anachronism' can be applied to histories of people from the scientific and medical disciplines. Merchant (2008) argues that many of Bacon's biographers simultaneously identified modern concepts in his works, while erasing anything that appeared superstitious or metaphysical, lest it tarnished the reputation of their subject. Consequently, while hindsight has created a gulf between Culpeper and Bacon–condemning the former as a superstitious quack while elevating the latter to the status of an intellectual luminary–when placed in their historical contexts and avoiding anachronistic and grand narrative methodologies, their arguments for the reform of learning are comparable.

Therefore, the science/superstition, philosophical/metaphysical, credible/gullible binary arguments do not fully explain why Culpeper's contribution to the reform debates were marginalised by his seventeenth century scholastic peers and almost ignored by twentieth century historians from the intellectual history disciplines. Consequently, something else must have occurred that enabled the esoteric elements of Bacon's philosophies to be erased or ignored while, conversely, similar beliefs identified in Culpeper's publications served to condemn him as an ignorant charlatan.

Boettcher (2003, pp. 77, 84) argues that Foucault's 'linguistic turn' and its relationship to concepts of power and knowledge contributes significantly to the re-evaluation and interrogation of the modernist interpretation of the 'production of knowledge'. Dreyfus and Rabinow (1983, p. 110) explain that Foucault recognises that knowledge production occurs in the contexts of rituals of power, domination and subjugation, which 'impose rights and obligations' and are to be found in the moral codes and laws that are controlled and manipulated by particular groups. Hence, as will be explored, the knowledge Culpeper was producing and distributing in his publications was disqualified and thus rendered as subjugated knowledge, not because it was deemed inadequate for the task in relation to its scientific validity (Foucault 1988). Rather Culpeper's knowledge was subjugated as a consequence of his conduct towards his gentlemanly peers, which resulted in him being ostracised from the centres of elite knowledge production. Therefore,

Nietzsche's concept of genealogy, as analysed by Foucault (1977), and his interpretation of power-relationships and discourse communities (Olsson 2010, p. 65) can provide explanations as to the fate of Culpeper and his publications.

Foucault rejects the search for origins, causes and historical grand narratives, in favour of perceiving history as a series of unconnected chance events and disparities (Kendall & Wickham 1999). By paraphrasing Foucault's approach to historical questions via 'conditions of possibility', Kendall and Wickham explain his aim was to 'describe the various bits and pieces that had to be in place to allow something else to be possible' (1999, p. 37). Nevertheless, in the context of Culpeper's life, it is less a matter of various bits and pieces that allow something else to be possible. Rather, Culpeper's personal life choices and historical contingencies actually impeded the manifestation of opportunities that, if realised, may have enabled his commentaries to be considered important contributions to the medical and social reform debates of the mid seventeenth century.

Culpeper and social status

While Marxist historians separate seventeenth century English society into upper, middle and lower classes, in actuality such classifications did not exist during that period. Instead of the Marxist interpretation of social classes, according to Slater (1976), Birken (1987) and Laurence (1994), social status was characterised by birth or ancestry, land ownership and patronage, or the lack thereof. It was believed that society existed in a type of divine hierarchy that reflected the natural world and the cosmos (Guthrie 1967). The belief in such correspondences between the hierarchy of nature and the social order can be traced as far back as the works of Plato and Aristotle, and persisted well into the seventeenth century. According to Guthrie (1967), the English philosopher Thomas Hobbes (1588–1679) compared the microcosmic hierarchy of the limbs of the human body to the macrocosmic structure of society: the head being princes and rulers, while common agricultural people were relegated to the feet. Culpeper's understanding of the structure of the Cosmos, as discussed in his *Treatise of* Aurum Potabile, is also an example of this hierarchy. Guthrie (1967, p. 62), citing a 'seventeenth century writer', explains that, 'the best comparison for the commonwealth is either 'the universal mass of the whole world' or else, 'the body of man, being the lesser world, even the diminutive and model for the wide-extending universal'. Thus, everything, from people to animals and even non-living objects had been assigned a place in the hierarchy, which was static, and to rebel was irrational as it defied God's plan (Guthrie 1967; Stone 1965; Heal & Holmes 1994).

In relation to its social application, at the pinnacle of the hierarchy was the monarchy. Immediately below were the extremely wealthy and powerful titled aristocracy and upper gentry, or nobility. Below them were the mere gentry who, Laurence (1994, p. 16) explains, consisted of 'men who were entitled to bear a coat of arms', but didn't hold any specific title. Below the gentry was the 'middling sort': ranging from wealthy professionals, merchants and shopkeepers, to tradespeople, including apothecaries and surgeons (Barry, 1994, p. 2). At the bottom of the hierarchy and consisting of the bulk of the population were the predominately illiterate rural and urban unskilled poor. Nevertheless, even at the time when the myth of the stable hierarchy persisted, English society during the sixteenth and seventeenth centuries was experiencing high levels of social mobility—both upwards and downwards (Stone 1965; Heal & Holmes 1994).

For centuries within the English legal system the oldest son was the sole heir to the ancestral estate (Birken 1987). Younger sons were excluded from receiving, and therefore benefiting, from the privileges a title or coat of arms conferred. The best they could hope for was to either seek patronage and/or financial assistance, or merely bask in the glory of their titled relatives. To preserve their status as gentlemen of means, younger sons were sent to university to study 'logic, grammar, rhetoric, mathematics, astronomy, music, and moral, natural, and metaphysical philosophy' (Axtell 1970, p. 145). Following this basic liberal arts degree, graduates then proceeded to undertake a professional degree, such as medicine, divinity or law. For example, Francis Bacon, the youngest son of Sir Nicholas Bacon, was sent to Cambridge with the view of studying law. Yet, an education was not all Bacon and his fellow students learned while at Cambridge. Axtell (1970) and Cook (1994) suggest an important function of the university experience was to mould the character of a man into that of a gentleman.

As indicated from the Culpeper Family Tree (Figure A.1) and discussed by Stockwell (1990) and Woolley (2004), while Nicholas Culpeper was descended from the titled gentry, his immediate ancestors were younger sons of younger sons. While maintaining social contacts and patronage with successive titled noble Culpeper contemporary cousins, his branch of the family had not been a member of the higher gentry for at least three generations (Stockwell 1990). Nicholas's grandfather and father, Nicholas Culpeper senior MA (1580–1616), maintained their gentlemanly status by obtaining university educations and entering the Church. Sir Edward Culpeper (1561–1630)–the heir to huge estates throughout Surrey, including the family seat Wakehurst Place–was Nicholas Culpeper senior's patron, offering him a parsonage at the local village of Ockley. According to Stockwell (1990), this permanent church appointment, or benefice, had been the responsibility of Sir Edward's family since the early sixteenth century and was usually awarded to younger Culpeper sons or minor relatives. This explains how Nicholas Culpeper senior became rector at Ockley.

Culpeper's maternal grandfather, William Attersoll, also a rector and gentleman, was determined to ensure that his grandson followed the Culpeper family tradition and study for the Church, via a Cambridge University education. Stockwell mentions that, during his childhood, Culpeper was a constant visitor to Wakehurst Place. It could be speculated that, through these frequent visits, Culpeper's mother and grandfather were ensuring that Sir Edward's son and heir, Sir William Culpeper (1602–1678) would pass the benefice onto young Nicholas.

However, Culpeper left Cambridge before he graduated, following a disastrous attempt at an elopement with a wealthy young woman (Woolley 2004, p. 29). In the light of Donogan's claim that a pastor was expected to 'try to live a traditionally virtuous life, living in love and charity with his neighbours and avoiding the usual sins' (1984, p. 86), Nicholas's youthful indiscretion had ruined his reputation and thus any chance of entering the Church. Additionally, when Culpeper's character is taken into account—his melancholic temperament; conceitedness; desire for, but squandering of riches; his irreverent jesting (Gadbury 1659 sig. B4v); as well as his dedication to the occult arts (Anon [Brooke] 1659, sig. C3r)—he would never have succeeded as a pastor, even if he had completed his studies.

In an attempt to salvage his status as a gentleman, Culpeper's grandfather secured him an apprenticeship with an apothecary (Woolley 2004, p. 116), a trade considered suitable for the younger sons of the gentry and gentlemen (Brooks, 1994). Yet, Culpeper did not complete his apothecary apprenticeship, which left him with no other suitable career choices. The Reverend Attersoll may have informed him that after the elopement debacle he was disinherited, because after his death in 1640, while he bequeathed four hundred pounds to his other grandchildren, Nicholas only received forty shillings (Stockwell 2006). The only option Culpeper had to enable him to maintain the material trappings of a gentleman was via a strategic marriage to the wealthy young Alice Field, daughter of a rich merchant (Anon [Brooke] 1659). As will be discussed in greater detail, Mr Field may have sought social elevation through marrying his daughter into a family with titled connections.

If Culpeper had modified his inclinations, graduated and then entered the Church under the patronage of Sir

Figure A.1 (Opposite): Culpeper's Family Tree (Stockwell 1990, frontispiece)

CULPEPERS OF BAYHALL, BEDGEBURY AND WAKEHURST

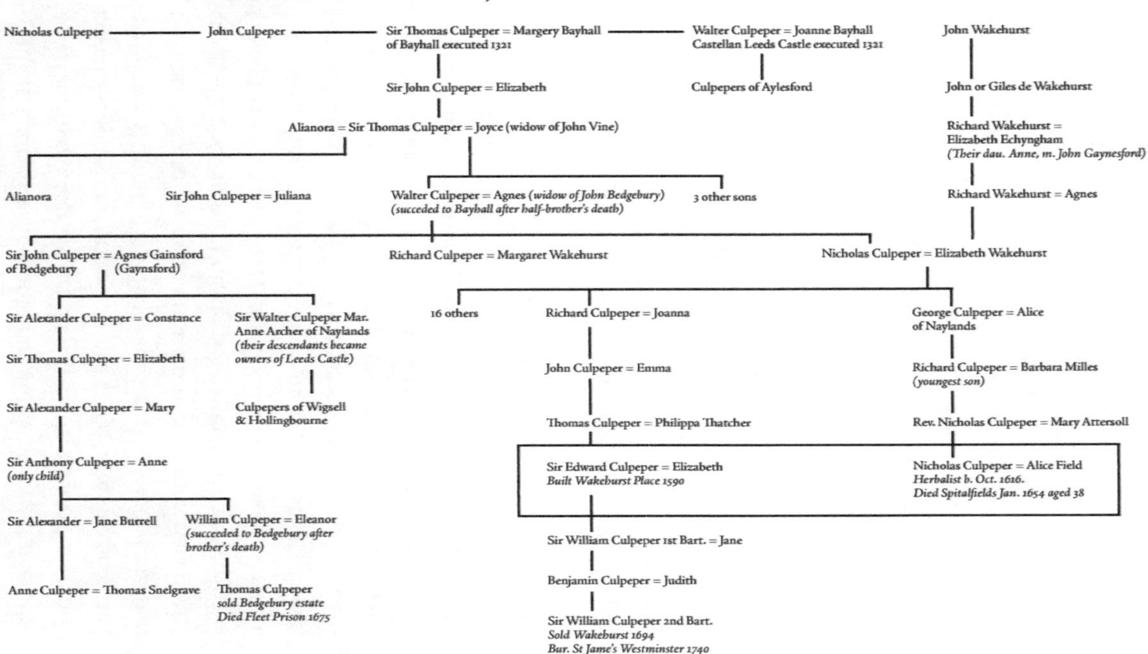

William Culpeper, he would not only have maintained the social status of a learned gentleman-cleric, a man of acknowledged authority and respect, but he could have also practised medicine within the law. Since medieval times, bishops had the authority to award medical licences to members of the clergy (Birken 1987). During the seventeenth century, the College tried to bar clergymen from practising in London. However, their complaints were ignored and so clergymen practised in defiance of the College (Harley 1998). If Culpeper had attained the status and education of a gentleman-cleric and licensed rural medical practitioner, his subsequent reputation and authority may have led to his publications receiving greater acceptance amongst gentlemen of learning, thus becoming a valid and insightful contribution to the contemporary reformist debates.

Why the potential difference in reception if Culpeper had finished his university studies and secured a position as a rural cleric-medical practitioner, thus preserving his status as an acknowledged learned gentleman? The status of a gentleman conferred many privileges. According to Cook (1994, p. 56), gravity, discretion and trustworthiness were essential qualities of learned gentlemen. Yet, of all the qualities a gentleman possessed, credibility was most important (Shapin 1988; Biagioli 1996). 'It was the acknowledged freedom of the gentleman's action, the honour accorded to his word, the moral discipline he imposed upon himself, and the presumed moral equality of the company of gentlemen that guaranteed the reliability of … knowledge' (Shapin 1988, p. 397). Furthermore, throughout the seventeenth century, Shapin states:

[T]he distribution of credibility followed the contours of English society, and that it did was so evident that scarcely any commentator felt obliged to specify the grounds of this creditworthiness. In such a setting one simply knew what sorts of people were credible, just as one knew whose reports were suspect (1988 p. 376).

Or to put it succinctly, it wasn't what one knew that was important; it was the high social status of the author or producer of knowledge, as well as the gentlemanly status of his peers that determined the validity, acceptance and durability of knowledge.

Culpeper's experience is mirrored by other intellectuals of the early modern period. Shapin and Schaffer (1985) re-examined Robert Boyle's (1627–1691) scientific successes and subsequent elevation to the status of scientific luminary, in comparison to his contemporary Thomas Hobbes's failures and almost erasure from history. They conclude that it was not a matter as to whether or not their knowledge and theories of the natural world were right or wrong; it was that Boyle had been a better communicator to the social elites that controlled discourse and knowledge production (Shapin and Schaffer 1985). Thus, Boyle presented himself and his ideas as being more credible and subsequently was remembered in the historical record, whereas Hobbes's contributions were forgotten, because of apparent character and communication deficits.

Similarly, According to Biagioli (1993), Galileo (1564–1642) was condemned by the Catholic Church and ultimately investigated by the Inquisition, not so much because of the nature of his ideas, but rather because he was inept in negotiating the discourse power relationships of the Court. Thus, Biagioli (1993, pp. 237–238) concludes, the advancement of science was not dependent on new ideas and inventions, but rather occurred as a consequence of the ability of the individual to negotiate power relationships and articulate their ideas in ways acceptable to the power elites.

Power relationships and the 'nasty clashing of wills'

On the eve of the English Civil War, Culpeper believed he was fighting a righteous cause by challenging the authority and legitimacy of the monarchy, gentry and the professions. Yet, the men who were the target of his criticisms, and responded with equal vehemence were, as far as Culpeper was concerned, his social equals. Culpeper described himself as having been 'born a gentleman and bought up a scholar [but hating] a sycophantic course of life' (1651c, n.p.). Hence, Culpeper is stating that, while he was born into a family of high social status, and therefore is a gentleman by right, he rejects the flattering, self-seeking pomposity of his social equals. It is this context of Foucault's social power relationships, or the 'catty fights, minor crudeness, ceaseless and nasty clashing of wills' (Dreyfus and Rabinow, 1983. p. 108), which provides an explanation for the marginalisation of Culpeper by his learned contemporaries.

The opening two pages of Culpeper's translation of the College of Physicians' *Pharmacopoeia*, reveals the extent of his contempt for members of the professions and especially that of licensed physicians. Deliberately establishing a provocative tone, he wrote:

[T]he liberty of our Commonwealth ... is most infringed

by three sorts of men, priests, physicians [and] lawyers …
The one deceives men in matters belonging to their souls,
the other in matters belonging to their bodies, the third in
matters belonging to their estates. Amongst these, physicians
walk in the clouds … Men [therefore] are led by their noses
… by a company of proud, insulting, domineering doctors
… The doctor's practice is to ask for gain, even at a time
when men cry out in pain (Culpeper 1649b, sig. A1r–A1v).

Culpeper liberally inserts personal comments into the
translation, which he called a 'worm-eaten Dispensatory'
(1649a p. 145). Attacking the competency, credibility and
intelligence of the licensed physicians, he lampooned their
bizarre and inappropriate recommendations for the use of
various herbs, by suggesting even more outrageous treatments:

As for the shell of walnuts, I know of nothing they are good
for, but only to make sport. For if you fill four of them full
of pitch, and shoe a cat with them and put her in a [room],
she will make pretty sport to please a melancholy [fantasy]
(Culpeper, 1649a, p. 22).

The common thread of many of the commentaries Culpeper inserted into his texts was the insulting and questioning
of the morals, credibility and competence of members of
the professions, who all considered themselves gentlemen
of learning. In the light of Shapin's (1988) and Biagioli's
(1993, p. 235) comments that gentlemen were bound to
refrain from seeking to discredit men of their own station,
Culpeper, therefore, had betrayed the code of honour that
united gentlemen. Consequently, he demonstrated to men
of his own station that he did not possess the qualities of a

gentleman, which may explain why he was ostracised from the sites of legitimate knowledge production.

Destabilising the hierarchy

Cook (1986, p. 29) describes the medical system in seventeenth century England as a 'medical marketplace', because of the diverse range of medical practitioners operating at the time. Most practitioners—from physicians to empirics—employed the orthodox medical system derived from the ancient classical works of Galen and Hippocrates (Cook 1986). A university medical education was primarily theoretical, based on a close study of the ancient classical works, with the aim of cultivating wisdom and good judgement (Cook, 1994). Practical skills, such as the making of medicines or undertaking surgical procedures, were left to the physician's subordinates: craftsmen trained under an apprenticeship system. Consequently, in order to protect their interests and separate themselves from the overwhelming number of competitors, physicians turned to their social status and qualities as learned gentlemen to promote their medical services. Cook (1994, p. 4) explains:

> The long university educations that marked physicians from all other medical practitioners therefore aimed not merely at transmitting information about healing, but at transforming the student into a physician of good character, who could exercise good judgement and advice: a man of learning.

Cook (1994, p. 71) also suggests that, while the College was a learned institution that provided public health-care advice to the Parliament, such as strategies for the treatment of plague, its 'one clear aim' was to preserve and promote the status of its members as gentlemen.

The skill that most separated physicians from other medical practitioners, and which enabled them to monopolise medical knowledge (hence Culpeper's translations) was the proficiency in reading, writing and translating Latin. According to Axtell, 'Latin remained the *lingua franca* of educated Europe' (1970, p. 149), and the ability to write, read and converse in the ancient language separated the physician from the apothecary and empiric. Some medical practitioners may have received an introductory education in Latin, if they had also attended grammar school (Axtell 1970). Yet, as McCarl (1996, p. 250) argues, few non-university-trained medical practitioners possessed the literary skills to comprehend the complex Latin medical texts written by and for physicians.

Culpeper, therefore, posed a serious problem for the College of Physicians, because its standard criticism of non-university-trained medical practitioners—their scant knowledge of Latin, limited formal education and dubious medical skills—did not apply to him. As Woolley (2004, p. 291) argues, Culpeper had humiliated the College by demonstrating that not only was he proficient in translating a complex Latin text into English, he was also able to correct the *Pharmacopoeia*'s many errors. Furthermore, Culpeper improved the text by adding many additional recipes sourced from local folk-lore, as well as orthodox medicines derived from the traditional classical authorities. Consequently, while not a university graduate, Culpeper proved to the College and (most especially) to his readers that his level of classical and practical medical education surpassed many learned physicians. Thus, Culpeper did not present himself as an ignorant empiric, but as a learned gentleman.

While the Fellows of the College responded to Culpeper's attacks with 'dignified silence' to the translation of the *Pharmacopoeia*, their supporters enacted revenge (Woolley 2004, p. 295). Culpeper's vulnerability was that he had not completed his university studies, nor had he finished his apothecary apprenticeship: facts his critics frequently emphasised. Unable to ridicule and condemn Culpeper's comprehensive medical knowledge, lest it cast shadows on their own practice, the College's supporters questioned his status as a gentleman by attacking his character, skills and educational shortcomings. Thus, the Royalist newspaper *Mecurius Pragmaticus* wrote of Culpeper's character:

> There is now extent a book entitled A Physical Directory …
> done (very filthily) into English by one Nicholas Culpeper …
> But because you may know who this our learned translator is
> … he is a son of a Surrey parson … he was bound apprentice
> to an apothecary … but ran away … from his master, upon
> his lewd debauchery… [He is] a most despicable, ragged
> fellow, and yet he looks as if he has been stewed in a tar-pit,
> being a drowsy-headed coxcomb not worthy the name of
> gentleman or scholar … (1649, n.p.).

The College's chemist, William Johnson (1652, p. 9), also attacked Culpeper's character, accusing him of using 'insolent language … against your betters'. Even ten years after Culpeper's death, the attacks on his character and credibility continued with the publication of a forty-page treatise titled *Culpeper's Character: or, A Character of Mr Culpeper and his Writings* (Mackaile 1664). The author claimed that Culpeper was neither a gentleman, nor did he have the skills or education to have written most of the works attributed to him Mackaile (1664, pp. 148, 156).

Culpeper's insulting commentaries, coupled with the vehement reactions of members and supporters of the College to his translation of the *Pharmacopoeia*, are quite interesting when Foucault's power relationships hypothesis is taken into account. Domination and subjugation, Foucault (1988, p. 97) claims, are not a manifestation of power of one distinct group or institution over another, but rather is a strategy of self-monitoring or self-assessment between members of a given group, 'at the level of those continuous and uninterrupted processes which subject our bodies, govern our gestures [and] dictate our behaviours'. Such monitoring, while separating a specific group from other groups, also constructs or maintains the identity of that group (Dreyfus & Rabinow 1983). Consequently, the conflicts between Culpeper and fellow gentlemen appears to have been a battle over defending one's right to be called a gentleman, and thus enjoy the privileges, power and respect that status conferred.

An explanation for this battle involving the power-plays of domination and subordination could be that, in relation to physicians, their status as gentlemen was not stable. It was in this context of power struggles over the legitimacy of status, that Culpeper posed most threat to the College of Physicians. Birken's (1987, p. 202) research indicates that, up until the 1970s, the overwhelming view amongst historians was that most physicians were the minor sons of landed nobility. Nevertheless, Birken (1987, p. 209) continues, later research has indicated that the status of physicians was not as high as once assumed; rather the older sons of merchants and yeomen filled the ranks of the College in the hope such a profession would provide opportunities for upward social mobility. Drawing on the research of historians, such as Ashley (1964) and Grassby (1982), Birken (1987, p. 203) suggests that the sons of the gentry often descended the social ladder by entering into apothecary and surgical trades, as well as commerce, business and politics.

The high status of the gentleman physician with all its qualities and privileges, therefore, was highly precarious. Apothecaries and surgeons were perceived as a threat to the College, as increasingly many of them were also the sons of gentlemen. Cook (1994) suggests the College subsequently tried to downplay the commoner origins of most of its members, by continually emphasising the gentlemanly status of the authoritative learned physician, as distinct from the subordinate status of the craftsmen apothecaries and surgeons, who they described as being undisciplined, lacking in judgement and of bad character.

Nonetheless, while members of the College of Physicians were perceived as gentlemen by their peers and the middling sort, acceptance into the gentry was not merely a matter of wealth or titles. For as far as the upper gentry were concerned, status could not be earned or bought: it could only be conferred by birth (Stone 1965). The rise of snobbery and attempts to reinforce titled privilege escalated during the Civil War and Interregnum, as it was an adverse reaction to a period when 'families were moving up and down the social and economic scale at a faster rate than at any time before the nineteenth … century' (Heal & Holmes 1994, p. 22). Consequently, while physicians may have attained the status of gentleman via a university education and even through receiving titles from the King, Birken (1987, pp. 209, 211) suggests it is questionable as to whether they would be welcome in the manors of the upper or landed gentry.

Citing Cressy (1976), Birken (1987, p. 2010) argues that gentility was a social condition identified as a state of mind and of conduct. It was, as Heal and Holmes (1994) describe, a mode of life characterised by qualities, appearances, subtle social behaviours or mannerisms, all of which were nurtured in a wealthy privileged environment. Furthermore, while wealth could buy titles and the appearance of gentility, a persistent and powerful element of a gentle status was lineage: the ability to trace one's ancestry back many generations. Thus, as Stone qualifies, 'birth and wealth ranked higher than virtue, education, or ability as indicators of status' (1965, p. 18). As mentioned, Stockwell (1990) claims the young Nicholas frequently visited Wakehurst Place to socialise with his titled betters. As a result, he would have been exposed to and raised in the manners thought appropriate for a gentleman descended from a distinguished, titled, estate-owning, genteel family.

It would have been very galling to the College to be reminded by Culpeper that he was related to 'Sir William Culpeper, Knight and Baron' (Culpeper 1652a, sig. A3r). By drawing attention to his lineage, Culpeper was participating in an activity that preoccupied the gentry during the Interregnum: proving and displaying lineages via the drafting of complex and often dubious genealogies (Heal and Holmes 1994). Culpeper had little to fear, because successive generations of his family not only held titles, but had participated in

Court and Parliamentary intrigues (Stockwell 1990; Woolley 2004). Hence the name Culpeper would have been well known in English society throughout the seventeenth century. Descended from and related to the landed gentry, Culpeper openly and with pride described himself as a scholar and gentleman. In stark contrast many members of the College being the sons of yeomen and merchants, could not make similar claims to justify their gentle status. As such, Culpeper's distinguished family name and associations must have been a source of humiliation to the College's august members.

Alienation and its consequences

Having graduated from Cambridge and taken up residence in Grey's Inn to practise law and later enter Parliament, Francis Bacon continued his studies into natural philosophy and writing his eclectic reformist tracts (Pérez-Ramos 1996). He was typical of the learned gentlemen of his age who, while independent of the universities, continued to produce valid knowledge in their role as solitary or independent scholars and philosophers. Nevertheless, according to Shapin (1988), by the mid-seventeenth century, (when Culpeper was writing and translating his texts) the independent scholar had fallen out of favour, replaced by small groups of like-minded learned gentlemen who discussed, debated and shared ideas. Thus, Shapin (1988, p. 378) writes, possibly as a consequence of the dubious practices of the mysterious and secretive alchemists, by the mid-seventeenth century, 'neither the individual philosopher in his study nor the solitary alchemist in his "dark and smokey" laboratory was a fit actor in a proper setting to produce objective knowledge.' Foucault refers to these specialist groups as 'discourse communities' (Olsson 2010, p. 65) which, as the seventeenth century unfolded, would come to dominate the production of knowledge and determined its truth.

During the mid-1640s, one such collection of like-minded men dedicated to the study of the New or Experimental Philosophy, established the Invisible College, later to become known as the Royal Society. According to Shapin (1988, p. 378), the most common meeting place for the members of the early Royal Society 'were the private residences of gentlemen' which provided a space for experimentation and the exchanging of ideas. Admittance to the group, Shapin continues, did not require 'any particular competencies … merely that [the applicant] was a gentleman of quality and merit, or held a distinguished title' (1988, p. 389).

In light of Dabhoiwala's claim that 'for those who regarded themselves as men "of honour" or "of quality", adherence to a specific code of honour set [gentlemen] apart from their inferiors' (1995, p. 203), Culpeper's damaging life choices, his contempt and breaching of the gentlemen's code alienated him from the men he considered to be his equals. As a consequence, while Culpeper contributed to the discourse on the reformist debates occurring during the Interregnum, he was excluded from the groups of gentlemen, such as the Hartlib Circle and the Invisible College, who were dominating these debates. Thus, in the context of Foucault's (1988) theories of discourse communities, the subjugation and domination of knowledge production as well as validity and truth, it could be argued that through Culpeper's own actions he alienated himself to the realms of the subjugated and silenced.

While history via hindsight is problematic, hindsight itself is a wonderful thing. However, it is not available to anyone when it is needed. If Culpeper had known the consequences of his life choices, he probably would have sought other ways and means to participate in the reformist debates of his time. Fate intervened when Culpeper chose to fight on the side of the Parliamentarians during the English Civil War, which ended with the execution of Charles I in 1649, followed by the founding of the English Commonwealth. Throughout the early 1650s, until his untimely demise in 1654, Culpeper consistently condemned supporters of the monarchy, as well as social elites, including the three dominant professions, physicians, clergy and lawyers, all of whom considered themselves learned gentlemen. Hence, Culpeper's anti-royalist and reformist commentaries reverberated throughout English society, rousing the common people to maintain their faith in Cromwell's revolutionary cause, while alienating his social equals and betters.

Yet, in early 1660, the Commonwealth collapsed and the monarchy was restored under King Charles II. Soon after the Restoration, Culpeper would be remembered as being on the losing side of the war and, as such, his reformist commentaries would have been considered treasonous. To make matters even worse, Culpeper had consistently breached the gentleman's code of honour, which effectively alienated him from the groups who soon came to dominate the production and validation of knowledge. Biagioli (1993, p. 235) suggests that within the Royal Society, facts or evidence were determined by the gentlemanly status of the scholar and constructed 'through a specific etiquette of inquiry'. Thus, following the establishment of the Society, the gentrification of the production of valid and objective knowledge intensified to such an extent that credible knowledge could only be produced by gentlemen, or 'in other words, gentlemen in, genuine knowledge out' (Shapin 1988, p. 397).

Alice Culpeper

The issues thus far discussed, ironically, are best explored in relation to Culpeper's wife and later his widow, Alice. It is for this reason that I both discuss Alice Culpeper in my thesis, and incorporate an examination of Alice in my novella as a sub-plot (see Noble 2016, pp. 67–73). By placing Alice Culpeper in her historical context–drawing on verifiable historical evidence of the roles and restrictions of women of the period–I provide her with a voice to explain her actions and motives. My aim is to present a plausible explanation as to why she conspired in the publication of the *Treatise of Aurum Potabile* and the selling of the universal elixir.

Nicholas Culpeper's alienation from his gentleman peers also cast a shadow over his wife. From the period just prior to Culpeper's death and continuing into the present era, Alice Culpeper has been cast in a very negative light. Greer (2007) claims that negative portrayals or interpretations of the wives or mistresses of notable historical men have had a long history within academia. Nevertheless, when Alice is placed in her historical context, and thus responding to the expectations, hurdles and stresses of life in mid-seventeenth century England, such negative representations are difficult to sustain.

Passing references to Alice Culpeper are to be found in

several texts, both contemporary of her era and subsequent historical interpretations. According to the biography in *Culpeper's school of Physick* (1659), Culpeper, being under the influence of the 'star' of Venus:

> Surrender[ed] all the powers and faculties of his soul to the virtues and beauty of Mrs Alice Field … at fifteen years of age, a gentlewoman, who as she was of a good extraction, so also, besides her richer qualities, had admirable discretion, and excellent breeding, she brought him a considerable fortune. (Anon [Brooke] 1659, sig. C5r–C5v).

Alice Culpeper was the second heiress that Culpeper courted because, as mentioned earlier, during his youth as a student at Cambridge University he had tried to elope with a young heiress. Tragically, on her way to their rendezvous a furious storm erupted, and this mysterious young woman was struck down dead by lightning (Anon [Brooke] 1659, sig. C2r). It could be assumed, therefore, that Culpeper's interest in potential brides was based more on the size of their dowry than on their demeanour or physical appearance!

Brooke states that, while Alice Culpeper 'so wisely de-meaned herself, as never to entrench on his prerogative, not in the least to disturb his prerogative … she only sought to maintain her own propriety in domestic feminine affairs', Culpeper instructed her in the medicinal arts in order that she be competent and independent (Anon [Brooke] 1659, sig. C5vr). Woolley (2004, p. 159) describes Alice as 'strong-willed, as well as an astute businesswoman', who generated respect amongst some of her deceased husband's associates, 'for loyally backing her husband in the face of often violent abuse'.

Nevertheless, Woolley also cast aspersions on Alice

Culpeper's morals and character by citing comments, made by Culpeper in his *English Physician* (1652c), about 'abusing women' and 'as drunk as a Bitch' (Culpeper cited by Woolley 2004, p. 323). Woolley (2004, p. 323) interprets these comments as indicating that the marriage between Culpeper and Alice was disintegrating because Alice 'may … have found another man.' Woolley (2004, p. 323) was referring to John Heydon (1629–c. 1667), who was a young lawyer and self-appointed Rosicrucian, and had taken up residence as a boarder in the Culpeper household during the period when Nicholas's health began to seriously deteriorate. Consequently, even though Woolley (2004) initially describes Alice Culpeper as a virtuous woman, he later portrayed her as a shrew and adulteress who contributed to the ruination of her deceased husband's reputation.

Initially, in my novella, I had intended to follow Woolley's example and portray Alice Culpeper as a conniving, self-centred, money-grabbing widow, who wished to exploit her dead husband's name for personal profit. Yet, after reading *Women on the Margins: Three Seventeenth Century Lives*, by Natalie Davis (1997) and Germaine Greer's *Shakespeare's Wife*, I re-evaluated Alice's life because, as Greer argues, 'history focused on the man the achiever [and] it was that the woman who slept in his bed would be judged unworthy of his company' (2007, p. 1). Davis (1997) and Greer (2007) analyse women in the context of their times, while refraining from judging them according to the values and expectations either of the patriarchal mores of the time or of subsequent historians' personal opinions. For as Skinner (2002) argues, it is only when taking context into account can the historian begin to understand the actions, aims and intentions of people from other eras and cultures. Thus, researching the lives of women, and especially widows during the mid-seventeenth century, I began to understand why Alice Culpeper may have acted and made decisions in relation to the various circumstances in which she found herself.

Even though Brooke (Anon (Brooke) 1659, sig. C5r) claims that Culpeper surrendered 'his soul to the virtues and beauty of Mrs Alice Field' it is unlikely that their betrothal was a love match. Rather, as was common practice of the period, it was a pragmatic business arrangement between Culpeper and Mr Field, Alice's father. According to Slater (1976), the head of the household usually arranged strategic marriages for their young teenage daughters. Woolley claims that Mr Field was a 'wealthy London merchant' (2004, p. 158), which probably meant that he was excluded from the status of gentry, but had gained influence through his wealth. Nevertheless, while of a lower social status to Culpeper, Alice's attraction was her dowry. Generally, prior to her marriage, either a woman's father or, in his absence, an elder male member of the family was in control of her assets, because women had few legal and social rights (Thompson 1993). Following marriage this duty was transferred to the woman's husband (Slater 1976). Alice's dowry was extensive enough for Culpeper to build a two-storey residence in Spitalfields, and enable them to live comfortably on the remainder of her dowry until the final years of his life (Woolley 2004).

Slater (1976, pp. 27–28) explains that a marriage allegiance was not only advantageous for the son or daughter, but also for her entire family as it expanded social relations and patronage. As mentioned earlier, Culpeper was not a man of financial means, having been disinherited by his grandfather. Therefore, Mr Field possibly agreed to the betrothal as a means for his family to rise in social standing by being associated with, and connected to the Culpeper name. Slater (1976) claims that, during the Civil War period, eligible marriageable gentlemen were rare. Thus, while Field must have known of Culpeper's reactionary and disruptive actions and commentaries, he may have overlooked these troublesome aspects of his future son-in-law.

Possibly, Field may have hoped maturity, marriage and fatherhood would have settled the impetuous Culpeper. Unfortunately, Alice's dowry provided Culpeper with the freedom to be even more radical and so attract the negative attentions of the press and those in authority, particularly the College of Physicians. Woolley (2004, p. 159) mentions that the marriage was 'troubled', which may refer to Culpeper's consistent unwise life-choices, which led him to the dire straits that left him almost penniless, alienated from and almost ignored by his gentleman peers. Thus, Alice must have been aware that Culpeper's lack of business sense would not guarantee their, or their surviving child, Mary's, financial security.

Realising that her much older husband was dying, Alice would understand that being a widow would not be a release; rather it attracted a whole set of new problems. Having few legal rights, widows were 'thus exploited … by men who were greedy for their dowries', and as there was a market for skilled and asset rich widows, they were under pressure to remarry immediately (Thompson 1993 p. 36).

How much of her dowry remained is not known. While not mentioned in the sources, it would appear that at some time Mr Field realised that the marriage arrangement was a mistake. Instead of receiving prestige from being associated with the Culpeper name, his family was now related to a trouble-maker who practised medicine illegally, as well as publishing unauthorised medical texts, thus attracting the ire of gentlemen of significant authority. As such, it would appear from Alice's actions during her widowhood, that she no longer received financial assistance from her family.

Alice Culpeper knew that she needed to maintain her family's security, in the knowledge that her husband's illness would soon lead to his death. Thus, in the social context of the period, realising she would soon be a widow, the family finances were drained, and coupled with her restricted legal rights and potential decline in social standing, it is understandable she sought some certainty in her life. Thus, oppressed by the presence of a diseased and dying husband, it is no wonder that a young, soon-to-be widow would be attracted to a debonair healthy gentleman boarder, of a similar age, who claimed (falsely) to be descended from European royalty. Furthermore, John Heydon's biography (Talbot 1662, sig. A4v) suggests he was even more of a ladies' man than Culpeper had ever been. In the light of Carlton's (1978) claim that young gentlemen exploited widows in order to set themselves up for life, Heydon's motives for courting and marrying Alice probably mirrored those of Culpeper: financial gain and security. Marrying the widow Culpeper, Heydon would have gained access to Nicholas's assets, which included the contents of the deceased man's library.

If Alice had enough independent finances when she became a widow, she could have enjoyed some freedoms that were denied other women. Carlton (1978, p. 126) claims that if they were financially secure, widows could be independent and even inherit their husband's assets and businesses. Yet these freedoms were precarious, because women, independent of the control or domination of men, were perceived as a threat to the social order. Hence widows were treated with scorn, often accused of being sexually promiscuous and so were objects of ridicule and mirth, as illustrated by their portrayal in theatre plays and literature (Carlton 1978, p. 127). According to Carlton (1978), many widows chose not to remarry, either because of a lack of eligible men, or a desire to maintain some independence, even though their reputations may suffer. Yet, whether a consequence of financial hardship and insecurity, or an infatuation with the young Heydon who beguiled her, Alice agreed to this second marriage. This time it was her decision to remarry, because widows did not have to seek permission from a senior male relative to make such arrangements (Carlton 1978).

As will become apparent in the artefact, by the time Zachariah began to make enquiries into Alice's involvement in the making and selling of *Aurum Potabile*, she had begun to realise that Heydon was not the man she thought she had recently married. As explained by Woolley (2004, p. 329), only a couple of years following her marriage to Heydon, Alice would sever it by having Heydon imprisoned for unspecified charges. Later Alice would become financially independent when she obtained a licence to practise as a midwife (Woolley 2004, p. 329).

Conclusion

Culpeper was not remembered as a gentleman by his peers. Through his life choices—his abandoning of his university studies and apothecary apprenticeship; his persistent vitriolic attacks on the College of Physicians and other professions; his breaking of the code of honour amongst gentlemen—all led to his alienation from the sites where valid and objective knowledge were being produced. As his political, religious and educational reformist commentaries were increasingly omitted from subsequent post-1660 editions of his medical works, simply because his reformist ideas could not survive in the new intellectual and political environment, all that survives into the eighteenth century and beyond are primarily his herbal themed publications.

With his credibility damaged, as indicated by Mackaile's (1664) criticism of Culpeper's character and works, physicians continued to discredit Culpeper's medical publications for years after his death. Eventually, I suggest, the claim that Culpeper was merely an ignorant superstitious quack overwhelmed the fact that he was actually well-versed in the medical and philosophical classical works, a skilled translator who participated in the reformist debates of his era. The detrimental construction of Culpeper subsequently became so entrenched, it enabled later historians of medicine (operating within a modernist grand narrative paradigm) to perpetuate and reinforce the earlier construction of Culpeper as merely an ignorant, unqualified empiric. Thus, Woolley (2004, p. 341) writes, 'A state of collective amnesia overcame the medical world when it came to Nicholas. Even his own works began to deny him.'

****

References

1. I will employ the Julian calendar that had been maintained by most Protestant countries, including Britain, until September 1752. Most of Catholic Europe had adopted the Gregorian calendar from 1582.

2. Description of Nicholas, in Gadbury, J 1659, 'The nativity of Nicholas Culpeper, student of physick and astrology', in Nicholas Culpeper, *Culpeper's school of physick*, N Brook, London.

3. Precursor to the natural sciences – the generic study of nature.

4. Culpeper, N 1649a, *A physicall directory, or, a translation of the London dispensatory made by the colledge of physicians in London …*, Peter Cole, London.

5. Anon., 1649, *Mercurius pragmaticus*, Sept. Pt. 2, No. 21, pp. 4-11.

6. Culpeper, 1649b, 'The translator to the reader', *Physical directory*, sig. A1v.

7. Anon., (Brooke) 1659, 'The Life of the admired physician and astrologer of our times, Mr Nicholas Culpeper', in N Culpeper, *Culpeper's school of physick*, N. Brook, London, sig. C7r. The document is not attributed to Brooke. However, Benjamin Woolley attributes it to him. See: Woolley, B 2004, *Heal thyself: Nicholas Culpeper and the seventeenth-century struggle to bring medicine to the people*, Harper Collins, New York.

8. There is no evidence to suggest this was so.

9. Woolley (2004, p. 323) implies that Alice brought Heydon into the Culpeper residence under the guise of a boarder, when in actuality they were having an affair. Woolley suggests Alice may have planned to marry Heydon to secure her future once she became a widow.

10. Culpeper, N 1656, *Mr Culpeper's treatise of aurum potabile: being a description of the threefold world …*, G Eversden, London, p. 50.

11. Anon., (Brooke) 1659, sig. C5v.

12. In modern terminology he would be referring to science rather than art – the term 'science' did not come into common English usage until the late seventeenth century. Prior to that, science was usually referred to as natural philosophy, book-learning, knowledge, or arts. Harper, D 2001-2014, *Online etymology dictionary*.

13. Zachariah Jenkin is a purely fictional character.

14. Sir William Culpeper (1602-1678), was a distant relative of Nicholas Culpeper. While Nicholas had claimed that Sir William was his patron, probably this was an exaggeration, especially considering Nicholas had sullied the ancient and titled Culpeper name with his radical and outspoken commentaries against the landed establishment.

15. Stockwell, C 1990, *Wakehurst Place: the Culpeper connection*, Richmond, Royal Botanic Gardens, Kew.

16. Woolley, 2004, p. 158.

17. 'RW', 1659, 'The preface', in N Culpeper, *Culpeper's school of physick, or the experimental practice of the whole art*, N. Brook, London, sig. A6r.

18. A newspaper or gazette. Woolley, 2004, p. 294.

19. Sanderson claims that Culpeper translated the *Pharmacopoeia* with his fellow apothecaries in mind, because most could not read Latin. Sanderson, J 1999, *Nicholas Culpeper and the book trade: print and the promotion of vernacular medical knowledge, 1649–65*, PhD Thesis, University of Leeds, p. 117.

20. Tobyn, G 1997, *Culpeper's medicine: A practice of western holistic medicine*, Element Books, Brisbane. Figure 3, p. 31. Silent reading, or reading to oneself was not a common practice at this time, even in private a reader would articulate printed texts. As aural reading was also a popular communal practice, a reader with an audience

of often illiterate listeners, it was an effective means of mass communication. See Jagodzinski, C 1999, *Privacy and print: reading and writing in seventeenth-century England*, University Press of Virginia, Charlottesville.

21. The handbill was signed Nich Culpeper and dated Jan 1653, nine days before Culpeper's death. As the handbill did not appear on the streets of London until 1655, it can be safely assumed that it was a forgery. McCarl, 1992, p. 239.

22. Tobyn, 1997.

23. Culpeper, N 1652a, *Catastrophe magnatum or the fall of the monarchie*, T. Vere and Nath. Brook, London.

24. Culpeper, N 1652a, sig. A3r.

25. Woolley, 2004, p. 7.

26. Woolley, 2004, p. 11.

27. Stockwell, C 1990, *Wakehurst Place: the Culpeper connection*, Royal Botanic Gardens, Kew. According to Stockwell, the young Nicholas was a frequent visitor to Wakehurst Place. It can be speculated that his mother sought to maintain the connection in the hope that her son would follow the family tradition and enter the church, thus being eligible to receive the Culpeper patronage. However, it is pure invention on my part that Sir Edward ever experienced any regrets regarding his uncharitable treatment of the widow, Mary.

28. Sir William's monetary support for Nicholas and Alice is pure invention on my part.

29. By the early seventeenth century, the apothecary trade had become respectable enough to be considered suitable for the second son of a gentleman. See Hill, C 1997, *Intellectual origins of the English revolution revisited*, rev. ed., Oxford University Press, Oxford.

30. Anon., (Brooke), 1659, sig. C4v.

31. Culpeper, N 1654b, *A new method of physic, or a short view of Paracelsus and Galen's practice*, Peter Cole, Cornhill, London. Originally published in 1625 in Latin by the Bohemian (German)

physician Simeon Partlicius (ca. 1590–after 1640) under the title *Medici systematis harmonici, in quo novo… discendae et exercendae medicinae methodus precepta brevis traditur, canones selectos illustratur, commentaria dilucta explicatur…* Prodromos. Partlicius also published works on history, chronology, astronomy, astrology and medicine. See Gilly, C 2008, 'The "Midnight Lion", the "Eagle" and the "Antichrist": Political, religious and chiliastic propaganda in the pamphlets, illustrated broadsheets and ballads of the Thirty Years War,' *Nederlands Archief voor Kerkgeschiedenis*, vol. 80, pp. 46–77. 'Chiliastic' is a Latinised form of the Greek *khiliasmos* and refers to millenarian doctrines. Harper, 2001–2014.

32. Culpeper, 1654b, sig. A2r.

33. Culpeper, 1654b, pp. 4–5.

34. Culpeper, 1654b, p. 6.

35. 'Middling sort' is, in modern terminology, the middle class and lower gentry. See: Walker, G 2005, *Writing early modern history*, Hodder Arnold, London.

36. Culpeper's New Model of Physic was based on his understanding of Hermetic astrological medicine, as distinct from the traditional Galenic system.

37. Thulesius, O 1992, *Nicholas Culpeper: English physician and astrologer*, St Martin's Press, New York.

38. The character of Jane Wilson is entirely fictional.

39. University educated, William Attersoll wrote several treatises on theology. Woolley (2004) describes him as a fanatical puritan.

40. The doctrines of election, salvation and predestination were conceived by the Protestant reformer, John Calvin (1509–1564), and later reinterpreted and popularised in England by the Anglican theologian, William Perkins (1558–1602). See Kendall, RT 1981, *Calvin and English Calvinism to 1649*, Oxford University Press, Oxford; and Durston, C & Eales, J 1996, *The culture of English Puritanism, 1560–1700*, St Martins Press, New York.

41. From the description of the symptoms, Woolley (2004) claims Mary probably died of breast cancer. Also see Culpeper, N 1653h, *Pharmacopoeia Londinensis, or the London dispensatory, further adorned* ..., Peter Cole, London.

42. Culpeper, 1653h, p. 166.

43. Gadbury, 1659, sig. B8v.

44. Nathaniel Brooke, a wealthy gentleman, commissioned the publication of astrological and occult titles during the mid to late seventeenth century. Not being able to find any biographical information on Brooke, my descriptions of his physical appearance and manner are fictional.

45. Culpeper, N 1655b, *Culpeper's last legacy: left and bequeathed to his dearest wife, for the publicke good, being the choicest and most profitable of those secrets which while he lived were lockt up in his breast, and resolved never to be publisht till after his death* ..., N. Brooke, London, sig. A2r.

46. Culpeper, 1655b, sig. A2v.

47. Culpeper, N 1651b, *A directory for midvvives: or, a guide for women, in their conception, bearing, and suckling their children* ..., Peter Cole, London.

48. TC, ID, MS, TB, 1656, *Compleat midwife's practice, in the most weighty and high concernments of the birth of man containing perfect rules for midwifes and nurses: as also for women in their conception, bearing, and nursing of children* ... *with instructions of the midwife to the Queen of France* ..., N Brooke, London.

49. TC, et al., 1656.

50. Very little documented evidence of this episode has been discovered, much of it derived from the 1659 biography 'The Life of the admired physician and astrologer of our times, Mr Nicholas Culpeper', in Culpeper N *Culpeper's school of physick*. Woolley suggests the young woman may have been the daughter of Sir John Shurley (1596–1631), who owned a manor in Isfield. See Woolley

(2004), pp. 29–31 and footnotes 52 and 53, p. 355.

51. Anon., (Brooke), 1659, sig C2v–C3r.

52. Early in the seventeenth century, it was discovered that the *Hermetic Corpus* had not been written by a single ancient sage, but were compiled in the late Roman era. However, either Culpeper wasn't aware of this discovery or, like his contemporaries, chose to ignore it. Modern historians have identified that the authors were primarily Christian Greek scholars living in Egypt between the second to fourth centuries AD. The *Hermetic Corpus* is an eclectic compilation of Platonic, Neo-Platonic and Egyptian philosophies, as well as a myriad of mystical religious and esoteric beliefs that had spread throughout the Mediterranean region during the mid-to-late Roman era. See Yates, FA 1964, *Giordano Bruno and the Hermetic Tradition*, Routledge and K Paul, London; Copenhaver, B 1988, 'Hermes Trismegistus, Proclus, and the Question of a Philosophy of Magic in the Renaissance,' in I Merkel and AG Debus (eds), *Hermeticism and the Renaissance*, Folger Shakespeare Library, Washington.

53. Anon., (Brooke) 1655, *Culpeper revived from the grave, to discover the cheats of that grand imposter, call'd aurum potabile. Wherein is declared the grand falsities therefore, and abuses thereby.* SN, London, p. 1. Poynter, (1972) and Tobyn (1997) claim Nathaniel Brooke was the author of this tract. See Poynter, FNL 1972, 'Nicholas Culpeper and the Paracelsians,' in AG Debus, (ed.), *Science, medicine and society in the Renaissance*, Science History Publications, New York.

54. Anon., (Brooke) 1655, p. 1.

55. Woolley (2004) suggests that Alice Culpeper and John Heydon were engaged in an intimate relationship during the last months of Nicholas's life.

56. Anon., (Brooke), 1655, pp. 2–3.

57. Anon., (Brooke), 1655, p. 3.

58. Anon., (Brooke), 1655, p.2.

59. Anon., (Brooke), 1655, pp. 2–3.

60. Anon., (Brooke), 1655.

61. Descriptions of Cole, his personality and state of mind are derived from Furdell, EL 2004, '"Reported to be distracted": the suicide of Puritan entrepreneur Peter Cole', *The Historian*, vol. 66, no. 4, 2004, pp. 772–792, and Sanderson, 1999, pp. 90–101.

62. Extensive lists of medicinal titles published by Cole were included in many of Culpeper's texts. Cole's *Rational Library* would not be published until the 1660s. See Sanderson, 1999.

63. Anon., (Brooke), 1659.

64. Gadbury, 1659, sig. B8v.

65. Anon., (Brooke), 1659, sig. C6r.

66. Anon., (Brooke), 1659.

67. Anon., (Cole), 1656, p. 2. The Norman Yoke, or the 'Tyrannical Yoak of King-ship' as Cole (1656, p. 2) calls it, referred to the eleventh century invasion of Saxon England by the French or Norman, William the Conqueror who imposed his foreign laws on the English people. Parliamentarians in the English Civil War justified their claim for the overthrow of the King and nobility because, they claimed, the nobility were direct descendants of these Norman usurpers. See Mulder, D 1990, *The alchemy of revolution, Gerrard Winstanley's occultism and seventeenth-century English communism*, P Lang, New York, pp. 74–83.

68. People who volunteered for the parliamentarian army to overthrow King Charles were often described as 'Saints' or 'people of God', because it was believed that through their selfless actions God would reward them with Election. See Parry, RH 1970, *The English civil war and after: 1642–1658*, Macmillian, London, p. 61.

69. Comenius, JA 1642, *A reformation of schools*. Facimile Reprint. 1969. Scholar Press, Menston, Yorkshire.

70. Up until the seventeenth century, it was generally believed that scholastic or university knowledge must be confirmed by their inclusion in an eclectic collection of ancient Greek and Roman

texts that randomly survived the fall of the Roman Empire. Hence knowledge production had all but stagnated. See Johannisson K 1988, 'Magic science and institutionalisation in the seventeenth and eighteenth centuries', in I Merkel & A Debus, (eds), *Hermeticism and the Renaissance: intellectual history and the occult in early modern Europe*, Folger Shakespeare Library, Washington.

71. Bacon, F 1620, 'The new organon (Novum organum)', in L Jardine and M Silverthorne (eds), 2000, *Cambridge Texts in the History of Philosophy*, McGill University, Montréal. Bacon was a philosopher and politician. He published many texts on a variety of themes.

72. Webster, C 1975, *The great instauration: science, medicine and reform 1626–1660*, Duckworth, London, p. 268. Sanderson claims that while Hartlib and Culpeper were not associates, their platforms for the reform of learning and dissemination of knowledge was complimentary. See Sanderson, 1999, p. 59.

73. The modern term is Armageddon, or the Second Coming of Christ.

74. Comenius, JA 1642, *A Reformation of schools*, Facsimile Reprint, 1969, Scholar Press, Menston, Yorkshire, p. 77.

75. Young, JT 1998, *Faith, medical alchemy and natural philosophy: Johann Moriaen, reformed intelligencer, and the Hartlib circle*, Ashgate, Aldershot, Hamp.

76. Comparisons can be identified between Cole's 1656 tract, *Mr Culpeper's ghost, giving seasonal advice to the lovers of his writings*, Peter Cole, London, pp. 1–5, and Culpeper's political commentaries in the prefaces of his 1649, 1650 and 1651 editions of Culpeper's *Physical directory*.

77. Culpeper, N 1652a.

78. The concept of the Fifth Monarchy was based on a Biblical interpretation popularised by extreme Puritans fighting on the side of the Parliamentarians. According to the Fifth Monarchists, their opposition to King Charles would herald the Second Coming

of Christ who would then reign for a thousand years. The Fourth Monarchy had been the Roman Empire, which had long since fallen. See Capp, 1972, *The fifth monarchy men: a study in seventeenth-century English millenarianism*, Faber, London.

79. Culpeper, 1652a.

80. Anon, 1652, *Black Munday turn'd white: or the astrologers knavery epitomized*, C. Whiting, London.

81. *Mercurius phreneticus*, 1652, 4:22 April, p. 28.

82. Anon. (Cole), 1656, p. 13.

83. Anon., (Cole), 1656, p. 15.

84. Anon., (Cole), 1656, p. 16.

85. Sanderson suggests that Cole was directly involved in the publication of the *Treatise*, but chose not to be publicly associated with it. He claims that Cole persuaded Eversden to publish the text in lieu of a payment of a debt. See Sanderson, 1999, p. 111.

86. Anon. (Cole), 1656, pp. 5–6.

Hippocrates (c. 460–c. 370 BC), is often described as the father of Western medicine, having established medicine as a skilled profession in its own right. Hippocratic medicine was based the doctrine of the four humours: yellow bile or choler, black bile or melancholy, phlegm and blood. Balanced humours resulted in a healthy constitution; however, illness and diseases were caused by the humours being out of balance. Medical treatments consisted of trying to rebalance the humours through diet and medicines, as well as bleeding the patient or causing them to vomit excess humours. Galenic medicine was derived a collection of texts written by a second century AD Roman physician, Galen. Yet, by the seventeenth century, Hippocratic and Galenic medicine would have been almost incomprehensible to the Roman physician, as the systems had assimilated medical practices from local Indigenous folklore, as well as an eclectic collection of other ancient Greek and Roman medical texts, which had arbitrarily survived the fall of the Roman

Empire. See Findlen, P 1994, *Possessing nature: museums, collecting, and scientific culture in early modern Italy*, University of California Press, Berkley and Los Angeles, Calif., p. 52.

87. Sanderson (1999) claims Alice exaggerated these numbers. McCarl (1996), pp. 263–276, provides a list of titles and multiple editions attributed to Culpeper between the years 1649 and 1700. However, as Sanderson and McCarl emphasise, following Culpeper's death publishers would fraudulently attribute new titles to Culpeper because of his saleable name.

88. A marriage allegiance was not only advantageous for the daughter, but also for her entire family as it expanded social relations and patronage. Therefore, Mr Field possibly agreed to the betrothal as a means for his family to rise in social standing by being associated with, and connected to the Culpeper name. See: Slater, M 1976, 'The weightiest business: marriage in an upper-gentry family in seventeenth-century England', *Past and Present*, no. 72, pp. 25–54.

89. During this period of high social mobility, both up and down the hierarchy, status could not be earned or bought, rather it could only be conferred by birth. While wealth could buy titles and the appearance of gentility, a persistent and powerful element of a gentle status was lineage: the ability to trace one's ancestry back many generations. See Stone, L 1965, *The crisis of the aristocracy: 1558–1641*, Oxford University Press, London. Heal, F and Holmes, C 1994, *The gentry in England and Wales, 1500–1700*, Macmillan, Houndsmills.

90. Woolley, 2004.

91. Second sons of the gentry were often better educated than first sons who had inherited the entire family estate. Second sons were expected to make their own way in the world, often having received very little inheritance and so many entered university to gain professional qualifications in either law, divinity or medicine. See Axtell, J 1970, 'Education and status in Stuart England: the London physician', *History of Education Quarterly*, vol. 10, no. 2, p. 145. Cook,

HJ 1994, 'Good advice and little medicine: the professional authority of early modern English physicians', *Journal of British Studies*, vol. 33, Jan, pp. 1–31.

92. Anon., (Brooke), 1659, sig. C9r–C10r.

93. Gadbury, 1659, sig. B6v; Anon., (Brooke) 1659, Sig. C5v.

94. Anon., (Brooke) 1659, sig. C5v.

95. Woolley, 2004.

96. Culpeper, A 1656a, 'To the Reader', in N Culpeper, *Nicholas Culpeper's treatise of aurum potabile …*, G Eversden, London, sig. A5v.

97. Culpeper, A 1656a, sig. A5v.

98. Talbot, F 1662, 'The life of John Heydon', in J Heydon 1665, *Elhavarevna or the English physician*, William Gilbertson, London, sig. A4v.

99. Talbot, 1662, sig. A1v.

100. Talbot, 1662, sig. A2r.

101. For a detailed history of the Rosicrucians see Yates, F 1972, *The Rosicrucian enlightenment*, Routledge & Kegan Paul, London; McIntosh, C 1980, *The Rosy Cross unveiled: the history, mythology and rituals of an occult order*, The Aquarian Press Limited, Wellingborough, Northhamptonshire, UK; Faivre, A 2010, *Western esotericism: A concise history*, SUNY series in Western esoteric traditions, State University of New York Press, e-book, pp. 43–46.

102. Anon., 1614, *Fama fraternitatis roseae crucis oder die bruderschaft des ordens der rosenkreuzer*, Kassel. (Germany); Anon., 1615, *Confessio oder bekenntnis der societät und bruderschaft Rosenkreuz*, Kassel. (Germany); Anon., 1616, *Chymische hochzeit Christiani rosencreutz anno 1459*, Strasbourg.

103. Yates, 1972.

104. Heydon, J 1662a, 'The Rosie Cros uncovered, and the places, temples, holy houses, castles and invisible mountains …', in John Heydon, *The holy-guide, leading the way to know all things past, present and to come, to resolve all manner of questions …*, TM, London, p. 7.

105. Heydon, 1662a, p. 7.

106. Heydon, 1662a.

107. Debus, AG, 1966, *English Paracelsians*, The Watts History of Science Series, F Watts, New York.

108. See for example: Ben Johnson 1610, *The alchemist*, in FH Mares ed., 1967, *The revels plays*, Methuen &Co LTD, London.

109. In 1652, the reformist sectarian Fifth Monarchist, Mary Rand, predicted that the philosopher's stone, 'would soon appear and herald the reign of Christ.' See Newman, WR 1994, *Gehennical fire: The lives of George Starkey, an alchemist in the scientific revolution*, Harvard University Press, Cambridge, Mass, p. 3.

110. Heydon, 1662a.

111. Read, J 1947, *The alchemist in life, literature and art*, Thomas Nelson and Sons, Ltd, London. Principle, LM 1998, *The aspiring adept: Robert Boyle and his alchemical quest: including Boyle's "lost" dialogue on the transmutation of metals*, Princeton University Press, Princeton, New Jersey.

112. Heydon, 1662b, *The holy guide, leading the way to vnite art and nature: In which is made plain all things past, present, and to come*, TM, London, p. 28.

113. Heydon, 1662b, p. 17.

114. Read, 1947.

115. Ryves, W 1658, 'On the famous and most renowned physician and astrologer, Mr Nicholas Culpeper, lately deceased', in N Culpeper 1659, *Culpeper's school of physick*, N Brooke, London, sig. C1ov. Historians differ as to the author of this work. Poynter (1962, p. 156), Thulesius (1992, pp. 156–157), Tobyn (1997) claim Ryves was the author, while McCarl (1996, p. 247) disputes this. See Poynter, FNL 1962, 'Nicholas Culpeper and his books', *Journal of the History of Medicine*, vol. 17, pp.152–166.

116. There is no evidence to suggest Ryves inherited any of Culpeper's manuscripts or books.

117. Ryves, 1658, sig. C11r. Ryves signed this epitaph: '[Culpeper's] quondam Servant'.

118. Culpeper, 1651b, p. 20.

119. Culpeper, 1653a, *The English physitian enlarged: With three hundred, sixty, and nine medicines made of English herbs that were not in any impression until this ...*, Peter Cole, London, sig. B4v.

120. Culpeper, N 1649b, 'The translator to the reader', in N Culpeper, *A physical directory...*, 1st edn, sig. A2r.

121. See Cook, H 1986, *The decline of the old medical regime in Stuart London*, Cornell University Press, Ithaca.

122. Nagy, D 1988, *Popular medicine in seventeenth century England*, Bowling Green State University Popular Press, Bowling Green, Ohio, p. 5.

123. Culpeper, 1649b, sig. A2v–A3r.

124. Parkinson, J 1640, *Theatrum botanicum: the theater of plant ...*, Thomas Cotes, London. Sanderson claims that it was known at the time of publication that much of Culpeper's *English physician* was derived from Parkinson's larger and expensive academic herbal. See Sanderson, 1999, p. 141.

125. Culpeper, N, 1652c, *The English physitian: Or an astrologo-physical discourse of the vulgar herbs of this nation ... 1st edn*, Peter Cole, London.

126. Culpeper, 1652c, sig. A2v. This extract could also represent a summary of the philosophy and ideas that are the foundation of Culpeper's *Treatise of Aurum Potabile*. See for example pp. 4–7, 22, 124–126, 158–165 of the *Treatise*. The significant influence of Paracelsian and Hermetic ideas as presented in Culpeper's translation, *A new method of physic* (1654b) are also evident in this extract. See for example pp. 424–426.

127. Capp, B 1979, *Astrology and the popular press: English almanacs, 1500–1800*, Faber, London.

128. Culpeper 1655a, 'Hermes Trismegistus, upon the first de-

cumbiture of the sick, showing the signs and conjecture of the disease, by the good or evil position of the moon at the time of the patient lying down, or demanding the question', in N Culpeper, *Culpeper's astrologicall judgment of diseases from the decumbiture of the sick: (1) from Aven Ezra by way of introduction, (2) from Noel Duret by way of direction …*, 1st edn, Nath Brooke, London, sig. A4r. Originally published in 1651 under the title: *Semeiotica uranica*.

129. Culpeper, 1655a, sig. A4r.

130. Culpeper, N 1652d, *Galen's art of physick*, Peter Cole, London, p. 22.

131. Culpeper, 1652c, sig. A2v. Also see Culpeper, 1656, pp. 17 & 169.

132. Culpeper, 1652c, sig. A2v.

133. Culpeper, N 1651c, 'An astrologo-physical discourse of the human virtues in the body of man …' in N Culpeper, *An ephemeris for the yeer 1651*, Peter Cole, London, Sig. K4r. An ephemeris was a booklet of astronomical calculations and astrological predictions or interpretations of the significance of the planetary movements.

134. Culpeper, 1653a, pp. 368–369.

135. Culpeper, 1655a.

136. Culpeper, 1653a.

137. Having undertaken an extensive analysis of Culpeper's texts, Poynter identifies similarities in language and terms between Culpeper's *Treatise* and his earlier texts. See Poynter, 1972, p. 214.

138. Heydon, 1662b, sig. A2v.

139. Culpeper, N 1651d, *Semeiotica uranica. Or the astrological judgement of diseases…*, N. Brooke, London.

140. Culpeper, 1654b.

141. Partlicius, 1625.

142. Culpeper had mentioned that he had completed the initial translation in 1642. See Culpeper, 1654b, p. 90.

143. Culpeper, 1654b, sig. A2v.

144. Culpeper, 1654b, p. 18.

145. Culpeper, 1654b, p. 424. Also see Culpeper 1656, pp. 15, 17, 20–24.

146. Culpeper, N 1651b, *A directory for midvvives: or, a guide for women, in their conception, bearing, and suckling their children* …, 1st edn, Peter Cole, London.

147. In modern terminology the womb or matrix is the uterus.

148. Culpeper, 1656, pp. 32–37, 47, 51–52, 59–65.

149. Culpeper, 1651b, p. 56.

150. Culpeper, N 1653g, *The anatomy of the body of man: Wherein is exactly described every part thereof in the same manner as it is commonly shewed in publick anatomies* …, published in Latin by Joh. Veslingus and Englished by Nich. Culpeper, Peter Cole, London.

151. Culpeper, 1653d, 'To his right worthy friend Samuel Hyland esquire; Nich. Culpeper wisheth encrease of grace in this world, and a crown of glory to come', in N Culpeper, *The anatomy of the body of man*, sig. A1r.

152. Culpeper, 1653e, sig. A1r. Similar phrases are also in *Mr Culpeper's treatise of aurum potabile*, pp. 17, 126.

153. See for example: Culpeper 1652c, 'To the reader', in N Culpeper, *The English physician*, sig. A2v–B1r, Culpeper 1653c, 'A premonitory epistle …', in N Culpeper, *Pharmacopoeia Londinensis*, sig. C1, Culpeper, N 1653a, *The English physitian enlarged*, sig. B3r–B4v; Culpeper, N 1653e, 'To his worthy friend Samuel Hyland esquire; Nich. Culpeper wisheth increase of grace in this world, and a crown of glory to come', in N Culpeper, *The anatomy of the body of man: wherein is exactly described every part thereof in the same manner as it is commonly shewed in publick anatomies* …, sig. A1v–A2r; Culpeper, N 1653f, 'To the reader', in N Culpeper, *The anatomy of the body of man: wherein is exactly described every part thereof in the same manner as it is commonly shewed in publick anatomies* …, sig. B1r.

154. Culpeper 1654a, *An ephemeris for the year 1654, being the second after leap-year*, John Macock, London, p. 21. This would have been the final ephemeris he would have drafted prior to his death.

155. Culpeper, 1652a, p. 50.

156. Culpeper, 1652a, p. 63.

157. Culpeper, N 1652b, *An Ephemeris for the year 1652…*, T Vere and N Brook, London, p. 16.

158. Culpeper, 1653b, *An Ephemeris for the year of our lord 1653*, n.p.

159. Culpeper, N 1653d, 'To the right worshipful Edward Hall, esquire …', in N Culpeper, *Pharmacopoeia Londinensis*, sig. B1v.

160. Culpeper, 1652b, sig. D2r.

161. Peter Cole claimed he had received correspondence from an unknown scholar who alleged to have recorded the views of Nicholas Culpeper's ghost. He reproduced this dialogue in his treatise 'Mr Culpeper's Ghost, giving seasonable advice to the lovers of his writings', included in the first edition of *Culpeper's treatise of aurum potabile*. McCarl (1996, p. 241) and Sanderson (1999, p. 111) claim Cole was the author. It is evident from its witty style that Cole's readers would understand the tract was a parody, not to be taken seriously as a message from beyond the grave. Culpeper's ghost must have been busy, because Thomas (1973, p. 715) reports that, according to Heydon, he appeared to his widow, Alice, 'bidding her to disown' forged works. Belief in ghosts interacting with the living was widespread in seventeenth century England. See: Bennett, G 1986, 'Ghost and witch in the sixteenth and seventeenth centuries', *Folklore*, vol. 97, no. 1, pp. 3–14.

162. 'Nicholas Culpeper's statement about John Dee's crystal, England, 1651–1658', *Science museum. Brought to life: exploring the history of medicine*, online.

163. Culpeper, 1651b, sig. Q6v, p. 217.

164. Woolley, 2004, p. 16.

165. Tymme, T 1605, 'The epistle dedicatory', in Joseph Du Chesne,

The practice of chymicall and hermeticall physicke, Thomas Creede, London, Sig. A4r. There is no evidence that Attersoll had a copy of this text, or that Culpeper had read it. However, Culpeper's understandings of the relationships between the accumulation of knowledge and salvation significantly resemble those of Tymme's. This quoted passage is almost the same as passages contained within two of Culpeper's publications: *Treatise of aurum potabile* 1656, pp. 185–186 and the prefaces of his 1653 edition of *The Pharmacopoeia Londinensis*.

166. Culpeper, 1656, pp. 159–160, 167–169.

167. The only known surviving examples of Culpeper's handwriting are the small three leaf manuscript that described the divination crystal that belonged to John Dee, as well an undated letter to a Mr Booker. See Sanderson, J 1999, p. 255.

168. These original hand-written manuscripts must have existed, but have not survived. Their description is purely my own invention.

169. Culpeper, 1656, pp. 20–21. Almost the same statement is to be found in the 'Premonitory epistle', in Culpeper's 1653 edition of the *Pharmacopoeia Londinensis*, sig. C1r, as well as his *Ephemeris for the year 1654*, p. 21.

170. Culpeper, 1656, p. 22.

171. Bayle, LC c.1613, *The practice of piety: directing Christians how to walk that he may please God*, 3rd ed. London, pp. 1, 10.

172. Culpeper, 1656, p. 27.

173. Culpeper, 1656, p. 17.

174. Culpeper, 1656, pp. 2–3.

175. Culpeper, 1656, pp. 167.

176. Culpeper, 1654b, pp. 10, 16, 20.

177. Culpeper 1656, pp. 17, 19.

178. Also referred to as the Kabbala or Kabbalah, it is an aspect of Jewish mysticism and popularised in Medieval Europe as a form of divination. See Dan, J 2007, *Kabbalah: a very short introduction*,

Oxford University Press, Oxford.

179. Culpeper 1652a, p. 75.

180. Culpeper, 1652a, p. 76.

181. Millenarian movements emerged during the English Civil War and were based on the belief that the events of the period were signs that God would return to Earth (and often specifically England) to establish a peaceful kingdom that would last for a thousand years. For more information on the millenarian movements see Capp, 1972; Mulder, 1990; Versluis, A 2004, *Restoring paradise: Western esotericism, literature, art, and consciousness*, New York Press, Albany, New York.

182. Culpeper, 1652a, p. 68. Culpeper repeated this claim in his *Ephemeris for the year 1652*, pp. 14–15.

183. Culpeper may have been aware that the Hermetic and alchemical philosopher, John Dee, had written a Creationist manuscript that was published after his death. Around the time that Culpeper was translating and writing his own works, other private contemplations had been published by Hermetic scholars. These include *Ortus medicinae* (1648), by van Helmont (1577–1644), and Robert Fludd's collection of treatises tilted *Utriusque cosmi* … (1617–1621).

184. Culpeper, 1652b, p. 27.

185. Culpeper, 1652a.

186. Culpeper, 1652b, pp. 15–21.

187. Culpeper, 1651b, sig. q7r–q7v.

188. Culpeper, 1654a, p. 24.

189. Culpeper, 1656, p. 187.

190. The cleric theologian William Perkins (1558–1602) popularised the notion amongst devout Puritans that a sign one was of the elect was a natural tendency towards self-improvement. See Kendall, 1981.

191. Culpeper, 1651b, sig. A5r.

192. Culpeper 1653c, sig. C1r.

193. Culpeper, 1654a, p. 23.

194. Culpeper, 1654a, pp. 21–24.

195. Culpeper, 1654a, p. 23.

196. Culpeper, 1651b, sig. Q6v, p. 217.

197. Culpeper, 1656, pp. 158–159. This phrase is repeated in Culpeper's, 'A premonitory epistle …', in Culpeper's 1653 edition of the *Pharmacopoeia Londinensis*, sig. C1r.

198. Anon. 1654, 'On the sad news out of Spittlefields; alas, alas, for my old acquaintance, Nic. Culpeper, Mortus est.,' *Mercurius democritus, Or a true and perfect nocturnall … no. 84, February 1–8*, pp. 461–462, London.

199. If a headstone had been erected on Culpeper's grave, it has long since disappeared. Hence the exact location of Culpeper's grave is not known.

www.ingramcontent.com/pod-product-compliance
Lightning Source LLC
Chambersburg PA
CBHW030401200726
48286CB00015B/2093